THE LADY
FOR RANSOM

Alfred Duggan

PHOENIX

A PHOENIX PAPERBACK

First published in Great Britain in 1953
by Faber and Faber Ltd
This paperback edition published in 2006
by Phoenix,
an imprint of Orion Books Ltd,
Orion House, 5 Upper St Martin's Lane,
London WC2H 9EA

1 3 5 7 9 10 8 6 4 2

A CIP catalogue record for this book
is available from the British Library.

ISBN-13 978-0-7538-1829-9
ISBN-10 0-7538-1829-9

Typeset by Deltatype Ltd,
Birkenhead, Merseyside

Printed and bound in Great Britain by
Clays Ltd, St Ives plc

The Orion Publishing Group's policy is to use papers
that are natural, renewable and recyclable products and
made from wood grown in sustainable forests. The logging
and manufacturing processes are expected to conform to
the environmental regulations of the country of origin.

www.orionbooks.co.uk

Alfred Duggan was born in Argentina in 1903, of partly American descent: his mother's father, Joseph Munro Hinds, was born in Illinois in 1843, and met the author's grandmother (born in Argentina of English parents) when appointed Consul General in Brazil. Duggan was taken to England at the age of two. After his education at Eton College and Balliol College, Oxford, he worked for the British Natural History Museum, collecting specimens. At the age of twenty-one he sailed in the 600-ton barquentine, *St George*, from England via Madeira, Trinidad and Panama to the Galapagos Islands, pursuing his job for the museum. In later years he travelled extensively in Greece and Turkey, studying Byzantine monuments, and in 1935 helped to excavate Constantine's Palace, Istanbul, under the auspices of the University of St Andrews. From 1938 to 1941, when he was discharged as medically unfit, he served in the London Irish Rifles (TA) and saw active service in Norway. For the rest of World War II he worked in an aircraft factory.

A prolific writer, Duggan turned out more than one book a year. His first was *Knight with Armour*, written in 1946 and published in 1950. Next came his novels *The Conscience of the King* and *The Little Emperors*, the latter dealing in lively fashion with the decline and fall of the western Roman Empire as it impinged upon the life of a British civil servant. 'As one novel follows another in pleasant succession', wrote Thomas Caldecot Chubb in the *New York Times*, 'it dawns upon this constant reader of historical fiction that in Alfred Duggan he has found an extremely gifted writer who can move into an unknown period and give it life and immediacy.' 'A specialist in decline and fall', in *Lady for Ransom* he dealt with one of the great crises of Byzantine politics. 'Mr Duggan's characters are sharply drawn', wrote Chubb, 'and, as always, he keeps his eye on the flow of history'. His 'cheerful cynicism' and satirical view of men and politics 'have introduced a refreshing new element into current historical fiction'. Orville Prescott wrote in the *New York Times*, 'Mr Duggan looks upon the past with a connoisseur's relish of villainy and violence'.

Alfred Duggan died in 1964.

By Alfred Duggan

Winter Quarters
God and My Right
Leopards and Lilies
Knight with Armour
Conscience of the King
The Little Emperors
The Lady for Ransom
Lord Geoffrey's Fancy
Thomas Becket of Canterbury
Three's Company
The Cunning of the Dove
Elephants and Castles
Founding Fathers
Count Bohemond
Sword of Pleasure
Devil's Brood
Besieger of Cities
Family Favourites
He Died Old

CONTENTS

INTRODUCTION

December 1096

Although I am not yet forty-five, and hope to serve God for many more Advents and Christmases, Lents and Easters, yet even in this short life I have witnessed great events and surprising reversals of fortune; notably the overthrow of a great Empire and the struggles of brave men to save something from the wreck. And now all the good knights of the West have set out on that journey which in my youth was seldom accomplished. Our cousins from Normandy are wintering here in Italy, and next spring Duke Robert, and our Count Bohemond ride together for Romania, and then, if God wills, to the Holy City.

Because I, alone of this community, have marched and fought from Thrace to Armenia and back again, our Abbot has commanded me to relate all that befell me. The scriptor will write it down, to be read to the young knights who keep Christmas here; they ride through Romania as allies, and it would be a pity if they offended their hosts through ignorance.

There is one point I must make at the very beginning. Everyone has his own name, in which he takes pride; calling a man by the wrong name can cause great ill-feeling. So don't call their Emperor 'the King of the Greeks.' It is a deadly insult, and he will not receive letters addressed to that title. His proper style is Basileus Autocrator, though we who pay due deference to the See of St Peter need not also call him Isapostolos, Equal to the Apostles, as his subjects do. But the people who dwell in the City of New Rome are Romans, their army is the Roman

1

Army, and their ruler the Roman Emperor. That seems queer to us, who visit the true Rome and have dealings with the true Emperor in Germany; but the Greeks feel very strongly about it. It does no harm to follow their custom, and in this narrative I shall refer to them as Romans. Oddly enough, the language they speak is called Greek, and nobody minds; in fact they are rather proud of it, because the Gospels were written in that language; though I believe time has brought certain alterations.

Very well then. Please pay attention, young gentlemen.

CHAPTER ONE

I Meet Messer Roussel

My father was Odo fitzRoger, a Norman of Normandy, who came on pilgrimage to St Michael at Monte Gargano and then served the fitzTancreds in their conquest of the country. He was not a gentleman, but neither was he a villein; he was a free craftsman, a smith. He carried his tools on a donkey, and boasted he could earn a living anywhere in the world where throats are cut with steel. He was not devout, but he kept his bargains and served his lord, in the field as in the workshop. He fought on foot, with a hammer of his own design, and said it was most interesting to find out by experiment whether strange armour was as strong as it looked.

My mother was Theodora Melitissa, whose first husband came to this country from Romania as smith and armourer to the troops of the Catapan. Nowadays the young men use a horrible slang word, 'Gasmule', to describe the son of a Frankish father and a Greek mother; if anyone called me that in the days before I entered religion I drew my dagger and made him apologise; because the word really means Bastard. I suppose people take it for granted that such a child must be the outcome of rape or seduction, but my parents were properly married, in church, before I was born. It was not exactly a love-match; but the Catapan's army had fled, and there was my mother trying to bury her husband single-handed, and heir to a well-equipped forge. By marrying her my father got a good title to the smithy, and settled down to shoe horses and mend ploughs at the crossroads instead of marching with the Norman army.

That was in the year 1051, and in 1052 I was born and christened Roger; I was the only child to survive the perils of infancy, though I had several brothers and sisters who lived a few weeks. When I was seven I began to help my father in the smithy, but this is a land of war, and I did not finish my apprenticeship. When I was twelve the Norman conquerors fought among themselves; Robert the Weasel was making himself ruler of all the Franks of Apulia, and some of his fellows were unwilling to take orders from him. A band of defeated rebels halted to sack our little settlement. My father rashly tried to defend his home, and when they killed him someone cut down my mother also; I suppose I should have helped my father until I was killed in my turn, but I inherit a sensible caution from both sides of the family; the forge was cold, and I hid up the chimney until the plunderers rode on. The stone chimney did not burn, though it grew very hot as the thatch blazed round it; when I came down there was not another living creature within miles.

I did not bury my parents. I know it is the right thing to do, but I had no spade, and was not feeling strong. Duke Robert the Weasel was coming up in pursuit of the murderers, and he always made his men bury casual corpses and in general keep his lands tidy. I am sure my parents did in fact get Christian burial; otherwise my mother would have haunted me in dreams, for all Romans set great store by a proper funeral; but she never has.

I was twelve years old, my clothes were filthy from my hiding-place and I had not a penny or a friend in the world. But I knew something of metalwork, and a good deal about the management of horses, because my father dealt in them as a sideline. If warriors have ruined you the obvious remedy is to become a warrior yourself; then you can plunder others; a groom who could also do simple repairs to a mailshirt would be welcome in any army. I began walking westwards, towards the coast.

In the evening I saw the coast-road below me, with Sicily on the horizon. That was where most warriors were at that time, for the infidels were besieged in Palermo. If I could beg a passage across the strait there would be gallant horsemen on the other side, needing grooms when they captured more chargers from the foe.

But I did not journey as far as the coast. That night I joined the household which I served for the rest of my life in the world. As I came down a little ravine I heard horses on my left; I hid in a bush, fearing brigands; but round a spur came a troop of Norman horse, led by a lady on a tall stallion. There were ox-waggons also, containing women and children, and a few waiting-ladies sitting sideways on quiet mules. I did not suppose a lady would be gathering recruits, but she would give me alms, especially if I appealed to her in French (at home I spoke Greek to my mother, but I am fluent in both languages). The Italian children in my native hamlet begged from every passer-by, whether they were hungry or not; my father beat me if he caught me copying them, but I knew it was done. I skipped among the prancing horses of the escort, crying.

'Gracious lady, spare a crust for a starving orphan. I have no father, I have no mother, my home was burned by brigands, and for three days I have not eaten.' As a matter of fact I had eaten breakfast that morning, but it was a pardonable exaggeration.

A sergeant knocked me over with the butt of his lance, which showed that the lady was charitable; otherwise he would have run me through with the point. I scuttled on all fours among the plunging hoofs, still begging at the top of my voice, until the lady raised her hand to halt the troop and called:

'Come here, you filthy little scarecrow. I can't think how you picked up all that soot in your short life. But how is it that you speak the decent French of a gentleman? Have you escaped from the sulphur-mines of the infidel?'

I was strongly tempted to pretend I was the son of some great lord, delivered as a hostage to the infidel and then condemned to the mines. But the lady spoke a very Italian French; she must have lived in Apulia for many years, and would be personally acquainted with every noble family. I lifted my eyes for a brief

5

glance at her face, and decided that, at least on this occasion, honesty was the best policy. For she looked competent, and more honest than charitable. She had the grey eyes and faded fair hair of a Frank, but her skin was so scorched by the sun, though she was not much more than twenty years old, that she must be of Italian birth; her nose was a commanding beak, very red from sunburn, and her mouth set in firm lines of decision. She was as big as a warrior, and more like a handsome man than a pretty girl. Above all, she looked as though she would stand no nonsense. I told her the truth.

'So although you are not a gentleman you are a Norman, or at least half one,' she said when I had finished. 'My lord will always help Normans in distress. You may come in my company to Sicily, and if you can really look after horses and mend mail we will find work for you in the household. You are Roger fitz-Odo, and you should know my name. I am the lady Matilda, wife to Messer Roussel de Balliol, who serves Roger fitz-Tancred. Since you have been hiding in a chimney I shall forgive your present appearance, but if I give you a clean shirt you must look very different by supper time. Go and help with the pack-mules until we halt for the evening, and then see me again. Here is bread and cheese to eat on the road.'

This speech was typical of the lady Matilda, as I got to know her later. I was so exhausted I could hardly walk, but she put me to work at once, for she hated her servants to be idle; on the other hand, she fed me immediately, instead of waiting for supper, because if her servants worked diligently she looked after them.

In the evening we halted by the roadside, just short of a walled seaport. In those days in Italy anyone who was worth a ransom did not care to enter walled places which were held by someone else. Duke Robert the Weasel called himself chief of all the Normans of Italy, but in practice they did not obey him very faithfully.

I threw away my sooty clothes, and a groom gave me a woollen shirt and a pair of pantaloons such as peasants wear, copied from the riding-chausses of their Lombard masters. I waded into a cold torrent and got myself cleaner than I had been for many years. Then, in my new clothes, I walked up to the main cooking-fire and asked a serving-maid where I might wait on the lady Matilda.

Without thinking I spoke in Greek, because at home I had spoken Greek to my mother and it seemed the right language for women. But the lady Matilda had come up behind me; she was always trying to stop the cooks stealing more food than was reasonable.

'What's that you said, boy?' she called. 'E Despoina Matilda? I know those words, though that's just about all I know. Can you speak Greek? Then my lord will certainly employ you. I suppose you can't read? A pity, though it's only natural. You can't be our interpreter if you can't read and write, but you will be a useful check on those rascally hired linguists; half of them don't really understand French, and they tell the Catapan anything that comes into their heads. You look quite present-able without all that soot. We'll see in the morning how you ride. My lord needs a lightweight page to ride his second charger, and one who knows Greek will be useful. You had better eat with my servants; then the sergeants won't steal your food.'

Four days later, when we landed in Sicily, I had begun to know my way about the household. There were more than three hundred men, women and children, of different races and speaking different tongues. But all had one thing in common; they had been uprooted by war, and they looked to further, unending war to provide their daily bread. The lady Matilda was the daughter of a Lombard noble, who had been killed in the breach when his town fell to the Normans. Messer Roussel married her that evening, as I learned from her women; I suppose he hoped for her father's fief in dower, but Duke Robert gave it to another knight. She was content with her fate. Noble ladies are always wedded to strangers, and never, as maidens, marry the man of their choice; though occasionally as

7

widows they do; at least it was a great deal better than being raped by the whole army and then thrown out to starve. Messer Roussel was of high birth, a cadet of the Balliols of Normandy, and he treated her with as much courtesy as if she had brought him a rich fief. Her women were local peasants; Italian was their native language, but some of them knew a little Greek. The men were more of a mixture. There were three Norman knights and about fifty Norman sergeants, who had arrived a few months before to seek their fortunes in Italy; it was to enlist this band that the lady Matilda had crossed from Sicily. Some of the grooms were infidel slaves, there were half a dozen Sclavonian mercenaries who had deserted from the Catapan, and ten horse-archers who came from nobody knew where, because their language was incomprehensible and they did not appear to be either Christians or followers of Mahound; no one could give them orders, but then they would not have obeyed anyway; they were crafty scouts and kept their horses very fit. I suppose they were nomads from the Danube, but we just called them the Foreigners. There was also one Saracen sergeant, who had been baptised; he appeared devout, and possibly his was a genuine conversion; but we all took it for granted that he had abandoned the faith of his forefathers to escape from slavery, and despised him accordingly.

Italian was the common language of the band, as it was of all the Norman forces in Sicily. A Frenchman of the north can make himself understood in that language, and other strangers had to learn it or remain silent.

Those Normans who were getting on with the war, instead of fighting among themselves or pillaging the open country, were at that time blockading Palermo; and Messer Roussel de Balliol awaited us before the city. By the time we got there my status had been fixed. I was luckily born with good hands, and even bad-tempered horses go quietly when I ride them; I rode a spare warhorse and led another. All over the world the great social distinction is between those who ride and those who walk, and I was a horseman. The food was good, and my lady had given me an old pair of riding chausses and two blankets. She said nothing about wages, but I gradually discovered that no one in the expedition was paid; the plunder we might take would be divided in fixed shares, according to the military worth of each man, and until we won plunder we would get nothing.

That particular attack on Palermo was unsuccessful; the town did not become Christian until several years later. When we arrived the army was already discouraged, and the camp was as foul and uncomfortable as unwilling troops can make it. But naturally Messer Roussel wished to make a good impression on the warriors his lady had collected to join his banner. We found him under a gay awning, with his knights standing behind in full mail.

If Messer Roussel had not been the man he was my story would be very different. When I stood by my horses, on the left of the line, my first impression, and I am sure the impression of everyone else in the band, was that we had found a friend. His hair was a foxy red, which was why he was called Roussel; I believe he had been christened William, but the nickname was so firmly established that everyone knew him by it; his skin was by nature very fair, but the Italian sun had burned it to a fiery scarlet; it never turned brown, and his nose was always peeling, so that in a crowd of southerners he stood out as a Frank of the Franks; he was straight and supple, with broad shoulders and a narrow waist; not the type of beefy musclebound champion who wields a mace no other man can lift, but obviously a good horseman who would be formidable in battle; he was about forty years old, and his red beard and red hair were clipped for comfort under the hauberk, though the sun made his skin so tender that he would never have his chin shaved. So far he was just a gallant Norman, like many other Normans in the following of the fitzTancreds. It was the smile which spread from his lips to his eyes that made him at once the trusted comrade of every man under his command.

How can I describe that smile? It was very friendly, understanding, and a little mischievous, as though you had been up to something you ought not, and he knew all about it; but as he also had been misbehaving your secret was safe and he would back you if there was trouble. He seemed to welcome us, not merely as faithful warriors who must obey his commands in the field, but as confederates in an amusing enterprise.

After he had greeted his lady he stood while the warriors came up one by one to swear fealty. We have no other form by which we can promise to obey a leader, but I wish some Count or Duke would invent a less binding substitute; for the perjury which ensues must greatly increase the population of Hell. Homage, fealty and allegiance are very properly due to a lord who gives land to his follower; a man who by rebellion imperils his fief has some encouragement to remain loyal to his oath. But a hired soldier swearing lifelong fealty to a commander who offers him pay or plunder for the duration of the campaign swears what he knows to be false; and this makes it easier for him to break what is actually the vulgar meaning of the promise, by deserting without notice to a more liberal paymaster. Even the Romans, who so frequently rebel against the Emperor they have chosen, reproach us with this levity; they have a saying, 'the race of the Franks is unfaithful by nature', and it has enough truth to make it sting. But all these warriors who had been engaged for the siege of Palermo swore fealty, putting their joined hands between the hands of Messer Roussel; because that was the only way in which they could enter his service.

After first the knights, and then the Norman sergeants, and finally the foreigners who did not know the obligation they were undertaking, had knelt singly before their new lord and gone back to stand by their horses, Messer Roussel walked down the line to inspect mounts and equipment. I stood on the left, holding my two chargers, and I stiffened and bit my lip when I saw he would inspect these horses also. They were fit and clean, because I had tried very hard and I do know how to manage horses; but at an inspection every commander must find fault with something, just to keep his men on their toes, and so far Messer Roussel had made no complaints. I feared to be turned adrift in that lawless camp, or at best given a flogging and told to do better next time; just because it was unwise to anger a real warrior and yet discipline must be maintained. He halted before me, looked the horses up and down, and ran his hand over the flank to find if any dirt came away. Then he gathered a handful of loose skin, to judge the beast's condition, and turned on me that charming smile.

'You are a good horsemaster, young man,' he said in rather stumbling Italian, 'and I see from your chausses that you can ride. That is all a sergeant does, and I wish they could all do it so well. You carry a knife. That makes you a warrior. Why did you not swear fealty?'

He seemed to mean what he said; even if he was making fun of me it was in a friendly way. I answered in French:

'My lord, I have no mail. But one day I will be a rich sergeant.'

'Oh, you are a fellow-countryman? You must have set out young on the pilgrimage to St Michael. The way to get mail is to kill a hero and strip him of his arms, but I might lend you a sword until you win a better. Come, lad, do you wish to follow my banner?'

There, in front of everybody, holding up the whole parade, he held out his open hands for me to put my clasped hands between them. I flopped on my knees, and gave the oath which I kept so long as he lived. I have never sworn fealty to any other human creature, and when I made my vow as a laybrother it was only the second oath I have sworn.

When I rose he seemed about to pass on to inspect the baggage-train. But I feared he would forget me, and his steward would not give me the sword. 'My lord,' I said with a rush, 'I speak Greek and Italian as well as French, and I know enough metalwork to repair damaged mail. Let me join your household and look after your arms.'

'Why not, if you want to,' he answered very graciously. 'My page is dead of camp fever, and it will be useful to have a linguist always in my tent. Can you read? No? What a pity. But the hilt of this dagger has worked loose. Bring it to me tomorrow firm enough to trust my life to, and you can leave those horses and be my page. It would be wasteful to give you mail which you will outgrow in a year, but you should start practising with lance and shield. Now I'm busy. See you tomorrow.'

Many people, when they heard I spoke fluent Greek, inquired at once whether I could read, and regretted that I could not. But no one ever offered to teach me, and I could not pay for lessons. Now my Abbot says I am too old to learn. I am sorry. I would have had a much more interesting life as a young man if I could have been employed as a real envoy in Messer Roussel's complicated negotiations, and the choir-monks here seem to enjoy the psalms they read much more than we who learn a few prayers by rote.

For six years I served Messer Roussel in the bloody wars of Sicily. My lord was not himself an independent chief; he followed Roger fitzTancred, one of the six original Hautevilles, and a younger brother of Duke Robert the Weasel. But our band swore fealty only to Messer Roussel, and if he had wished to join another leader we would have followed him. You are familiar with the course of that slow and bitter conquest, in which we were finally successful after many setbacks and disappointments. My own dear lord once led a victorious charge when even Roger and the famous Serlo shrank from the throng of infidel horse who dared us to come on. But it was not the kind of war that will be remembered by posterity. There were too many hangings of hostages, broken oaths, and massacres of the defenceless, for a gallant knight to win immortal fame in it. I grew up in a tough school, but it did not make me a hardened scoundrel, as it might easily have done; it is nothing to be proud of, only the Grace of God for which I must always be thankful, that even by the winter of 1069, after I had seen so many ugly things, I could still be shocked by brazen wickedness.

I was then seventeen, and had risen to be chief page to my lord. I saw that his mail and weapons were in good order, though I did only simple repairs myself; but the armourer had to follow my instructions if there were new scales to be fitted to the mail or new rings to the hauberk. In battle I remained in the rear; I wore no mail, to spare my horse, but I carried sword and shield; for it might be my duty, if my lord was unhorsed in the mêlée, to ride through the enemy and see him safely mounted on my horse. Luckily that had never yet happened; Messer Roussel was a gallant knight, and several times his horse was killed under him; but his men always backed him up, and by the time I arrived there was never an enemy within reach. I slept at the door of my lord's tent and ate the remains of his dinner, which meant that I was better lodged and better fed than the common sergeants. It was a job with no future, for an unarmoured page cannot win fame in battle, and so knighthood and eventually a fief; but while it lasted my comfort was the envy of my comrades; and no youth of seventeen worries about a penniless old age.

But the great advantage, in my eyes, was the constant companionship of my master. Messer Roussel took his family on campaign, because there was nowhere in all Italy where he might leave them in safety. The lady Matilda had now borne him two sons and a daughter, real fair-haired Franks who would make handsome young corpses or rule great fiefs if they lived; there was a great household of men and women, from Lombard waiting-ladies of good birth to the infidel slaves who pitched the tents; and I, connected with weapons though not actually a warrior, had an honourable position in it. In an emergency I would do anything that had to be done, but in normal times no one ever asked me to wash dishes or gather fuel. I lived more softly than if I had finished my apprenticeship and become a skilled smith.

My lord had no secrets from anyone who spoke French; probably he would have been just as free with the infidel slaves if he could have spoken their language, so it was not really a compliment. But it was pleasant, all the same, to sit in a corner of the tent, polishing a helm, and listen while he discussed his plans with my lady and the knights. My lord and my lady were very good friends. They were both brave to recklessness, but with a saving common sense which showed them exactly what risks they were running; neither had a home to go back to, or any preference for one patch of ground over another, though they were determined to get hold of a fief somewhere and found an enduring house of fitzRoussel. My lord was very generous with his followers; he plundered with avidity, but scattered his treasure as soon as it was gathered. My lady was more careful, and that was the only subject on which they sometimes disagreed. Messer Roussel would say there was no point in heaping up gold in a land so ravaged by war that no merchant dared to bring luxuries for sale, and that if he was known to be wealthy someone would cut his throat for his goods. The lady Matilda answered that occasions sometimes arose when a mule-load of money would buy a way out of a tight place; but she was really thinking of the more settled conditions in which she had been brought up. Sometimes an infidel chief would offer to free a captive for ransom; but usually he did not keep his word; after the silver had been weighed out the captive would be hanged all the same, and the world would laugh at the simplicity of his family, who were now impoverished as well as bereaved.

The excuse for all our warfare was that we were rescuing Christian lands from the unbelievers, but religion did not in fact play a great part in our lives. Even in my youth I liked to hear Mass whenever I found myself in the company of a priest who had been silenced by excommunication; but there were not many of them about. It was fifteen years since Pope Leo had excommunicated the Patriarch of Constantinople, and since then many of the clergy had incurred the anathema from carelessness or ignorance; the clerks who wrote Messer Roussel's letters were often out of communion with both Rome and Constantinople. Sometimes our band halted near a cathedral or monastery on a feast day; then we would attend the principal Mass in state, to show which side we were on. I think the lady

Matilda believed nothing, and would have gone just as cheerfully to a ceremony of the infidels, from politeness or convenience; but Messer Roussel, though a sinner, would have faced martyrdom. He had been baptised, and he was not a deserter.

We were a very happy and united household. My lady saw that we did our work, and punished the lazy; but we were so fond of Messer Roussel that very little supervision was needed.

In Advent of the year 1069 we were wintering in Calabria, camped in a substantial stone-built village; though since it contained no manor-house my lord lodged in his handsome tent, which could be heated with braziers. One evening I was crouched in a corner, binding waxed thread round the hilt of a sword; in another corner the steward clicked his abacus as he divided our plunder into fair shares for the Christmas livery; an infidel groom had brought in a mare to give birth to her foal at the far end (the infidels always try to arrange that a warhorse shall be born in a human habitation; they say first impressions are important, and that a horse born in these conditions will be friendly to the human race); Ralph, my lord's seven-year-old son, was teaching his five-year-old sister how to hood a falcon, while little Osbert crawled on the floor and various servants hung about to tend the torches or separate the dogs when they began to fight. But otherwise there was no one in the tent except Messer Roussel and the lady Matilda. We were unusually private, and convenient to receive a messenger.

He came in a fortunate hour; for my lady was complaining that we were poorer this Christmas than we had been a year ago, and urging my lord to think of some new venture. Messer Roussel always listened to advice, and answered courteously. I put down my work to hear what he said, and he smiled to include me in the conversation.

'We have had a very bad year,' he began in his friendly voice. 'Not because this is a bad country to fight in, but because we share the misfortunes of a weak leader. Twelve years ago, when I made my pilgrimage to St Michael, the six sons of Tancred were on an equal footing; it was by chance that I swore to serve the lord Roger. But nowadays the Weasel has outdistanced his brothers; he takes all the profit of the land, and my lord must put up with his leavings.'

'Then you must leave Roger, and swear fealty to the Duke,' said my lady. 'Or gather more men and make war on all the fitzTancreds. They don't help one another, and you might set up your own County.'

'I don't like to desert poor old Roger, who has never done me harm. He is very unhappy to see his brother surpass him in everything, and it would break his heart if his own men joined the Weasel. I may go right away, to some other land; but if I stay in Italy I could not ride against Roger's banner in the field.'

'You could make yourself independent, without fighting him.'

'Perhaps, my dear. But where will I find an army? There are plenty of mongrel mercenaries, outcasts from every nation under Heaven, but brave Norman horsemen no longer make a pilgrimage to Monte Gargano. Every Norman who would rather fight than plough now crosses the Channel to serve Duke William in England. No, the Weasel is too strong to be overthrown, and too greedy to leave anything for his brothers. Would it be better to try our luck in England, where we must obey Duke William, or in Spain, where the infidels are powerful but there might be room for an independent County?'

Just then a sergeant came in, leading by the ear a dishevelled-looking man in a linen tunic. 'This fellow crept up to your tent and tried to wriggle under the flap, my lord. He says it was only to deliver a message in secret, and when I searched him I found no weapons. So I spared his life. Shall I sit him on the brazier? Then he would tell the truth, in few words.'

We all crowded closer, leaving our various occupations. If they were going to burn a spy until he told all he knew it would be a pity to miss the comical expression on his face at the beginning, before he screamed himself senseless. But Messer Roussel would have none of it.

'Let go of the poor brute,' he commanded. 'If everyone who

comes secretly is tortured to death I will never get warning of the plots of my enemies. I was not expecting a message, but people do in fact send them secretly, and the first of the series is bound to be a surprise. Here, you, drink up this wine, get over your fright, and then tell me your news, now, while I am alone.'

The messenger looked in surprise at the score of people in the tent, and I guessed he had been reared in Romania; for my mother had told me that where she came from even those of the middle sort, skilled craftsmen like her first husband, had a private room which strangers did not enter. She never got used to our Norman custom of doing everything amid a crowd of interested bystanders. But compared, say, to a Christmas drinking party, or a council of war, Messer Roussel was more or less alone.

'Noble lord,' the man said in stumbling Italian, with a Greek accent, 'I was told to deliver my message to you personally, and to make sure that the lord Roger brother of Robert did not hear it. But it is not very secret; your household may hear. The Emperor wishes to recruit Franks for his army, and he ordered the Catapan of Bari to send his letter to a suitable leader. The Catapan chose you, since you are already thinking of leaving Italy. Here are the letters. When your clerk has read this one, which is in Latin, I can explain more fully.'

'Well, that seems quite friendly,' my lord said with a flash of his charming smile. 'Roger fitzTancred would not like it if he knew that in Romania he is called nothing better than "brother of Robert"; but that is the only mistake you have made so far. Naturally the Catapan would know that I intend to leave Italy before I have made up my own mind; his spies tell him everything. This, I suppose, is the official letter from the Imperial Chancery. What a handsome bit of painting! Since no one here can decipher it I shall hang up all those gold-haloed saints as an ornament in some chapel. Master John, what do you make of the Latin version?' He threw it across to the steward, who puzzled over it for a few moments in silence.

'This is not a letter from the Imperial Chancery,' he said in the end. Of course a clerk does not as a rule read out a letter written in Latin, for a layman might not understand it; he paraphrases it in Italian or French, and you have to trust his honesty and intelligence to give you the right meaning. 'It purports to be sent by one Crispin the Bestiarius. Is that the man in charge of the Emperor's wild animals?'

I saw the chance to display my qualifications. If we were all going to Romania now was the time to remind them that I spoke Greek.

'Try "Vestiarius", Master John, an official of the Emperor's wardrobe. The Romans cannot distinguish between those two sounds.'

'That's it, of course,' the steward agreed. 'Crispin, some sort of courtier. He says they have a new Emperor, an experienced warrior who appreciates the worth of Frankish horse. Next summer they will campaign against the Patzinaks and he is authorised to take into pay a troop of three hundred well-equipped and well-mounted Franks, with rations but no pay for a reasonable proportion of followers. He would prefer to enlist an organised band, and he asks the Catapan of Bari to send his letter to a Norman knight with about the right number of men. Then follows a long passage about rates of pay, the oath they must take, and conditions of service in general. I can't tell you that off-hand. I must work it out on my abacus.'

'There you are, Matilda,' said my lord with a grin. 'Romania is a richer country than England or Spain, and once we are over the Adriatic I cannot find myself fighting Roger fitzTancred, to whom I swore fealty.'

'Besides,' my lady interrupted. 'Romania is a wide realm. If you go carefully you may win a fief far from the City, which would be practically independent.'

'That's as may be. I keep my oaths. We'll see when the time comes. Now take the messenger to the kitchen, young Roger, and see him well treated. If I accept I must work out some way of exchanging hostages with the Catapan. How all my friends would laugh if the Emperor hanged me as a brigand when I thought I was about to take service under his banner!'

So I missed the interesting free-for-all discussion which ended in Messer Roussel accepting the offer; but at the same time I was promoted to be a kind of confidential interpreter, trying to find out over a jug of wine what was in the minds of properly accredited envoys.

CHAPTER TWO

Romania

The Catapan was a senior commander, empowered to conclude agreements without reference to Constantinople. His official title was Catapan of Langobardia, which had once, before the sons of Tancred visited St Michael, included all Italy south of Rome. In 1069 he held nothing but the town of Bari, and two years later, while we were in Romania, even that fell and there were no more Catapans. We were only just in time to negotiate with the last Imperial official who had a staff of clerks able to write in both Latin and Greek. Nowadays you young pilgrims will find it much more difficult, for Latin is almost unknown in the great City.

By Christmas we had Roger fitzTancred's permission to leave Italy, and negotiations could begin openly. Messer Roger was probably glad to be rid of us, for Messer Roussel was now so popular that he might have ousted his lord from even his subordinate position under the Weasel. Our band camped in a fortified ruin a few miles from Bari, and the lady Matilda with her three children entered the town as hostages for our good faith; in return they sent us the sons of some prominent burgesses, for the Catapan was unmarried. My lady was a willing hostage; she liked to meet distinguished foreigners, and since her husband valued her she knew he would not imperil her life by a treacherous attack. The negotiations were concluded in three weeks, and on the second Sunday after Epiphany we entered the town of Bari to embark for Romania.

The agreement specified that for every two men, mounted

and in full mail, whom he could show to the paymaster, my lord would draw three gold pieces on the first day of each month; with half-pay for the sick or wounded who possessed horse and arms but were not at the moment fit for duty, up to a total of three hundred men and four hundred and fifty gold pieces. This, we were told, was a high rate in the Roman army; it should enable us to live like gentlemen. There would also be bread, meat and wine for a thousand persons all told, but no pay for anyone who lacked the full equipment of a Frankish warrior. So my lord discharged the javelin-men and horse-archers who had been our scouts and skirmishers in Sicily, and engaged a few more Norman sergeants; our women and servants easily made up the thousand, and in fact a number were weeded out, for the men hoped to pick up prettier girls in Romania. But the lady Matilda would not permit them to abandon wives who had been genuinely married before a priest; married women always stick together, and make it as hard as they can for any husband to evade his obligations.

I myself had no concubine. I won't pretend I remained a virgin until I entered religion, but I never met a woman whose face I wanted to see first thing in the morning every time I woke up; my lord's servants cooked for me and mended my clothes, and I was more at ease with my lady while I lived chastely.

It was taken for granted that I would go with Messer Roussel, for my knowledge of Greek would be very useful. But my lord, with his usual kindness, arranged that I should also draw pay. 'Young Roger,' he said to me one evening, 'when we are oversea I shall still want you to look after my weapons, though since western warhorses are scarce in Romania I cannot spare a second charger to wait behind the battleline. But the Emperor won't pay you unless you are armed. Would you like my spare armour? It's good mail, worth all of twelve gold pieces. Give me one gold piece a month and at the end of the year it is yours. You will still draw a gold piece every two months, which is more than your father ever earned at his forge.'

I was delighted to close with this generous offer. It is always difficult to get hold of good mail; no smith would spend months making such an elaborate piece of metalwork without a definite order, and even if you order it good smiths are busy men, and you may have to wait a year. That is why mail is usually got by stripping a dead man on the field, though probably it won't fit the new owner and may have an ugly hole in it. But we were to make war on men who did not wear armour of our fashion.

I had only three days for practice before we embarked, but I found I could ride in mail quite easily, once I was accustomed to the enormous weight above the waist which makes it unsafe to lean sideways out of the saddle. My father had taught me the warrior's way of riding; if I touched the reins with my right hand he made me get off and lead the horse home. In the Hippodrome of Constantinople I have seen acrobats perform feats that no Norman could accomplish; but they had nothing to do but ride, with one rein in each hand. A Frankish warrior is fixed in his seat by the high wooden guardboards on his saddle, his right hand holds the lance, and the weight of the shield hampers his left arm. He must control his horse with the finger-tips of one hand. The Romans admit that this style of riding is beyond them, and the highest compliment they can pay to one of their own nobles is to say he rides like a Frank. The fact that the Emperor was hiring us at such a high rate reminded us that we were, by universal consent, the best warriors in Christendom. We embarked for Romania determined to prove our value.

We sailed in Venetian ships by the short passage to Durazzo, because a long voyage means loss among the war-horses; though since Thessalonica was our destination we could have avoided a toilsome march by sailing the whole way. The country round Durazzo is very like Apulia, a little more mountainous and even more thoroughly harried, for masterless Sclavonians slip over the hills on foot and retreat with their plunder by ways no horseman can follow. All this district is very lightly attached to the Empire, and the Romans hold only the great road to Italy and the west.

My lord was nervous about entering the strong walls of Thessalonica. (They resemble in outline the walls of Rome, but are continually kept in repair; no vegetation grows in the cracks, and if a stone decays it is immediately replaced by a fresh one, cut to the right shape and set in good mortar. They look as steep and sharp as when they were first made; a strange sight to our eyes, accustomed to mighty buildings patched with clay and timber.) But my lady told him he must make up his mind, once and for all, that Romans were comrades to be trusted; or go back to Italy if he lacked courage to trust anyone at all. I was there and heard her say it. Not many ladies would dare to speak so to their lords, and most husbands would beat a wife for such frankness; but my lord has an easy temper and would always heed advice, no matter how strongly expressed; to my knowledge he never lifted his hand against my lady in all his wedded life. He laughed, saying she was quite right; but begged her never to appeal to his courage, or he would do something cowardly to show he was not a child who could be dared to pull the tail of a mule. We entered the city unarmed, and took up the quarters assigned to us.

The town of Thessalonica is unlike any place in the western world. It is crammed full of people, who live, without ploughing, by the practice of various crafts; on every day of the year it looks like a holy shrine on a feastday. At first I expected it to empty tomorrow, when the fair ended; but presently I discovered that the fair did not end, and that all these people were dwelling in their permanent homes. The other odd thing about it, and about all the towns of Romania, is the way money continually changes hands. My father was hardly ever paid cash for his ploughs; the peasants would split a tally with him, and at harvest discharge the debt in flour and wine. But everyone in Thessalonica goes shopping with a purse full of small coins. I don't mean that everyone is rich; the lower classes spend their little copper coins as fast as they earn them; but all this money floats about in the market-place, continually changing hands in a way to make you dizzy. At first some of our men grumbled;

when they explained who they were and promised to settle by Christmas the stallkeepers would not part with their goods, and that seemed a reflection on the honour of respectable Frankish sergeants. But we had been given one month's wages before we left Bari, so that with money in our purses we should not plunder friendly villages; we found that these magnificent gold coins, of very pure metal and all the same weight and size, went a very long way; for the Catapan spoke truth when he said our pay would keep us in comfort. It is the only gold in the world which bears Christian symbols; the Emperor of Romania is the only Christian prince who can afford to mint gold, and those other pieces, covered with squiggly marks, are struck by the chiefs of the infidels.

Thessalonica is not a place where Franks feel at home. There are foreign merchants in plenty, but they come from the unknown north; some are even heathen Lithuanians who journey south because they will not trade with their German neighbours; they speak no Frankish tongue, and the Christians among them follow the Greek rite. As for the Romans themselves, they never speak anything but Greek, and despise all foreigners who have not learned the only language in which civilised men can converse. Our people could not make themselves understood in the wine-shops, and sometimes got into trouble with the watch for wandering near forbidden parts of the fortifications. Of course I was all right, and some of our women knew enough Greek to haggle over a lettuce; but it was only because my lord kept good discipline that the first few days passed without a riot.

We landed on a Tuesday, and by Sunday the men were so discontented they refused to attend Mass, saying all the priests in the town were bloody Greek excommunicates. This was nonsense, as they knew very well. One Patriarch has been excommunicated, but he is dead and in Hell; the Eastern Church as a whole is not affected, and you young gentlemen must attend eastern Masses while you ride through their country. Luckily, Messer Roussel found a western church down by the harbour, where a Latin Mass was said for the Venetian sailors. The Romans build good seagoing ships, but they never voyage west of Corfu; ostensibly because they fear the pirates of the Adriatic, but really, I suspect, because the Emperor does not like his merchants to sail beyond the control of his tax-gatherers. Our band rode in state, but unarmed, to the Italian Mass; and that evening, since the horses were not fit after their journey, my lord went to sup with the Strategus of the Theme, to discuss the coming campaign.

Although there was business to be discussed this was also a party at which it was hoped we would make friends with our employers and allies. My lady came also, and the ten knights who were gentlemen by birth. I went as cupbearer to my lord; that is usually the work of a boy and I was rather big for it; but I was needed, because I could understand confidential asides which the official linguists did not choose to translate, and my lord told me, as tactfully as possible, that he did not think my manners and the natural awkwardness of my disposition would allow me to pass as a knight.

By this time we were all very puzzled about the composition of the Roman army, and the position of this Strategus of Hellas. In the force that was gathering there were other bands of mercenaries, Sclavonians and Patzinaks, though we were the only Franks; they served for gold as we did, and there was no mystery about them. But there were also native bands, horsemen who wore mail of a kind, though it was lighter than ours; they carried bows as well as swords. These sergeants, though they served their natural lord, lodged together in barracks and held no land; or if they did they must neglect it shockingly. The Strategus himself lived in the middle of the town, and we had seen his servants buying food in the market, as though he too were landless; which was absurd, for he was the equal of a Count. My lord told me to find out as much as I could, especially what made the sergeants live together all the year round and appear on parade every day; he might have asked these questions himself, but he thought that would seem too inquisitive.

The party was held in the great hall of the Strategus, a fine room with a vaulted roof and a floor patterned in precious marble. There are places like that in Italy, but all have been repeatedly sacked and burned; this hall stood exactly as its designer had planned it. There were long tables ranged on three sides of a square; about thirty guests sat on the outside, and waiters carried dishes and distributed wine on the inner side, without confusion or crowding. The more important guests had each his own cupbearer standing beside him, on the outside where in fact there was nothing for us to do. But we would be handy to carry messages if needed, and the real, though unacknowledged, reason for our presence was to guard our masters against assassination.

My lord had the place of honour on the right of the Strategus, who was named Nicephorus Bryennius. When everyone was talking loudly I chatted, under cover of the noise, with the cupbearer beside me. The lad answered readily, but with a slight accent, and when I mentioned it he said at once that Greek was not his native tongue. That introduced the first surprise of the evening. He told me, as though he were proud of it, that he was Russian by birth, and had been captured in childhood and sold into slavery; he had recently been promoted to be cupbearer to the Strategus, and evidently considered himself a personage, worthy to chat on a footing of equality with a freeborn Frank. As tactfully as possible I made some remark about the treatment of slaves in the Sicilian sulphur-mines; he took my point at once, for he was quick-witted, and explained that in Romania some slaves, at least, were as good socially as anyone. This was because there are strict laws for their protection; so strict, in fact, that if you want someone to do hard and unpleasant work it is cheaper to pay wages to a free man; thus no one makes a profit from the labour of slaves, and since they are nothing but a sign of the wealth and luxury of their masters they are treated as pets, even as friends. He clinched the argument by reminding me that he had been captured when he was seven years old, too young to defend himself; though he agreed that it would be dishonourable for a grown man to accept mercy and servitude.

Once he had put himself in the right he was eager to answer my questions. He was delighted to astonish a foreigner from the barbarous west. I first inquired about the ladies among the guests, for I remembered my mother had told me that in her home there were separate female apartments. She had been quite accurate, but I had misunderstood her; the Romans do not keep their ladies hidden away in the infidel manner. There was a Gynecaeum in this house, as in all respectable houses; but that meant a place whither ladies might retire if they wished to be alone; no one might enter it, but the ladies might come out whenever they wished.

By this time the party was going well. Neither my lord nor my lady were in the habit of getting drunk, except on occasions like Christmas when custom makes it practically obligatory; our knights also stayed sober, out of respect for their lord. But everyone took enough to be talkative, and the two or three linguists were busy translating toasts and banal expressions of goodwill; while the Chartularius of the Theme, a dignified old gentleman who sat on my lord's right, explained in Italian the plans the Strategus had made for the campaign. Even the Romans were enjoying themselves, for they do not habitually feast like Franks and to them the party was a rare treat; though they made a complicated business of their eating, for each held a pronged instrument in his left hand and used it to transfer small portions of meat to his mouth, never touching the food with his fingers. You can't really enjoy a meal if you eat in this finicky fashion; for one thing you can't get your mouth properly full; but undoubtedly it is a very courteous custom. After each course servants carried round bowls of scented water, but only the Franks needed to wash their hands thoroughly; the Roman ladies, and even some of the smart young men, dipped their fingers very gingerly; for their faces were painted in a rather

27

attractive, though startling, manner, and a drop of water on the cheek would have spoiled the effect. My lady's crimson nose and wind-cracked lips stood out in this dainty company, but I don't think it worried her.

Occasionally I leaned over my lord's chair as though to take a message, and listened to what was said. But each time the Chartularius was repeating in Italian exactly what the Strategus said in Greek; the interpreting seemed honest and there were no revealing asides. I continued my questioning of the slave who was my equal and companion.

I was anxious to clear up this business of great leaders who bought their food instead of growing it on their own land. I was polite, but I hinted that the Strategus could not be a very important person, since he lived in a town instead of on his own fief. This got the slave boasting about the glories of the house of Bryennius, which was what I had intended; he told me that the lord Nicephorus was head of his family, and owner of wide lands in the district of Adrianople; the Emperor never appointed a noble to rule the Theme where lay his own castle, for fear of rebellion. This was the first I had heard of the *appointment* of a Strategus; I had taken it for granted he inherited his place. I suggested that an Emperor who feared rebellion would choose men of low birth to serve him. The slave agreed that this might be true in theory, but said that the present ruler, the brave Romanus Diogenes, was a mighty warrior, beloved by all the army; he appointed great nobles, and the Bryennii were very noble indeed; 'not like some officers of the late Emperor Constantine, who weakened the army to please the Treasury'. This was interesting. To us in Italy, where half a dozen bands squabbled over the taxes of every village, the Empire of Romania seemed a very united realm, though we knew that if an Emperor misgoverned he was swiftly over-thrown. Here was a hint that there were two parties in the state. A civil war is more profitable to a mercenary than a straightfor-ward foreign campaign, because he can threaten to change sides unless his pay is increased. I determined to find out more about the recent history of the Empire; though not at this banquet, in case I aroused suspicion of my lord's fidelity.

I was still not at all sure the Strategus was really a great man by birth, since all servants exaggerate the importance of their masters to increase their own standing. I asked again how it was that a nobleman who held a great fief had to send to the market to buy mutton. The answer was a surprise; it appeared that the tenants of the lord Nicephorus paid a fixed sum of money every year, and held their land by that tenure only, without suit of court or any other service! So instead of getting ox-carts laden with his own provisions the Strategus received this money from his tenants, and used it to buy food, or anything else he needed, in whatever market was convenient.

In short, in the Empire of Romania everything is done by money; not only are the necessities of life always for sale in every town, but all obligations may be discharged by silver. I had stopped asking questions, but the boy was talkative, and kept on giving information until the end of the feast. He said there were thirty-eight Themes in the whole Empire, and some of those in Asia were very much greater than Hellas; and every sergeant, in every Theme, was a paid soldier, who remained with his band all the year round. Certain men, therefore, did nothing but drill and fight; and others did nothing but work and pay taxes, never fighting at all, though they were reckoned free. You young gentlemen, who perhaps never handle money from one year's end to another, must understand that in Romania you may meet respectable men who walk about unarmed and don't even keep a sword at home, but think themselves as good as you because they pay someone else to do their fighting for them.

When the party broke up, quite late but with everyone sober and Franks and Romans on very good terms, my lord and my lady made me sit on their bed and tell them what I had found out. As usual, they talked very freely before me. Messer Roussel assured my lady that the proposed campaign was nothing to worry about. The Patzinaks whom we were to fight were light horsemen armed with bows, who never dared to stand against even the Roman sergeants of the Themes. They live north of the Danube, and only invade the Empire as plunderers, never to conquer land and settle it. We would march north in a body as far as the great river; we would give those heathens a good fright, and perhaps catch a party who were slowed up by driving raided cattle. But there was no likelihood of a great battle; in any case a horseman can only use a very weak bow, since it must be short enough to clear his horse's withers when he draws it in the saddle; arrows from such bows would not penetrate Frankish mail.

'That is what you were told,' answered my lady. 'But if it is the whole truth, and these heathen raiders are contemptible foes, why has the Emperor hired us at such an expensive rate? Perhaps after you have grown accustomed to taking his orders he will send you to reinforce the Catapan. Then in spite of your precautions you will find yourself making war on Roger fitzTancred, unless you are recreant to your oath.'

'A sound point, my dear. It occurred to me also, but the Chartularius answered my suspicion before I could mention it. This campaign is a preliminary, to get us accustomed to working with Roman troops, and to scare the Patzinaks so that next year they will leave the northern frontier in peace. The Emperor is now on the border of infidel Syria; the eastern provinces are much richer and more important than the European Themes, and the Asiatic army is said to be stronger than the western. But they are bothered with a new foe, horse-archers like the Patzinaks but apparently braver and more numerous. These Turks are descended from certain devils who long ago were shut away behind a wall by a famous knight of those days called Alexander. A few years ago they found a way round their wall, and began to ravage eastern Romania. Next year the Emperor plans to march east, restore the plundered cities of Armenia, and deliver battle against the King of the Turks wherever he may catch up with him, if he has to chase him to the rim of the world. He will take us with him. So far everything is quite straightforward. But then the linguist became confidential, and rather hard to follow. He was obviously passing on a hint, but I am still not sure what it was about. Apparently, there is a Frankish band in the Army of Asia; it was led by that Crispin who dictated the letter I received in Italy. Who that is I don't know. The linguist could not tell me the name of his father or of the fief where he was born. It seems that the band of this Crispin made a nuisance of themselves by plundering a friendly countryside, and the Emperor thought of dismissing them. But Messer Crispin died suddenly, and now his men behave better. The Strategus was insistent that the linguist should tell me all about the unknown Crispin before he went on to say that next year, when we campaign in Asia, his men will be added to our band. Do they imagine he was some disreputable relative of the Balliols, that I should be interested in his death?'

'Perhaps they imagined all western knights are cousins,' I said, joining in the discussion as my lord always permitted.

'No, Roger,' said my lady with decision, 'this was not social gossip about births, marriages and deaths. These Romans never talk idly. If what they say seems pointless you must just think it over until you understand why they raised the subject. They told you the Emperor was annoyed because these troops ravaged the territory they were supposed to protect. That may be a warning that you must behave better, but surely you could have guessed it without being told. What else? Messer Crispin was not killed in battle, or by a riding accident; the normal ways in which death comes to a knight. He had a sudden disease of the stomach, and I suppose acute pain as well? Just so. And this happened immediately after he had vexed the Emperor by disregarding his orders. The man was poisoned by his own employers, because they dared not arrest him in the midst of his band. The story was told to remind you that even when you are at the head of the strongest force in the army they have means to keep you in order. Now you understand do you think it would be wiser to resign, and go back to Italy, where there is nothing but steel to fear?'

'Has no one ever been poisoned in Italy?' said my lord with a laugh. 'I agree with your interpretation, my dear, but the warning was hardly necessary. I shall earn my pay by fighting for the Emperor. Or circumstances may arise in which I fight against him. But whoever I fight for I shall not plunder the subjects of my paymaster. A mercenary who cannot be trusted to do his best is not worth hiring. So long as they supply me with these splendid golden coins I shall be loyal to Romania, and in my old age I hope to return home and build a really strong castle, that the Balliols may defy the Duke of Normandy and found an independent fief.'

My lord meant what he said. He had a reputation for fidelity. If Romanus Diogenes had enjoyed a long and prosperous reign we would have died in Normandy wealthy and respected, when we were too old for war. But then our story would be hardly worth telling.

'Anyway,' said my lady, 'that was a very enjoyable party. Tomorrow I shall start practising with one of those eating-prongs. Of course in the end we shall found a fief of our own; it would be disgraceful to die landless. But meanwhile I like sitting among those clean, smiling young men. Perhaps one day I shall learn enough of their language to talk gracefully at table as they do.'

In a few days we marched north, with the bands of the Theme and a body of Sclavonian mercenaries, miserable savages who use no mail and fight on foot with javelins; but in that country they were useful because they could skip over the mountains by ways where no one could take a horse. They cooked their own very queer meals apart, and we had few dealings with them. But we saw a lot of the regular sergeants of the Theme, since when we camped our horses were picketed with theirs, to economise guards. We had left behind us the Italian sailors of Thessalonica, and there was no Roman in the army, except the few official linguists, who spoke any tongue our men could understand. I was kept busy composing the numerous quarrels that arise when men feel they are doing more than their fair share of stable fatigues, and seeing that our horses were not neglected when forage was short. I got to know the junior officers of the Roman cavalry, who posted the guards and allotted the camping grounds; in fact I ate with them, because if I lay down by our cooking-fires I had to get up ten times in an hour to answer the familiar cry: 'Where's young Roger fitzOdo? This bloody Roman wants me to do something, but I can't make out whether that tool is for cutting grass or burying the dead.'

I could never make up my mind whether the sergeants of the Roman army were extremely well looked after, or savagely oppressed. The officers see they get their full rations, don't steal their pay, and send them to visit the physician if they appear to be suffering from disease; there is even a body of noncombatants attached to the train, who carry bandages and a flask of strong wine; their sole duty is to take wounded men, on their led horses, to the nearest surgeon; for this they receive a regular wage, sufficient to keep them without doing any other kind of work. The life of a trained horseman of the Themes is considered extremely valuable.

But in return he must put up with endless nagging. His safety depends on the good condition of his weapons, and that should be enough to induce him to keep them properly; but he is constantly inspected by someone in authority, who does not care whether his sword has a sharp edge so long as the blade shines. He must go to bed when the trumpets sound, and get up, leaving his bedding neatly rolled, at a very early hour; he must ask permission before leaving his quarters; and if he gets drunk, even off duty, he can be punished. This routine continues even if there is not a foe within a hundred miles.

So Roman sergeants get into the habit of obeying orders, and can be trusted to stay in their ranks, advancing and retiring as the trumpet signals or the officer commands. But though they never do less than their duty they never do anything more. A hostile champion may ride down the line shouting insults, and no Roman will offer to take him on; if the officers are killed the men retire, in good order, towards the nearest wine-casks; they have a custom of feigning sickness to dodge a ceremonial parade, and if some of the faint-hearted try the same game on the morning of a battle their comrades think none the worse of them. The regulations of the Emperor have made fighting a task, instead of the thrilling pastime it should be; as a task it is performed reluctantly, and a wise man stops when he has done his stint.

But I discovered that there was more in common between their system and ours than at first appeared; since land is the only thing really worth fighting for, any realm, even one that uses money as does the Empire of Romania, must in the long run allow the most fertile fields to come into the hands of the best warriors. Many troopers came from small farms which their fathers or brothers held free of tax, on condition one member of the family served continuously in the army. The soldiers drew pay as well, like every other soldier in the ranks, but if he deserted the land would be forfeit; there was no nonsense about going home after a fixed period of knight service.

The senior officers also drew pay, though they came from families of landowning gentry; but their estates were managed by hired bailiffs, since Romans do not care for country life. The clerks in charge of supplies were very lavish about feeding noncombatants; it was the settled policy of the Emperor to keep his soldiers fit for battle by allowing them numerous servants; certainly it is a great help to a mounted force, for a man who must feed and clean his own horse after the march can very seldom enjoy even an hour's leisure. Our three hundred warriors drew rations for a thousand mouths, which meant that every fighting man had a woman and a groom. There was no pinching over this, though the paymaster was strict that only genuine warriors should get those handsome gold pieces. The

Emperor of Romania was in those days a very generous employer.

The chief paymaster was not only a civilian and a clerk; he was a eunuch. We do not see this queer class in the west, though I need not explain their characteristics to young knights who are always telling smutty stories about the home life of the infidel. The only one I had met hitherto was at the storming of an infidel castle in Sicily. On that occasion a very fat and foolish-looking eunuch attempted to save his elderly mistress from insult; one of our grooms, revolted by his gross appearance, kicked him on the backside; he showed such abject fright that I gave him another kick to make him squeal louder, then my companions joined in, and in ten minutes the wretch was dead under our feet. I have always been ashamed of that unnecessary murder; for even eunuchs are God's children, though they have not been left as God made them. I was prepared to be civil to Basil the Protonotary, who must always be wincing under insulting reminders of the wrong that had been done to him.

Christian charity sometimes appears to be wasted, though that is no reason why you should not display it for the good of your own souls. Our paymaster was quite satisfied with his estate, and the Romans held him in honour. They told me that when we visited the City I would see numbers of well-dressed eunuchs; if I met one in the street I would be wise to stand aside and salute him, for probably he would have power to imprison friendless foreigners. Furthermore, they said our paymaster had not been mutilated by a slave-dealer. His own father, a poor cadet of the noble house of Ducas, had hired a fashionable surgeon to alter his son's constitution, that he might be the more fitted for a high position in the civil service. It was thought right that senior officials of the Treasury, and even, disgusting though this seems to us, Bishops and other dignitaries of God's Church, should have minds undistracted by the lusts of the flesh. Also they would have no families to support, and therefore would be the less tempted to seek bribes. (Here the Romans are wrong; eunuchs are notoriously avaricious.)

The officers also described another class of these half-men; of very high birth and considerable fortune they dwell in fine houses in the great city, amusing themselves by writing poetry and painting pictures. It is their high birth which is the cause of their disability, for they are inconvenient and ambitious relatives of the Emperor, or dangerous heirs of a former Imperial house. When I said it seemed harsh to mutilate a man for no crime, just because he was the son of a too noble father, they answered that on the contrary it proved the Imperial government was extremely merciful; in other countries pretenders to the throne suffered death, not a minor amputation which fitted them very well for a career in letters or the arts.

There is some force in this answer. Although the Romans obey canons drawn up by eunuch bishops, and pay the levies of eunuch tax-gatherers, of course they do not employ eunuchs in the army; and the chief function of the Emperor is to command the army which defends Christendom. The Imperial throne is often vacant and the Romans may find difficulty in choosing a suitable candidate, but so far they have never considered a eunuch.

These Romans are not in their private lives any more godly and righteous than Franks, though of course there are holy men among them, as among us. But their Emperors take the teachings of religion rather more seriously than do our western princes. They are extremely reluctant to inflict death, either on foes in war or on convicted criminals. The law lays down the death penalty for many crimes, but the actual punishment is nearly always commuted to blinding, with sometimes castration in addition; and on campaign they are all quite genuinely reluctant to fight a bloody battle if they can compel the retreat of the foe by other means. The effusion of blood is regarded as an evil, even though it be hostile blood.

They were well satisfied with our campaign of 1070. The barbarians fled before our mighty army; the provincials were delivered from raiders, and confirmed in their loyalty; but there was very little slaughter of the heathen. (By heathen I mean savages who worship miscellaneous idols; the followers of Mahound I call infidels.) We marched north-east, and soon linked up with the troops of the neighbouring Theme of Thrace. This is the most important Theme in Europe, and its Strategus should have commanded the whole force; but since our Strategus was head of the great house of Bryennius he was treated as equal commander. Even among the Romans, who lay down on paper all sorts of rules about precedence and seniority, a great noble receives respect and obedience, even though perhaps mere birth without other qualifications is not so highly regarded as in the west. But Nicephorus Bryennius was a good soldier as well as a great magnate.

Without any serious incident we marched right up to the great river; my lord impressed the Romans by riding down a chief of the Patzinaks who turned to fight when he could not get away; he was not a formidable antagonist, but the Roman troopers hung back when he faced us, and were glad that a Frank took up the challenge. They are brave enough when they have to be, but they fight without the inspiration of glory. Their holy men regard all warriors as bloodthirsty murderers; death in battle, even against the infidel, is considered a regrettable accident, not something for your sons to remember with pride. This chief wore a very rich belt of linked gold plates, wrought in the shape of deer and horses, which Messer Roussel gave to my lady.

We did not cross the river, although no hostile army gathered to dispute the passage. The Romans have no desire to conquer heathen barbarians, who must be baptised and taught Greek before they can be of value to the state. In those days they fought tenaciously in the east, to protect their Greek-speaking fellow-Christians; but in Europe they only wished to hold their cities; they would not undertake the difficult business of enslaving their nomad neighbours, whom they would then be compelled to protect from the even fiercer nomads who lived beyond them. We camped by the river, caught a few incautious raiders who tried to slip through our pickets, and in the autumn marched to join the great Army of Asia under the personal command of the Emperor.

CHAPTER THREE

The Politics of Romania

Ɛ

It is a long journey from the Danube to the great city, and we travelled slowly to spare the horses. It was Advent, and there had been flurries of snow, by the time we reached Constantinople. We had seen Thessalonica, and we had some idea of what to expect; but our first sight of that mighty metropolis filled us with awe, and, I must admit, some terror as well. As we marched over a rolling plain I made out, a long way ahead, a level horizontal scar across the landscape; it was so level and so long that it looked like a body of water, and I thought it must be the strait which hereabouts separates Europe from Asia. Then I heard a Roman trooper call to his comrade: 'There it is, Costa. If we reach the gates before they close you will see your grandmother tonight.'

'Show me the city,' I called. 'Is it on that shore?'

'What shore?' he answered. 'Those are the walls, the sacred walls of Constantine and Anthemius. They were built to keep out barbarians, but perhaps if you ask humbly the gatekeepers will let you enter.'

I have noticed that the sight of the great city has a bad effect on the manners of all Romans. They may have been talking to you quite politely, to show they are broadminded and don't despise fellow-Christians who have the misfortune to be mere Franks; but when they see those mighty walls they at once begin to boast of their invincible fortress, and of the hosts of Arabs, Avars and Russians who were foolish enough to lay siege to it and of course perished by thousands. But perhaps I would be just as proud if my forefathers had built such a superhuman fortification.

The odd thing is that, in another mood, they will placidly discuss whether it will be your sons, or some other barbarians, who will eventually batter a way in. Most things in this fallen world are destined to destruction, and the great city is no exception. It is engraved on the heart of every Roman that one day it will fall (unlike the true Rome, which will endure to the Day of Judgement). There are countless tales to this effect, but the most convincing is that a famous necromancer, Apollonius of Tyana, buried under the Column of Constantine the Great a list of all future Emperors, and the list is more than halfway completed. To my mind this unescapable future lends dignity to Roman warfare. It is more honourable to fight stubbornly in a lost battle than to charge, cheering, to fore-ordained victory. But I seem to have been led away from my story.

We were marching in company with the bands of Hellas, who were also to join the Emperor for the great campaign to the eastward. The Strategus of Thrace had been left in charge of the depleted garrison of Europe; but we had frightened the nomads of the Danube, and it was unlikely they would raid next year. When we were within two miles of the gates we could clearly make out those amazing defences, five miles long, three walls in depth; we dismounted to prepare for our ride through the streets. For us Franks that meant no more than wiping the mud off our shields and rubbing up our bridles; we wore full mail, but naturally we did not attempt to burnish all those little scales. But for the Roman sergeants it was quite a business to put on the right clothing, and even more difficult to make sure they were not wearing something forbidden by the regulations; every warrior likes to show a trophy taken from the foe, to prove he has really been in action, and many of them had muffled their ears with Patzinak fur-caps, or swathed their thighs in thick barbarian breeches. But the Emperor, who pays his soldiers all the year round and gives them horse and weapons, considers that in return for this paternal care he has the right to supervise their daily lives; what they should wear on parade is laid down in writing, and money is stopped from their pay if they cannot produce everything they should possess; while it is a grave offence to appear in civilian or barbarian apparel, even if the correct equipment is underneath.

Every sergeant must wear a leather corselet fortified with long but narrow plates of polished steel; this is nearly as strong as Frankish mail, but it only reaches his waist and elbows; on his head is a polished steel cap, but there is no hauberk and the corselet is cut low on the shoulders; this is comfortable in the heat of Asia, but it exposes a vital part of the body. On his feet are boots of soft leather reaching to the knee, easier to walk in than our pointed shoes and padded chausses; in fact a very sensible mode which some of our men copied. His legs above the knee are covered with thin woollen breeches, which are also comfortable on foot but allow the saddle to chafe on a long ride. His weapons are a long sword hanging from a baldric, a bow and a sheaf of arrows in a double quiver tied to the saddle, and a small round buckler. Officers carry no bow, but a very deadly iron mace hangs from the saddletree as a badge of rank, so that strange soldiers will recognise their authority. But I have not yet mentioned the most important part of their dress, which gives them more trouble than armour or weapons; each man *must* wear a coloured tuft of wool on his helmet, and a coloured cloak fluttering behind where it gathers mud and cannot keep him warm. Each band wears these things dyed in a uniform colour, and the effect as they wheel into line is undoubtedly impressive; but, as I said, they seem to collect all the mud or dust in the air, and they are never clean enough to satisfy the officers. If a man has brushed his cloak really clean, which is more work than grooming a horse, the officer will probably condemn it as too faded beside its neighbours.

You can see from all this that the prospect of riding through the city, under the eye of the Emperor, was more trying to our comrades than a skirmish with the Patzinaks.

Eventually the officers were satisfied that their men were as smart as they would ever be. I heard one say that since we had been in the field all summer the spectators would make allowances. But his companion replied that the Varangians of the Guard, who never left the cobblestones of the city, spent eight hours a day polishing their axes and never made allowances for anybody.

It was still the grey daylight of a winter afternoon when we entered the Gate of Adrianople; for *seven miles* we rode through the wide straight streets of the incomparable city, while burgesses thronged the windows and the narrow pavements. Then the Roman soldiers were dismissed to the enormous barracks which lie round the great palace, but we Franks were ferried across the harbour and quartered in roomy stone-built barracks in the suburb of Galata. In those days it was not the policy of the Roman government to allow foreign mercenaries within the walls of the city; except the dismounted axemen of the Varangian Guard, who found sentries for the palace and did not march on campaign. These were Northmen from Russia, with a few English exiles who had fled from our Duke William, and the theory was that they made good sentries because they were brave warriors but at the same time too stupid to conspire against the Emperor. They look very fine, in gilded armour with masses of jewellery, and of course a dismounted axeman is well equipped to guard an inner door. They turned up their noses at the shabby state of our mail, and we regarded them with awe, for they were reputed invincible. When I heard, a few years ago, that the first time they took the field they were utterly defeated outside Durazzo by our Count Bohemund I had to remind myself pretty sharply that I am a monk, who may never rejoice in the death of Christian men.

We lived comfortably in our barracks; our rations were provided punctually and in full, for the Emperor employs a number of honest and competent clerks in his Treasury, who see that his money does not trickle away in commissions and bribes; these clerks never draw the sword, but they contribute greatly to the strength of the State.

As I said earlier, the Romans do not like their merchants to sail to foreign ports where there is no Roman tax-gatherer; yet the city is the centre of the Christian world, and churches in Denmark and Ireland must get their altar-furniture from its workshops. These luxuries are brought westward by Italian sailors, so there is a large Italian colony by the harbour; of course they need a church of the Latin rite, and provosts from their home towns to settle disputes when they cheat one another. Nobody feels safe shut in by the walls of a foreign city; the Italians live together in the suburb of Galata. We found a good Frankish armourer, and since there were also Frankish wineshops and brothels our men had no occasion to cross the harbour and enter the city.

When we arrived the Emperor was in his palace, but soon afterwards he returned to his army, far eastwards in Asia. We were to follow when the grass grew in spring, and in summer we would chase the infidel Turks over the rim of the world. But one of our knights, who went to stare at the great Church of the Holy Wisdom, noticed that the guard on the palace was still at full strength; someone else saw a purple litter in one of the main streets; my lord was puzzled, and when he inquired the local Italians told him there were *two* Emperors of the Romans, or rather two and a half, for the Empress-mother also enjoyed great power. This second Emperor and his mother never left the city.

My lord was not very interested. This was just another queer custom in a land of queer customs. But my lady, who always frowned if someone said 'Bloody foreigners, no telling how they will behave', thought the situation should be investigated. One evening, when I was explaining to my lord that the armourer demanded high wages because in this great city money did not go very far, she took me up.

'In this great city, indeed,' she said crossly. 'What the Hell do you or any of these bumpkins know about the city? We have been here six weeks, but we have seen nothing except the Hippodrome and Holy Wisdom. Our Emperor, the one who

43

pays us, may have fled because his colleagues sought to slay him; or the people may be about to revolt, as we know they do sometimes. We eat Roman meat and drink Roman wine, and allow these Romans to wander all over our quarters where they could cut our throats any day, and we none of us have the faintest idea of what goes on in a Roman head. We should bar off part of the barracks and make it into a private castle.'

'What's that?' said my lord, smiling cheerfully; my lady expressed herself strongly, as usual, but as usual she spoke wisely. 'You told me, my dear, outside Thessalonica, to make up my mind once and for all to trust these Romans. Why have you altered your opinion?'

'Because I have two sons and a daughter, too young to defend themselves or to run away. The soldiers who follow Bryennius are certainly our comrades, but there may be others who think differently.'

'That is true. Within a few miles of this barracks are hundreds of thousands of Romans, and it would be odd if they were all agreed on every question. There have been conspiracies in the past, and there may be one brewing now; but I have made up my mind to keep out of plots in this strange country. Otherwise the plotters may persuade the Frankish mercenaries to do all the killing, and then leave them to carry back the empty pitcher.' (This was a slang expression, current among our sergeants.)

'But we ought to know more,' my lady persisted. 'Can't you pay a Roman officer to tell us what they think of the Emperor, or send spies to hear the gossip in the taverns?'

'That's no good, my dear. The informer could tell us anything he chose, since there would be no checking his story. As to sending spies, who can we send? Young Roger, you at least speak the language. Could you pass for a native Roman?'

'No, my lord,' I answered regretfully. 'I can't manage their fiddling little eating-prongs, and most Romans who dress as well as I do can read and write.'

'You must be observant, or you would not have noticed so

44

much,' said my lord with his usual kindness. 'But I agree that you could not pass as a Roman. Language isn't everything. What marks a man as a stranger are all sorts of little personal habits, how he handles his money, what he stares at in the street. But at least you can overhear what they say. You could go out openly, as a young Frank who happens to speak some Greek, and chat in a wineshop about the present state of the country. You will not learn any secrets, but they would tell you the news.'

'Someone with a sense of humour might tell him very startling news,' my lady objected.

'I have a better idea,' I said. 'I make my confession once a fortnight. Next Saturday I shall go to Holy Wisdom and find a Greek father to shrive me. Give me two pieces of gold for an offering, and I will chat with the priest afterwards.'

My lady agreed. We would not learn more than was known to any porter at the docks, but at least we would no longer be stumbling through a completely unknown world. And a priest who had just absolved me would not fill me with a lot of nonsense as a practical joke.

So on Saturday I rode three miles through packed streets to the Church of Holy Wisdom, (a very remarkable building, but you will all see it next summer, if God wills, and I spare you a description). After I had been shriven I took my confessor aside and offered a gold piece for the altar. I kept the second piece; that was not dishonest; my lord knew I would, otherwise I would not have asked for two; my inquiries deserved a reward, and often it is more tactful to take your reward than to demand it. Then I sat down with the priest in the porch of the church, where you can see the Hippodrome and the palace and the beginning of Coppersmith's Street, the finest view in that city of fine views; and he told me as much of the recent history of the Empire as a foreigner could understand.

This was what I told my lord that same evening: the great weakness of the Roman Empire was the lack of a rule of succession. When an Emperor died, in theory his successor was appointed by the Senate and Army; if he left a grown son there need be no argument, and in fact any relative of the Imperial house had a fairly strong claim. But sometimes, in fact much too often, the commanders of different armies fought among themselves for power. This was seen to be a disadvantage, and to avoid it they had hit on the device of appointing a co-Emperor, who did not rule, but arranged an orderly succession when his senior partner died. This co-Emperor might be a child, or even a woman. At present the Romans had both. The last Emperor, Constantine Ducas, had left a young son, who now reigned as the Emperor Michael though he was too young to rule. His mother, the Empress Eudocia, had very sensibly married the most dangerous potential usurper, the Domestic of the Schools or commander of the guard, our paymaster Romanus Diogenes. So he held, by right of his wife, a pretty strong title; but young Michael Ducas would one day claim the throne in right of his father. If both Emperors lived there would probably be civil war in about ten years.

But the situation was even more complicated. There were, as I had surmised at Thessalonica, two parties in the state. The army of regular sergeants was extremely expensive. The great nobles, who held high command in it and saw their estates protected from barbarians, thought it worth the expense. But the clerks of the Treasury, and those citizens who never saw a raider, complained that the country was ruined by high taxes. Constantine Ducas had listened to the clerks and reduced the army; but *his* predecessor, the Emperor Isaac Comnenus, had been a great soldier, beloved by the army; he had abdicated to enter religion, and he left no sons; but the soldiers hoped that one day his young nephews would attain power and make those greedy merchants pay up. Meanwhile Romanus Diogenes, to whom we had given our fealty, must soon win a great victory to secure his position; for though he was himself a good soldier he represented the taxpayers' party, and his underpaid army was discontented.

My lord tried to follow the outlandish names, and then

summed up: 'Don't puzzle my poor brains with a soldiers' party and a taxpayers' party. There are no peaceful taxpayers in Balliol. The house of Ducas holds the Empire, the house of Comnenus held it once and hopes to hold it again; like Carolingians and Capetians in France in the old days. My own lord, the present Emperor, is guardian of the Ducas heir. I suppose that puts him on the Ducas side, at least until young Michael comes of age. I shall follow his banner. I don't understand these people well enough to meddle in their politics. If they start a civil war I may demand higher pay as the price of not changing sides, but I shall not carry the threat into effect. A mercenary who sells himself to the enemy is usually betrayed by his new employer, with the applause of every honest man.'

'That is wise,' said my lady. 'It is better to take the honourable course, so long as you don't really lose by it. But there is one thing I don't understand. If our Emperor represents the house of Ducas, which is supported by the Treasury, and the merchants, why must he win a great victory to make his throne secure?'

'The priest explained that,' I answered. 'The late Emperor Constantine might reduce the army because he did not live among his soldiers. The Strategi of the Themes held the frontiers and the Emperor sat in his city and did justice. But these new barbarians, the Turks, have broken the eastern frontier; the Emperor must lend his army against them, and unless he proves himself a good general the soldiers may set up another commander. Besides, he is not himself a Ducas; the citizens support him, but only until young Michael comes of age. He must make a great name in the next ten years, or he will be compelled to enter religion like his predecessor Isaac Comnenus.'

'Ah, there is our weakness,' the lady Matilda said quickly. 'We follow the Emperor in possession, the wisest course for strangers. But he is only a temporary Regent, who must win a victory to secure his power. Leaders who *must* win a victory sometimes lead very desperate charges.'

47

'Very well, my dear,' said my lord. 'Before you remind me that I am responsible for the safety of three little Balliols I promise of my own free will to look very carefully before I follow the Emperor into the thick of the foe.'

'I wish you would,' she said, smiling at him. 'But that red hair of yours gets into your eyes when you hear the war-cry. Have you ever taken a pull at the reins when the foe rode to meet you?'

'Once, sweetheart, in Sicily, when Roger fitzTancred set the example.'

'Exactly. Then you halted for ten whole minutes, while the leaders were discussing the best line of retreat. When you charged alone the infidels fled. But don't think you can do it every time you try.'

I wandered away to a corner of the room. My lady was no longer talking politics, she was making love to her husband. Messer Roussel was proud of that charge, which was in fact a very gallant feat of arms; whenever he was depressed by the knowledge that he was only a mercenary, who must kill his lord's enemies without inquiring into the rights of the quarrel, he would comfort himself by recalling that once he had been a knight-errant, fighting the infidel for the love of God. My lady reminded him whenever she wished to cheer his spirits. She loved him, which was understandable, though unusual between husband and wife; for no one could know Messer Roussel without loving him. What was strange was that he in return loved his large, masculine, sunburned wife. I think it had begun as a punctilio of honour, when he was disappointed of the Lombard town which should have been her dower; she was his lady and the mother of his children; he thought it unknightly to let the world see he had married her only to get possession of a fortress; he had to pretend affection, and then, because although she was plain she had wit, good manners, and a sense of honour, in time the pretence had become reality. Now the battered adventurers cooed to one another like two adulterers, not a wedded man and wife.

Presently Messer Roussel called me. 'Come here, young Roger, we are not telling secrets. Matilda is set on finding out more about our Emperor, and she wants us to pay social calls on Roman gentlemen! You must do all the talking, unless I ask the Treasury to lend me an official linguist. Do you think we shall be received as friends, and will it be very boring if we are?'

'Surely they will receive us,' said my lady. 'We are not used to people like them, but they are used to people like us. There is always a leader of the Emperor's Franks. There was that Crispin who invited us and got himself poisoned, and before that there was a Messer Hervé.'

'My lady is right,' I said. 'The paymaster told me that they will soon appoint you Frankopole, commander of the Franks. It is an official post, carrying the rank of Vestiarius, if you should want to see the Emperor wear his crown in state. There is rather a large fee to the clerk who draws the patent, but a Vestiarius receives a salary, which pays for it in a few years. You should accept, my lord.'

'Of course you should,' added my lady. 'As Frankopole and Vestiarius you will have a place in the official table of precedence; that may not interest you, but I should like it. In the end they may give us a castle; then we can found a noble house out here, and invite the other Balliols to join us; a much safer way of rising to independence than fighting the Duke of Normandy.'

'Very well,' said my lord. 'Tomorrow the three of us will put on our best clothes and go visiting.'

The Romans have a system whereby acquaintances gather to eat and drink in one another's houses. These parties are not like our Frankish feasts, given by a great man to his dependents; they are gatherings of equals, and though there is dainty food and rare wine no one settles down to cram his belly in silence, or drinks until he is carried off to bed; the company meet to exchange opinions – usually about theology or literature – topics which fascinate all educated Romans; but sometimes, if their fellow guests can be trusted, they talk politics as well. You indicate that you would like to be invited to these parties by making a round of visits, calling at the front door of a great mansion, sending in your name by the porter, and perhaps entering to salute the owner if he is at leisure to receive you; but you only stay long enough for a cup of wine and a formal salutation. If the host approves the bearing and repute of his visitor, in a few days he will send a written invitation to supper.

As a matter of fact Romans get on worse with Franks than with any other foreigners, because we do not reverence their civilisation wholeheartedly; in some things we are superior, we ride better and our monasteries keep a stricter rule; whereas a Sclavonian or a Patzinac naturally admires everything he sees. And I am afraid we have a bad reputation for being drunk and quarrelsome. But it was known that my lord would soon receive his patent of Vestiarius, and if he was good enough to attend the Emperor he was good enough for any company. No porter rebuffed us, though the only great man who actually invited us to supper was our old commander, Nicephorus Bryennius.

My lord decided to do the thing in style, and hired closed litters. February is a wet and windy month in the city, and Romans do not normally ride in their best clothes; of course in that huge place the distances are too great for walking, and the porter would despise guests who arrived on foot. Some of our knights watched us start, and naturally they passed a few remarks when Messer Roussel climbed into a litter, like a pregnant woman or a gouty Bishop. But my lord answered cheerfully: 'I would rather be laughed at by my comrades than mocked by the rabble as a nomad barbarian who can't get unstuck from his horse. That is what they would call after me if I rode to a party.'

We were dressed very magnificently, for our pay continued all the winter and we had more money than we could spend. Matilda wore the trailing silk gown of a Roman lady, the heavy embroidered kerchief, and a silver coronet set with imitation pearls on top. Since she could not look beautiful, she said, she would at least look dignified. In fact she looked rather odd; her fierce nose emerging from the silk kerchief made her resemble a warrior disguised as a nun. But our hosts took it for granted that all female barbarians looked odd, and they were pleased that a foreigner should try to copy their costume.

I wore a tunic and close-fitting chausses of fine scarlet cloth; my lady lent me her gold Patzinak belt to carry the dagger and towel that marked my office of cupbearer, and one of the women of our band had set my hair in curls with a hot iron. I looked very dashing, but not in the least like a Roman.

My lord had intended to wear complete Roman dress, but he balked at the last minute. His embroidered robe came down to his feet, on which were boots of soft green leather; but when he tried on the towering Roman head-dress, a foot high and nearly as broad at the top, he found that in such an outfit he could not bend his head to eat; instead he wore a little cap of red cloth, with a ruby dangling on his brow. This marked him as a foreigner, among those stately Romans whose tall gauze mitres swayed and bent like flowers in the wind; but short-haired Franks look ridiculous in Roman mitres, which need flowing locks to carry them off; and of course no Frank who wears a hauberk can grow his hair long.

The lord Nicephorus had assembled about a dozen guests to meet us, chiefly senior officers and their elderly wives. There were no pretty girls, which was in one way a pity; but it made things easier for me as interpreter, since it is a great nuisance if something you say to a young lady, out of politeness, is taken as undue familiarity. No one could imagine my lord was being too gallant to these matrons.

Ladies and gentlemen sat alternately at the supper table, and I took position behind my lord, as a cupbearer should. But apparently it was not correct to bring a cupbearer to a friendly informal supper. The lord Nicephorus told me with a smile that I must consider myself a real linguist; he ordered his servants to fetch another chair, and I sat at the foot of the table.

An elderly veteran who had served the Catapan had been found to sit next to my lady; he spoke a little Italian, and they made laborious conversations about the weather and the public buildings of the city. My lord was not so lucky; his two old ladies talked across him, chiefly about hairdressers and popular preachers, while he ate in silence. But Messer Roussel was a man of great self-possession, and he was not abashed by what must have been a trying ordeal. Nobody spoke to me; I was only an upper servant, and my neighbour, who had the lowest place among the invited guests, was naturally more on his dignity than a great man like Bryennius.

I could understand the talk, but it was not very interesting; chiefly about the failings of other officers, and the curious decisions of the clerks who arranged postings and promotions. After a short meal, with very little wine, we moved to another room; my lady's partner stood at a lectern, reading aloud from a book he had just written concerning the Italian campaigns of the famous Maniakes. Our host went straight to a little table in the corner, and beckoned my lord to join him. Then he called to me: 'Young man, there is no formality in my library. Bring a stool and sit by the noble Frankopole. We won't listen to the wars of Maniakes. He fought against the Franks, which makes it an awkward subject. I want you to tell your master in Italian exactly what I say in Greek. That isn't easy, even when you know both languages. So take your time and make sure you get it right.'

'Now, sir,' he began, 'I command the bands of Europe in our great campaign to the eastward, and I want to know all about your Franks. Are they skilled in siegecraft?' and so on, a technical discussion which I will not relate in full. I had no difficulty with the translation; the two leaders were talking seriously on a subject I understood, and that is always easy to render into another tongue; it is when great men make meaningless conversation, full of delicate nuances of friendship, that a linguist needs all his skill.

These Roman officers study the military art very seriously; as juniors they undergo a thorough training in the correct system of tactics for each branch of the service, heavy lancers, light horse, mailed infantry, and skirmishers on foot; there are books on these subjects, and they read them in their spare time, since every Roman gentleman, and many common soldiers, can read and write fluently without making hard work of it. The lord Nicephorus soon grasped the strong and weak points of Frankish knights, and summed up:

'You can ride down any horsemen in the world, and of course any foot who should dare to stand against you. But those big-boned chargers of yours don't cover the ground as fast as light ponies, and the weight they bear tires them in a long skirmish. The Emperor must get you into position, with the foe up against some obstacle so they can't scatter and let you charge empty air; then you will win the battle. You agree, lord Frankopole? Unfortunately the Turks don't like fighting hand to hand; but now we know what to do we shall manage it.'

My lord nodded when I passed this on. He was getting bored with all this professional discussion; why spoil a good party, he muttered; they could talk it over later on, during the march.

He looked round the room. Most of the ladies were discussing absent friends; the men had gathered round the lecturer, moving little tokens about a map to represent the marches of the Italian campaign (in those days the Romans had not given up hope of reconquering Italy). My lord spoke quietly:

'That's enough tactics for a social evening. Now say this gently to the lord Nicephorus, but stop if you see it angers him. Why must the Emperor force a battle against those Turkish plunderers? Is it because his soldiers will rebel unless he gives them victory?'

I translated in a low voice, lest the company should overhear. But Bryennius listened calmly. He rose, took my lord by the arm, and walked out to the paved court that lay in the midst of the great rambling mansion; as they strolled arm in arm I dodged from side to side, translating as hard as I could.

'You probably know there are two parties in the state,' Nicephorus began, 'the Treasury officials who say the army is

53

too expensive, and the nobles who say it is too weak. This division would hamper any Emperor, for if he leads one faction the other will oppose him. But Romanus Diogenes is in a very unfortunate position; he has managed to incur the hostility of both sides at once. He is a soldier, so the taxpayers know he would like to increase the army. But he has not in fact increased it, for the Empress Eudocia, who raised him to the Purple, will not let him. So the soldiers are disappointed.'

'Then how the devil did he get to the top, the Purple as you call it, if nobody loves him?' asked my lord.

'Oh, the Ducates put him there, but they are beginning to change their minds. You see, if the Purple is hereditary we may be ruled by a fool or a weakling; if it isn't, the generals fight endless civil wars. So when Constantine Ducas died we all promised to obey whoever the Empress-mother chose as her second husband, and she took Romanus. But he is only a stopgap until young Michael comes of age. The Comneni lead the soldiers, the Treasury look to the Ducates. But the head of that faction is not the young co-Emperor, who is deficient in family feeling; the real leaders are the Caesar John Ducas, Michael's uncle, and his son Andronicus, second in command of the Army of Asia. That is a sign of weakness. Young Andronicus is too junior for such a post. But the Emperor is afraid to leave him behind, and a man of his birth must have an important command, or his family will make trouble.'

'I thought when we came here,' said my lord, 'that it was to serve the Empire of Romania. If I had known we were to follow Romanus Diogenes against the rest of the Romans and the Turks as well, I might have left my family safely in Italy.'

'Perhaps I paint too dark a picture. I was only answering your question,' Bryennius replied. 'When we have won our battle the Emperor will be supreme. Young Michael will experience a vocation for the life of religion, and may go blind if he delays. The Empress Eudocia will also take the veil, unless she dies of a sudden pain in the stomach. And you and I, my lord Frankopole, will be the trusted advisers of a mighty ruler.'

'All because we win one battle?'

'Yes, if it is a really famous victory. Romanus should be supreme, since the army is at his disposal. He isn't, because his men would not follow him against Comnenus or Ducas. But they would stab their own mothers if those were the orders of a soldier-Emperor who had cleansed the eastern Themes of those infidel Turks.'

'That is another point. Suppose when we meet the Turks *they* beat *us*?'

'Don't worry about that. I didn't think Franks were so cautious. The Turks are plunderers. There are a lot of them, and they move astonishingly fast. But whenever our bands catch up with them we ride straight through and out the other side. A Turk who lingers within reach of a Roman soldier is a dead Turk. We shall have a very long march before we corner them. But they have begun to make the mistake of garrisoning the cities they capture; that gives us a target to aim at. If they don't stand, and we chase them to the rim of the world, that will do just as well.'

'I understand. I am sorry about the long marches. My men are no use unless their horses are fit. There is one other thing. My wife will not ride with us. She wants to settle down and educate the children. But there may be trouble in the city. Would you mind if she passed the summer in your castle of Adrianople?'

'She would be welcome, but I don't advise it. No one lives in that castle except my bailiff. Why doesn't she board in a comfortable convent of nuns, here in the city? No rebel who depends on popular support would violate the enclosure of a convent. In fact we do not usually molest women and children if they take sanctuary. If we did there wouldn't be a noble family left in Romania, after all these rebellions and civil wars.'

So at last we knew where we stood, in this strange land, among people whose language and customs were unknown to us. The really important discovery, to Franks who regarded the Emperor of Romania as the most powerful monarch in the world, was that there were two great parties, and a number of noble houses, all attempting to seize the Purple by force. That night our orders arrived; we were to cross the Bosphorus on the Monday after Septuagesima. But before we set out there were serious discussions in our barracks by the Golden Horn.

It was gradually borne in upon me that the real leader of the Band of St Michael, as we called our company, was Matilda de Balliol. Messer Roussel was a very gallant knight; but he did not plan for the future, though he had a vague wish to end his life as ruler of a great fief, whether in Spain or Romania or the land of the Franks. My lady had made up her mind: she had been reared in Italy, the borderland between east and west, and after seeing both systems at work she was convinced that our Frankish way of life was better than anything the east could offer; we had only to show it to the peasants and burgesses of Romania, and they would be our faithful vassals.

'These people pay enormous taxes, and see their fellows condemned by judges appointed from the city; instead of fighting for the land they plough, and sitting on juries of equal peers,' she said to my lord one night. 'Let them see how they ought to live, and they will fight for you even against the Emperor whom they blasphemously call the Equal of the Apostles. It's a pity you told Bryennius we are not skilled in siegecraft; you stormed my father's town, or I should not be here. But if you capture some strong place you must install your own provost and introduce western customs. Then, without actually making war on Romania, you will find yourself lord of a rich town, merely because the burgesses are content with your rule.'

'My dear,' Messer Roussel answered gently, 'you must not preach treason among these knights who have sworn to obey me. You wouldn't like it if they set up another leader, or went off to found an independent band. For the present I am a mercenary, and a mercenary who will not fight for his paymaster is not worth the forage of his horses. Besides, for many centuries these people have been subject to Romania; they

56

often try to set up another Emperor, but for some reason I don't understand they all want to remain under the rule of the city.'

'I'm not saying you should betray your paymaster. Nothing lasting comes of that. But when the Emperor has won his battle the infidels must retreat, and the boundaries of Christendom will be enlarged. Out there in Armenia they don't like Romans; I know that. They will need a Christian ruler to protect them, and if you behave tactfully they may choose the house of Balliol. Young Ralph is eight, and it's time you looked out for a fief he can inherit.'

'Plenty of time for that. No one left me a fief. My father gave me arms, and food for three days; he said that if by the fourth day I had not won more I deserved to starve.'

'Ah, my dear Lord,' she said, with a loving smile which took all sting out of the reproach, 'you are a Norman pirate, and red-headed too, which makes it worse. I wish I could get you to see that you live more comfortably among your own fields than by laying waste those of your neighbours.'

'I haven't done badly so far,' my lord answered placidly. 'When I am too old to charge it will be time enough to look for a castle.'

But I knew that in the end he always followed my lady's advice. After we had fought our great battle, or marched to the eastern rim of the world, the Empire of Romania would have trouble with Messer Roussel de Balliol.

CHAPTER FOUR

The Eastern Rim of the World

The Themes of Europe contains rich towns, richer than any you will see in Italy; but the open country has been many times overrun by raiders. The Themes of western Asia, through which we marched to Imperial headquarters at Caesarea, were the heart of the Empire of Romania, and there was nothing like them anywhere in the world. As you young gentlemen rode south you will have admired the mighty buildings of Provence and Italy. No man of this degenerate age can build in that fashion, and it is all we can do to prop up, with beams and rubble, the carved stones that remain. But in Optimaton and Bucellarion, the inland Themes which were garrisoned by the Emperor's guard, the great heathen temples, the aqueducts stretching over hill and valley, the steep curtain-walls set with towers which surrounded every town, the paved roads bordered by stone gutters which ran straight as an arrow to some notch on the horizon, even the carved tombs as big as houses where great kings were laid who had died before the Incarnation, all stood as fresh and fair as when they were first designed, in the wicked but prosperous world which obeyed the great Caesar on the Palatine.

Even the open country was one great garden, the fields of each village joining those of the next. They were cultivated right up to their stone fences, and the drains and irrigation-channels of cut stone were clean and in good repair. The olives and vines were obviously of great age, but carefully pruned and tended. I describe what I saw less than thirty years ago, though you will not recognise the land from my description. But if you do your duty it will return to Christendom; it is a land worth fighting for.

We rode by easy stages along a smooth paved road, carried over the smallest stream by stone culverts strong enough to bear a loaded wagon; each night we camped in stone-faced barns, where prosperous peasants awaited us with forage and provisions. No one sought payment, for we rode on the Emperor's service.

Once as we topped a rise my lord drew rein and looked about him. 'See, Roger,' he said, 'twelve ploughs at work, and all drawn by fat oxen. The ricks stand unfenced and there are silver vessels in that chapel by the cross-roads. Peace reigns everywhere. This is a fairer land than Balliol, or any fief of the Franks. Yet the taxpaying slaves who till it never draw the sword. I shall teach them to live as free men, and one day the house of Balliol shall rival Comnenus or Ducas among the magnates of Romania.'

He had come round to my lady's point of view, as I knew he would sooner or later.

After three weeks we reached the great Army of Asia. In the Theme of Charsiana, of which Caesarea is the capital, we saw traces of the Turks. Last year there had been a confused campaign, unusually incoherent because the various Turkish bands were at war with one another as well as with the Empire. A Turkish chieftain, known to the Romans as Kiss of Gold, had rebelled against his sovereign; to escape punishment he led his men westward and ravaged the Theme of Sebaste; young Manuel Comnenus marched against him, but was captured in a skirmish. Meanwhile the King of the Turks had sent an army in pursuit of the rebels; Kiss of Gold changed sides in the inconsequent manner of these barbarians, put himself under the orders of his prisoner Manuel Comnenus, and offered to fight for the Emperor. No one trusted him, and the offer was refused; so he and his men took service with the King of Egypt, who was at war with the King of the Turks. Meanwhile the other

Turkish captain, seeing his prey had escaped, filled in the summer by sacking Iconium, and then, since he feared to return to his master unsuccessful, wintered in the snowbound Taurus. This leader was Afsin the Guardsman, who a few years before had sacked Amorium, hundreds of miles from the frontier in the peaceful Theme of Anatolikon. Yet the King of the Turks considered himself at peace with the Emperor, and envoys frequently passed from one court to the other. The politics of Romania is complicated and no Frank can understand them.

In those days the Turks rode swiftly, in fear of the Romans, and their passing did little damage. These infidels are extremely avaricious, and indifferent to bloodshed; they will cut a woman to pieces to strip off her ornaments, and they strangle any captive who cannot offer ransom; but they brought no wagons, and they dared not linger to waste the fields. The town of Caesarea was little damaged, though the inhabitants were poor.

The great Army of Asia was in itself a moving city. There were more than sixty thousand horse, lancers of the Imperial Guard, sergeants of the Themes, mesnies of great nobles, and mercenaries in Roman pay. With servants, artificers of the siege-train (there was one mighty ballista drawn by a hundred yoke of oxen), women, and the clerks of the Imperial House-hold, there were more than two hundred thousand mouths to be fed every day; and such was the wealth of the Empire, as yet hardly damaged by infidel raids, that food was always forthcom-ing in abundance.

My lord sent forward a linguist to announce his arrival. Almost at once, for the Romans do these things very efficiently, the man returned with another band of more than five hundred Franks. These were the followers of the late Crispin; all winter they had camped, leaderless, among the Imperial Guard, and they were extremely glad to swear fealty to a competent western chief; for they had been very frightened, isolated in a strange country and dreading that every morsel they ate would send them to join the late Frankopole. They were not such decent men as my lord's own followers, and they had allowed their horses to lose condition. But they soon settled down, and my lord smartened them up. We camped in great comfort on the left wing of the army.

Next morning my lord rode to the Emperor's tent to give his oath of fealty. Of course everything was done through an official linguist, but as Frankopole my lord was entitled to an escort, even in the presence of the Emperor, and he took me to make sure he was not committed to anything more than he said in French.

We set off with great anticipations. Every Italian child is brought up on wonderful tales of the Emperor of Romania; the golden trees swaying in the breeze, the golden nightingales that sing, and the golden lions that roar, while he sits on his throne to dazzle barbarian envoys. We were disappointed to find none of these things. The Emperor wore a magnificent crown and his embroidered robes gleamed in the lamplight; but he sat on a wooden chair, and his tent was no better than some I have seen in Sicily. My lord suspected the Romans might be tricking him into swearing fealty to some subordinate. He whispered to the linguist: 'Where are the golden lions?'

The clerk answered quite naturally, speaking at his ease, though the Emperor awaited us. 'Do those tales linger in the west? To see the lions and nightingales you should have come a century ago. In those times the Equal of the Apostles sat in his city, and the barbarians who gazed on his majesty withdrew peaceful and abashed. But this fallen world grows worse every year. Nowadays we choose as Autocrator the bravest soldier we can find, and in the field he lives as a warrior. Golden lions would not frighten the Turks. In fact when you have made your prostration and given your barbarian oath you will be permitted to seat yourself, in the Imperial presence, while we discuss the campaign.'

So it was. After we had touched the ground with our foreheads, in the Roman manner of saluting the Emperor, a priest brought forward a very holy picture, Our Lady of Blachernae; Messer Roussel gave oath on it, and the Emperor rose from his throne while my lord did fealty, putting his joined hands within the Imperial grasp. Then a table and stools were brought in, and half a dozen of the chief commanders sat with the Emperor. I stood behind my lord, though the official linguist translated.

To a stranger all these Roman officers look very much alike. They wear their hair and beards long, they are darker than Franks, and a common system of education and a common code of manners have given them a common cast of expression. The Emperor and his chief captains might have been cousins. Then I recalled that the Emperor was a noble like the rest of them. It brought home to me the weakness of his position; if the Empress Eudocia had chosen to marry another lord Romanus Diogenes would have been wearing one of those nodding gauze mitres and Bryennius or Palaeologus the pearls of the Imperial diadem.

The Emperor took pains to set us at ease, though of course the company waited for him to open the council. 'Gentlemen,' he began, while linguists whispered into the ears of the barbarian mercenaries, 'we are here to decide on measures to end these everlasting Turkish raids. Even Romania cannot keep sixty thousand horse in the field year after year without great oppression of the tax-payers, whose welfare is dear to our heart.' (Some captains looked a little sour at this excellent sentiment.) 'We must force the Turks to fight before autumn. Do you all agree?'

Bryennius interposed. 'Your majesty, the Turks will not meet this army. The ruler has no wish to fight us; the foe he hates is the King of Egypt. Can't we frighten him into sealing a treaty?'

The Emperor answered politely, as though to an equal. 'We have an excellent treaty at this moment; it defines our boundary, and the King of the Turks has ordered his followers to respect it. They keep the treaty as well as plundering nomads ever observe such an agreement. But every Turk who doesn't like him flees over our border, and he seems to be faced with constant rebellion. Kiss of Gold was a rebel, who thought the more damage he did the more eager would we be to pay him to fight on our side. He was disappointed, and I wish we could have hanged him; but young Comnenus got himself captured and I had to observe the terms which set him free. Other rebels will take the same road; at this moment Afsin the Guardsman is quartered in the barren Taurus, technically on our side of the frontier. We must frighten *all* the Turks, not merely their King. Joseph, you are a Turk. Do you think your cousins would meet us if we marched into Armenia and laid siege to Chliat?'

A Roman noble, just like the other Roman nobles, bobbed his head and replied. He was the famous Tarchaniotes, a Turk of good family who had been genuinely converted to the True Faith; he had served the Empire for many years, and he answered in fluent Greek.

'Your majesty, the Turks will be very reluctant to stand. Alp Arsian, their King, is now bickering with the Egyptian garrisons of Syria. But if you menace Chliat he must fight, for the Caliph has appointed him Sultan and protector of all the cities which acknowledge Baghdad. It is a sound plan. He must meet you.'

'For Heaven's sake, Romanus, if you intend to besiege Chliat, go there. Don't lead the army by forced marches all over Cilicia, turning aside at every rumour of Turkish raids, as you did last summer.'

I was astonished at such bold speech, for my mother had told me that the Emperor of Romania was obeyed in silence. But, like her stories of golden lions and nightingales, this information was out of date. When the Emperor replied I understood.

'Andronicus,' he said, 'it is just because that campaign wasn't good enough that I wish to fight a battle.'

So this sneering young man was Andronicus Ducas, cousin of the co-Emperor Michael, the magnate who was too powerful to be left at home. Well, at least he was eager for battle; though he must have great power if he dared to speak so to his Emperor.

Alyattes, Strategus of Cappadocia, raised a tactical objection. 'Your majesty, you can't lay siege to Chliat until you have taken Manzikert. The Turks may not fight there, but its walls are strong, and you may be held up most of the summer. You can't campaign among the mountains after the first snowfall; so this year will be wasted and next year we must reduce the army. The citizens cannot pay such a great host for more than one season.'

The Emperor was annoyed by this second objection. 'My intention is to march on Chliat,' he said firmly. 'But this army is strong enough to invest two little hilltowns at once. Manzikert lies on what will be our main line of supply, and we are too numerous to live off the country. But while we batter its walls we can send forward a detachment to blockade Chliat. When Manzikert falls we will bring up the siege-train, and Chliat will already be hungry. We shall capture both towns, and beat the Turks in open battle, all in this summer. We should be on our way home by Michaelmas. Any more questions?'

Young Ducas muttered: 'There he goes, just like last year! The Empire sweats blood to gather this great army, and then he divides it in the presence of the enemy!' The Emperor pretended not to hear, while the other Romans fidgeted uncomfortably. Of course the linguists did not translate this criticism, so my lord was unaware of the passing awkwardness. He spoke up, with that tiresome itch to make a point of his own which afflicts every member of a council of war:

'I don't know Armenia, but you talk of mountains. I must make it clear that my Franks are heavy cavalry, who need level ground for their charge. If I order it they will dismount to hold a wall, though that is not how they fight best. But they cannot scramble up hills on foot.'

'That will not arise, lord Frankopole' said Bryennius before the Emperor could answer. 'You never see a Turk without his shaggy pony. The story goes that their women ride also, and that when they make love the ponies trot side by side, while the riders do in the saddle everything that Christians do in bed. That may be an exaggeration, but you won't find Turks offering battle on foot.'

Someone laughed; there is nothing like a smutty remark to

end a conference on a note of good humour. Nobody had more to say, and the captains took leave of the Emperor.

That evening my lord talked things over with his knights. Everyone was pleased; the Emperor seemed to be a friendly warrior, instead of the unapproachable despot whom we had expected; and the plan of campaign was of the kind that appeals to every knight. We had heard so much about the scientific methods of Roman warfare that we had feared a boring summer of complicated counter-marching; but we were to invade the enemy's land, and challenge him to stop us, that is the Frankish way of waging war.

In a few days the great army marched north-east, up the valley of the upper Halys. We left behind the rich and peaceful lands of western Asia; the districts we passed through have been on the frontier since Mahound brought his devils out of the desert. There were no more prosperous farms in the valleys, no more wayside churches full of silver candlesticks; the land was ploughed, but the peasants lived on the hilltops. But a land of war is a land of warriors; the local barons brought their followers to the army at their own expense, as western knights serve for their fiefs. We Franks thought to ourselves that men who fight for hatred of the infidel, taking no pay for what is after all the elementary duty of every able-bodied Christian, must be more formidable than hired sergeants. But the Romans prefer drilled hirelings, who obey the trumpet from long practice on the parade-ground; they held it against these volunteers that they could not keep in line at full gallop, or change direction together. They were placed in the second division of the army, under young Andronicus Ducas. The drilled regulars formed the first division, under the immediate command of the Emperor.

Of course neither we nor the Turkish mercenaries were in either division. Joseph Tarchaniotes and Messer Roussel would obey any reasonable instructions that came from the Emperor himself; but neither Frankish knights nor Turkish light horse would carry out the orders of a young gentleman who thought that because someone had given him an officer's mace instead of a sergeant's bow he belonged to a different and superior branch of the human race. To prevent friction the mercenaries marched on the flank of the army.

We did not camp with the Turks, whose manners make it impossible for civilised men to associate with them. But we rode beside them on the march, and I spoke with the few who knew a little Greek. It was rather pleasant to talk to people who spoke worse Greek than I did. I had been puzzled that the Romans should take such a large contingent of mercenaries to fight against their own cousins; but I discovered they were not the same kind of Turk as our foes. The Romans call anyone a Turk who lives in the saddle and fights with a short horseman's bow; but such people dwell in all the lands of Magog that lie to the north and east of Christendom; they speak more or less the same language, and have the same customs; but they do not all serve the same lord. Our foes were called the Children of Seljuk; only a generation ago they had suddenly appeared over the unknown eastern rim of the world. Our mercenaries were Cumans from north of the Black Sea; for centuries they had traded with Romania, and they had some idea of civilisation. At home they were idolaters, but the Romans encouraged them to undergo baptism, since Our Lady of Blachernae could not be expected to aid a heathen army. They should have been very good Christians, for it is their custom to be baptised every time they re-enlist; the priests then give them the white robes of innocence, and they regard this as a valuable livery which it would be a pity to forgo just because they have received it already; some of them have been christened eight or ten times, but in a tight place they still call on the North Wind.

Their leader, Joseph Tarchaniotes, was a genuine convert, who had lived many years in the Empire without revisiting his home. I was told he could never go back, for he had shot his own grandfather out hunting and his family would impale him if he fell into their hands. Turks are never convinced by a hunting accident, especially if it is the heir who removes the owner of

67

numerous flocks. All the same, Joseph was an honourable knight; perhaps his grandfather really did look like a deer.

In the Theme of Colonea we left the headwaters of the Halys and marched due east by the southern branch of the upper Euphrates; all this land is so mountainous that our heavy train must keep to some valley. Here is the Theme of Mesopotamia, and to the east lie the principalities of Armenia, which used to pay tribute to the Empire and now pay tribute to the Turks. The Armenians are Christian, and we expected them to join us. But though they always tell you proudly that Armenia was the first kingdom to become Christian, a few years before Constantine saw in the sky the Cross in whose name he would conquer, they have fallen into heresy; I don't know exactly their error, or whether they have more than one; but both Pope and Patriarch are against it. The Emperor, therefore, has rightly forbidden these heretical practices within his dominions. But infidels take tribute from all who do not follow their false prophet and then allow them to worship God or the Devil, whichever they prefer; and this tribute is no more than the Emperor's taxes; so the Armenians would rather submit to the Turks, who do not close their churches, than obey the laws of the Empire. They did not join our army, and where they were strong enough they closed their gates against us.

We gathered a few recruits, for a minority among the Armenians follow the True Faith and look to the Emperor to protect them from persecution by their fellow-countrymen; but we had to leave large detachments guarding our line of supply, and on balance the army was weakened. In particular we could not scout the steep mountainsides; our whole army was mounted, and the Emperor had planned to raise local foot to picket the heights. In the latter part of our advance we marched blind, for our horse could only investigate the valleys and a hostile army might be just over the next ridge.

All these matters were discussed at frequent councils of war. It is a Roman custom to hold such councils, and the Emperor listened patiently to his senior officers; he had to keep the army

68

contented, for if the soldiers rebelled he would get no help from his supporters in the city, hundreds of miles away.

I told my lord, quite truthfully, that the Roman officers did not mind being completely out of touch with the Turks. We had invaded their land to provoke a battle, and it was for them to seek us out; they were horsemen like ourselves, and could not surprise us by charging down from a snowbound peak; if we met their whole force round the next corner of the valley, that was what we had come all this way to do.

By the second Sunday after Pentecost we lay before Manzikert, the first town where we could be sure of finding armed Turks. Like all these little towns in the war-torn March of Armenia it is very strongly fortified. The Emperor sent an envoy, offering to permit the garrison to depart unharmed if they would render the fortress; but they closed the gates against us.

It was interesting to watch our army preparing for the siege. Most Romans can read and write, and it is much easier to calculate if you can jot down figures than if you have to carry everything in your head. On the first day the engineers did nothing but ride round the walls, making notes on their tablets. On the second day all the followers of the baggage-train dug at once, in dozens of different places, and by the third day the lines of circumvallation were linked up, without gaps or awkward corners. That is the sort of work only Romans can accomplish.

The mercenaries were to ride forward to blockade Chliat while the engines battered the walls of Manzikert. But there was no hurry; for a few days we remained in the main camp. When the good news came I was lucky enough to hear it at first hand.

There was the usual council in the Emperor's tent, and I walked there with my lord. We did not expect an interesting meeting. There was nothing to be discussed while the army lay halted; but the Emperor had been reproached for not taking the advice of his officers during the futile Syrian campaign, and he was determined to give no opening for the same complaint this year. As we approached the standard which marked Imperial headquarters we both noticed that the common troopers seemed unusually pleased with themselves; outside the tent even the gilded Guardsmen of the Schools grinned and stuck up their thumbs, a Roman sign of victory; this annoyed my lord, for these sentries were supposed to hold themselves rigid, and by taking such a liberty they showed they did not consider the Frankopole a real officer. We guessed that the whole army had heard of a Christian victory; perhaps the Duke of Antioch had routed a band of plunderers.

The Romans often began their council without waiting for us, and my lord was apt to be late on purpose, to emphasise his dignity. But on this occasion the Emperor was just giving the formal greeting which opens the proceedings. My lord prostrated himself while Romanus was still speaking, to show he was as good as anyone in the tent; but Romans overlook bad manners in a Frank, rather contemptuously, because they think we could not be courteous if we tried. As my lord took his seat and the linguist came up to translate, the Emperor concluded: 'The Vestiarius Leo Dabatenus will address the council.'

The man who rose was a stranger. His long official robe was creased, and under it he wore riding-boots; but he was not a military courier; his smooth painted face and pendent stomach showed him to be a eunuch. He spoke in the high voice such creatures use, but slowly and distinctly, to allow the linguists to interpret, and I could follow all he said.

'Your majesty, my lords: I serve the Logothete of the Dromos, as accredited envoy to barbarians and linguist in Arabic and Turkish. About Septuagesima I was sent to the Sultan, to discuss a proposed rectification of the frontier. The negotiations are not important; the Sultan demanded recognition of his conquest of Manzikert, and my instructions forbade me to concede anything of the kind. But I was also instructed to remain near the Sultan, in case he offered submission when he heard of the approach of this mighty army; so I discussed ransoms, and the exchange of captives, and did not give a definite refusal. About Pentecost the Sultan lay before Aleppo, whose infidel ruler serves the Caliph of Egypt. The Sultan serves the Caliph of Baghdad, and his dearest wish is to destroy the rival Caliph and unite all the followers of Mahomet.' (The creature was a true pedant of the Dromos, and took great pains to call these filthy infidels by their correct titles.) 'While the Sultan battered Aleppo a courier arrived from the Beg of Chliat, telling of your majesty's advance. The Sultan summoned me to learn why there had been no declaration of war, and I explained that we were not at war with the Caliph of Baghdad. Your majesty merely wished to arrange for the administration of Chliat and Manzikert, which are part of the Roman dominions; if the brigands of those parts offered resistance that would be a breach of the treaty, and the Caliph would be the aggressor. The Sultan replied that he was the Sword of the Caliph, and that his Begs would resist. So Romania was at war with Baghdad. I prepared to leave the infidel camp, but the Turks moved before I could pack my baggage. Your majesty, their march was a frenzied flight. Everyone had heard of the great army of Romania, and thought only of putting the River Euphrates between himself and the just vengeance of the Emperor. They did not wait for ferryboats, they swam their horses and baggage across the stream; many were drowned, as I saw with my own eyes. The Sultan is a brave warrior, but his followers will not face the lancers of Romania. I rode here at once, to tell of the utter demoralisation of the Turks. Oh, and one other thing. On the way I heard that Afsin the Guardsman had broken up his camp on Taurus, and is marching east at full speed. Already the plundering infidels have begun their retreat to the rim of the world!'

When the eunuch had finished the whole council rose and acclaimed the Emperor. Wine was brought, and there was no more discussion. The mere rumour of our approach had already won the war.

Next day the Frankish and Turkish mercenaries rode past beleaguered Manzikert, a long day's march to Chliat, the next fortress. This is a very strong place, and our division, heavy mailed Franks and bowlegged Turkish horse-archers, had no means of harming its thick stone walls; but we camped two bowshots from the main gate, compelled the infidels to man the battlements without rest, and pillaged the neighbouring farms. Our food was brought up by pack-mule, since Manzikert blocked the only road by which wheels could pass; but the Romans are good at arranging convoys and we suffered no privations. We were the furthest advance guard of the Christian army, deep in the land of the infidel; but our stay before Chliat was an interval of rest after the long marches which had carried us to the edge of the Christian world.

Our Turkish allies lived apart, for they devour raw sheep in a way which revolted our sergeants. But Joseph Tarchaniotes dined with my lord, since he had lived many years among civilised men and even used a Roman eating-prong. Our knights dined in the same tent, and I was always present to interpret for the Turkopole.

Joseph was the only man in our army who thought we had advanced too far. He was always pointing out that we were not in contact with the enemy; if the Sultan was the wily leader he was said to be our first news of him might be of a counter-raid. Remember, he would say, the interior of Romania is defence-less; the whole regular army, and the mesnies of all the nobles, are gathered before Manzikert. But that did not worry Messer Roussel; Romania was not our land, and we did not care if it was ravaged.

For six weeks we remained in this pleasant situation. Then one day our horse-archers, who rode far afield in search of unravaged barns, reported strong bands of hostile Turks. They had exchanged arrows at long range, in their usual manner of fighting, and then fled at full gallop to avoid being surrounded. Their foes followed cautiously, and halted when they caught sight of our camp. While we discussed this a messenger rode in from the main army, a eunuch of the Dromos, very frightened and saddle-sore; he said he had been chased by a hostile patrol, though we were not sure he was telling the truth, for these eunuchs sometimes panic at sight of friendly mercenaries. He bore good news; Manzikert had capitulated, and tomorrow the Emperor would march on Chliat; though with his great siege-train he would be at least two days on the road we had traversed in one.

At dusk a band of infidels raided the stream from which we drew water; they cut down some women who were filling their pots, but did not meddle with the horse-guard who watered our animals farther downstream. Then they fled into the darkness, and pursuit was impossible; but our sergeants, especially those whose concubines had been slaughtered, felt angry and a little frightened. It had been a very neat raid, obviously planned by cool veterans. The Turks were not so demoralised as that silly Dabatenus believed.

Our camp was unfortified, and some knights suggested it would be a good idea to dig a trench. My lord pointed out that if we dismounted to hold a palisade we threw away the advantage of the irresistible Frankish charge; but he reassured the nervous by reminding us that the Emperor and his great army were only two marches away. We had made this long journey to provoke a battle, and we should be glad that at last the Turks had come to meet us.

The Turkopole was worried. He complained that these Seljuks, who spoke a language his Cumans could understand, had been calling out that the great Atabeg Alp Arsian, Sultan to the Caliph, welcomed all Turks and would lead them to rich plunder. Cumans are notoriously fickle, and they might accept the offer; though the real bother, as we saw it, was that neither we nor the regular Roman soldiers could distinguish between friendly Cumans and hostile Seljuks; for both were bundled up in sheepskin and dirty woollens, and rode in the distinctive Turkish manner with short stirrups and a long rein. We stood to our horses for most of the night, though the Turks who approached the camp always turned out to be Cumans.

No convoy arrived next day, and Messer Roussel put us on half rations. The Turks were scattered over the countryside, cleverly concealed in folds of the ground. They had the legs of us, and galloped away if we rode at them; but our patrols were continually shot at by an elusive foe who would not stand and fight. Our camp was a little island of safe ground amid a wide ocean of infidels.

We passed an uneasy night, sleeping in mail; which is like trying to sleep on a harrow. Under cover of darkness the enemy crept up and shouted to our Cumans, who answered in the same language. It sounded like an exchange of insults, but of course we could not understand; our allies might plot treachery at the top of their voices, so long as they called in a tone of anger. We could not send out our horses to graze, and we had very little forage; when that was finished we must feed them on our own barley-bread, or find ourselves afoot in the heart of the enemy's country.

Next day was the Assumption of Our Lady, which encouraged us; on that day the defenders of Christendom should be able to count on aid from Heaven. All morning we stood to our horses, watching the valley fill with scattered bands of Turks; they threw a convoy of provisions into blockaded Chliat, so our work of the last six weeks was wasted. Our Cumans held the open ground for half a mile round the camp, and the Turks never drew into one body to challenge us to battle; but nothing is more tiring than standing to arms without fighting. Messer Roussel put a brave front on it, but I could see he was worried; the Turkopole was more cheerful, for he told us that if his men had intended to change sides they would have done so last night; anyway, the main army should join us that evening.

But at sunset there was no sign of the Emperor; dustclouds hung over the level ground between the mountains, but they were as likely to mean Turkish ponies as Roman chargers; we looked for the twinkle of polished mail, since the infidels wear woollens even in battle; the valley ran straight for several miles, but we saw no friendly gleam. We had now fortified our camp with a trench; it was only big enough to stop a horse, since Turks never attack on foot, but it should give us a peaceful night; yet the sergeants grumbled that such toil was beneath the dignity of mailed horsemen.

That night my lord sat in his tent, talking to Joseph with me as linguist. About midnight he had a look at the weather, which was very dark. During the day a stray arrow had killed a child, and his mother was mourning him in a high-pitched wail that got on our nerves, though my lord was too kind to silence her. We were getting jumpy.

My lord flung himself crossly on his stool. 'This can't go on,' he grumbled. 'In a few days we shall all be too frightened to face the Sultan's mother-in-law on a donkey. Roger, ask the Turkopole if these blasted infidels fight well in the dark.'

Joseph answered without hesitation: 'There is nothing they dislike more. They fear ambush, and if they can't see to shoot they will certainly not charge.'

'I don't expect an attack,' said my lord. 'Men who make all that noise are not preparing to charge. The point is that on a dark night a horseman could gallop past them without being shot, and if they barred his way any Frank could ride them down. I must have news of the Emperor. He changes his plans on impulse, or so says young Andronicus. He may be marching on Antioch for all we know. Roger, I want you to ride back. We know Manzikert now has a Roman garrison, and if you start at once you should reach the gates at dawn. Will you try it? Say frankly if you think it too dangerous, and I shall get my clerk to write a despatch. A Cuman might get through unnoticed in daylight. But I would rather send the only man in the band who can understand my instructions and repeat them to a responsible Roman officer. Well?'

It was a very dangerous mission, the sort of thing no veteran undertakes; our sergeants had a proverb that they were paid to do their duty, but volunteers were always dead by payday. But I was young, and I loved Messer Roussel. I said I would go.

'Good lad,' said my lord. 'You shall ride my best horse. That's Whitefoot, isn't it? Charge straight into anyone who tries to stop you. Their arrows will miss in the dark. When you reach the Emperor, or the commandant of Manzikert, tell him this: Chliat has been revictualled and it is useless to continue the blockade. Our horses cannot graze and the men are getting hungry. Tomorrow is Tuesday, if no orders reach me I shall retire on Friday. I shall march north of west, not to bring these Turks against Manzikert, which must be weak after its battering. I shall send messengers to the cities of the north-eastern Themes. Mesopotamia, Colonea and Sebaste. Let the Emperor send my orders to any fortress in those parts and I shall obey as soon as I receive them. If there are no orders tell the commandant of Manzikert to send me news of the Emperor. He must be marching south-east, perhaps on Baghdad itself. These dirty little skirmishers couldn't stop him if he was trying to join us. But that is not part of the message. Now have a good drink; and I shall arm you myself.'

My lord was brave, and he inspired courage in others. He was trying to lend me some of his own resolution.

In an hour I set out. For the first half-mile a score of sergeants rode with me, driving the Turks before them. When they wheeled back to camp I continued alone; they made noise enough to drown my hoof-beats, and the enemy never realised that a single messenger travelled the winding mule-track which had been trampled by our convoys.

My greatest fear was that my horse would come down, leaving me to be discovered on foot when day broke. But Whitefoot was a very good horse, and he knew, as horses always do, that his rider was frightened; he wished to escape the threatened danger, and scrambled over the rocks as though a leopard were after him. Yet a ride in the dark never goes as you expect; presently I lost the track and blundered across a boulder-strewn hillside. I got off to lead my horse downhill. That is what you should do when lost in the mountains, but it does not always work. I found a noisy torrent, but my way was then barred by a precipice and waterfall. Dawn came with a thick white mist, and I knew I must hide until dark; but there was a way down the precipice, and a large wet cave behind the

76

waterfall. I gave my horse a long drink, led him into the cave, and hobbled him closely, back and front, with my baldric and the saddle-girth. Presently the sun dispersed the mist, and I found myself looking out over a wide valley, with an enormous encampment a thousand feet below.

It was a Turkish camp. No one could mistake the haphazard squalor of the nomads for a neat Roman bivouac. Men saddled their horses and rode out in scattered parties, in the barbarian manner; but none climbed my hill, which was too steep for their tactics. I kept very quiet, muttering prayers to overcome my hunger and fear. The Emperor could not be far away. Three days ago he had been within twenty miles, seeking the King of the Turks. I could see a rambling collection of many tents joined by covered passages, which must be the moving palace of a great chief of the nomads; the Romans had scouted very badly, but the great battle would not be long delayed.

I peered down, lying on my stomach in the mouth of the cave. I sweated, and every little scale of my armour made a separate bruise on my ribs. But no one can arm himself alone, so I dared not disarm. I could see about three miles down the valley, but then a bend cut off my view. About midday I realised that something was happening round the corner. Many infidels galloped that way, and I thought I could hear war-cries. After about two hours most of them rode back again, not with the haste of beaten men, but at their ease. They carried some kind of trophy. There had been a skirmish at the outposts.

As it grew dark I fixed in my mind the easiest way down. Then I unhobbled my horse, and led him about until the worst of his stiffness had worn off. Whitefoot was a gallant charger, and though he had not eaten all day he had another gallop left in him. The mist rose with the night, and presently I mounted and rode quietly down towards the distant bend where the skirmish had been fought that morning.

The whole grassy valley was full of Turkish ponies turned out to graze. Whitefoot was a stallion, and I was pestered by mares which trotted up to make friends; but no trained warhorse neighs in the dark, and the infidel pickets were all in front, facing the enemy they knew; barbarians scout slackly when they know where the foe is encamped. But there would be Turkish sentries near the bend in the valley. I was about to spur Whitefoot, to gallop past before they could shoot, when we encountered some obstacle, and he grew very excited. There were no mares about; this must be something that worried all horses. I dismounted and peered closely. When I discovered what lay before me I was as upset as my horse. It was a heap of dead men, all headless, wearing the brief corselets of Roman troopers. There must have been a hundred of them, lying together behind a barricade of dead horses, every carcass bristling with arrows. A Roman detachment had been surrounded and shot down to the last man. So Romans did not *always* gallop straight through a Turkish army and out the other side!

Horses hate the smell of blood, but chargers are trained to face it. I led Whitefoot wide of the sinister heap, and when I mounted he galloped with a will. Further on was a line of Turkish pickets; three suddenly loomed ahead of me, but before I could couch my lance Whitefoot knocked over one little pony, then reared on his hind-legs and struck out at another; the smell of blood was all around, and he was maddened by it. The second Turk went down in a heap, and the third fled. My horse wanted to stay and savage the fallen bodies, but I got him on the move, and as we turned another bend I saw before me a line of watchfires. I pulled up where the firelight would glint on my Frankish mail, and shouted 'Agiostavro', Holy Cross – which had been the Roman watchword when we left the army. Six troopers, their arrows on the bowstring, led me to the Roman camp.

CHAPTER FIVE

The Great Battle

I was taken straight to the Emperor's tent, without any refreshment. Romans habitually go to bed much later than Franks, and they have a stringent rule that a commander must be interrupted, no matter what he is doing, when a messenger arrives. The tent was crowded with senior officers, while at the far end a choir intoned passages from the Holy Scriptures in one of those interminable all-night services which the eastern church regard as the most acceptable form of intercession; these easterners say Mass in the morning, of course, but for anything special they begin at vespers and continue to daybreak.

The laymen were standing or kneeling, following the service in little books; for you must remember that all well-born Romans read with ease. My arrival caused a sensation. The priests continued to chant, but the Emperor at once heard my message, without interrupting. That is an excellent Roman custom; they never hector a messenger or break into his tale with questions; they wait until he has quite finished before saying a word.

Then the Emperor spoke: 'I don't understand. I sent six couriers to the Frankopole, and none of them could get through. Yet a single horseman rides here without difficulty.'

'My lord,' I answered, 'there were certain difficulties, though since they were not part of the message I did not relate them. But I took two days to cover fifteen miles, and only good luck brought me here. May I tell the whole story to one of your officers?'

'The lord Bryennius will hear your adventures presently. Wait first while we talk over this news. The Frankopole is right to abandon the blockade of Chliat, since he is himself blockaded. But why retire to the north-west? If he fell back the way he had come the whole army would be united.'

I answered hotly: 'We thought that if the army was still in these parts your majesty would join us before Chliat. That was the plan. My comrades are only fifteen miles away, and they will not start before Friday. It is now Wednesday night. You may still join them. Surely the great Army of Asia can march where it wills?'

'That's what we thought, last week. I'm afraid it isn't true any more. Yesterday Basiliakes lost the band of Theodosiopolis, trying to march where he would. I expect you passed their bodies. But we shall fight our battle in a day or two, though only God knows how it will turn out.'

The clergy were continuing their intercession at the far end of the tent, and as the Emperor ceased speaking the lector came to a fortissimo passage. 'Whosoever killeth you will think he doeth God service,' he chanted in a thunderous bass. Some officers winced at such an appalling omen.

Then the lord Bryennius took me to his quarters, where I might disarm and eat. Two mighty armies were encamped within an hour's ride, but so far we had no orders to draw out in line of battle, and he advised me to sleep on what must be the last day before the collision.

I did not wake until afternoon. The whole army was fussing over horses and weapons with the bad-tempered restlessness which warriors display at the approach of a desperate action. I lay on a pile of cushions until Bryennius entered.

The lord Nicephorus Bryennius commanded the whole European wing of the army. But he was a courteous gentleman, and he might take liberties with a Frankish mercenary which would have been unseemly with soldiers under his command. He invited me to share his meal, and talked freely.

Naturally I inquired what had happened while I slept.

'Nothing much,' he replied kindly, 'and none of it good. Before dawn Tamin the deputy-Turkopole led his men to the Sultan's camp. That was to be expected, and since such scoundrels will not be trusted by the other side it's no great loss. But they were the last of our light horse; if the Sultan retires we shall never find him again. Oh, and this morning we very nearly made a treaty; but in the end we didn't.'

'What's that, my lord?' I said in alarm. 'I thought last night that the council were losing heart. But surely the Emperor of Romania did not sue for peace?'

'Good heavens, young man, I believe you are frightened. In strict confidence, so am I. But I never thought a Frankish knight knew enough to recognise a tight place when he was in it. Of course the Emperor did not sue for peace; Andronicus Ducas would have his eyes if he weakened. No, the Sultan is as nervous as we are, now that a hundred thousand horse are met to dispute the lordship of Asia. There was in the barbarian camp a holy man of the infidels, an envoy from their Caliph, and this morning the Sultan sent him to us; he offered peaceful possession of Manzikert and Chliat, and the old frontier of Christendom, if we would make a firm peace.'

'Well, isn't that what we want? Why did the Emperor refuse?'

'It was tempting, certainly. But the council would have none of it, and they may be right. In the first place, a treaty with the Sultan won't stop these plundering raids; he would say rebels made war against his will. We must frighten the common barbarians if the eastern Themes are to reap their harvests unburned. And though at this minute our army would be very glad to go home, as soon as they felt safe they would complain of the Emperor's cowardice. Michael Ducas will be sixteen next winter, and Romanus will be overthrown unless he wins renown in this campaign.'

'But won't he gain renown by forcing the Turks to sue for peace? The Sultan will be dishonoured if he yields two strong cities without a battle.'

'Such a treaty would be a moral victory, as I pointed out. But the Emperor wants more. He said the terms were satisfactory in themselves, but that he must show the world that Alp Arslan sought mercy and the Romans granted it. If the Sultan retired from the camp he now occupies, and allowed us to encamp there, that would be a symbolic triumph, apparent to all Asia. Unfortunately the Sultan also must think of his good name, if he wishes to remain King of the Turks. On that little point negotiations broke down, after we had agreed on a frontier and everything else. So the Caliph's envoy left in a huff, and we fight tomorrow. Pity they chose a Friday. It's the holy day of the infidels, and the Devil may grant them more aid than on other days of the week.'

'So we fight without the Frankopole. Couldn't the Emperor retire north-west to link up with my lord? Then the horses would have a good feed before the battle.'

'No, Roger. Your comrades charge gallantly, but eight hundred Franks will not win or lose an encounter of myriads. We must fight at once if we fight at all. So far east the Sultan can gather reinforcements quicker than we can. There are two things in our favour. Since our light horse deserted we know that every Turk is an enemy; and since the Sultan made such a point of protecting his camp we have something to aim at, without chasing those little ponies half-way to India. Now I must rest. Of course you want to charge in the great battle. You may ride with the escort of my standard.'

On the Friday within the Octave of the Assumption, the 19th of August 1071, the great army of Romania was still sixty thousand strong, though all the Turkish mercenaries had deserted. But not more than half the men were drilled soldiers, and the balance was made up of eastern nobles and their mesnies, who could not keep station when formed in large bodies. It took several hours to array the line of battle, which is very exhausting to men made nervous and excited by approaching danger. But the final effect was tremendously imposing.

In the centre rode the Emperor Romanus Diogenes under

the holy battle-flag, the Labarum which appeared to Constantine the Great as he marched to make Rome Christian. He kept full state, as though for a review; his charger was buried under a purple housing, and the only foot in the entire army were the sergeants who bore aloft the two ceremonial Swords of State; these are carried on either side of the Emperor, and of him alone, when the Equal of the Apostles takes the field. The Schools, and the garrisons of Bucellarion, Optimaton, and Opsikion, who are household troops of lesser rank, made up twelve thousand armoured lancers; they formed the centre of the front line, the immediate command of the Emperor. On the right Alyattes, Strategus of Cappadocia, led the Themes of Asia, another ten thousand men, trained sergeants who would obey the trumpet; they were armed with bows, but they wore strong corselets and heavy sabres; they could skirmish with the Turks on level terms, and crush them at close quarters. My lord Nicephorus Bryennius, Strategus of Hellas, led the Themes of Europe on the left wing; for in the Roman army Asia always takes the right of the line. The Europeans were also armoured bowmen, eight thousand strong, in everything except precedence equal to the men of Alyattes. They were ranged in eight ranks, and the whole line of thirty thousand horse stretched for three miles.

For centuries the Romans have fought mounted nomads; it is a cardinal rule of their tactics that there must always be a second line, to baffle the usual barbarian method of encirclement. This second line, thirty thousand men and more, was made up of nobles and their mesnies under Andronicus Ducas. Their duty was to keep station two bowshots from the front line, so that if the Turks got in our rear they would encounter the arrow of both lines; our formation was practically a square, though the sides were arrows, not men. But the little mesnies had not been drilled as large units, and Andronicus was their only commander, with no subordinates. Since his line was also three miles long he would not find it easy to control them; but his only duty was to keep station, conforming to the movements of the great battle-flag which all could see. In fact, as my lord Bryennius remarked, the Emperor had cunningly given the young cub a splendid command, but no chance of winning renown in the battle.

It was mid-morning when the holy image of Our Lady of Blachernae had finished her progress down the line and we were ready to move off. We could see Turkish pickets at the bend of the valley, but the enemy had not shown himself in force. The Emperor advanced at a stately walk, and we walked also, a mile to his left; though we sometimes had to trot or halt for a few minutes, since even drilled troops cannot keep their dressing in such a long line without altering pace. We arrived at the bend in perfect order, without loosing or receiving an arrow.

Even here this great valley was wide enough to hold our line, but we had to change direction and that took time. We Europeans broke into a gentle trot, while the right of the Asiatics halted. It was not an easy movement, though for me personally it was a relief, since Whitefoot did not understand this business of marching to battle at a slow walk. He had been fighting his bit in a manner very tiring to both of us; now I could let him out, and he quietened down.

As we looked up the new reach of the valley the Sultan's camp should have been in plain view. But there was nothing but Turks; they stretched as far as the eye could see, though it was difficult to estimate their numbers as they surged to and fro. To look at they were more ugly than imposing, for their only mail is of greasy leather; most of them fight in loose woollen wrappings. The day was very hot, and our own army smelled, but the reek of that Turkish host took me by the throat. On their heads were tall fur caps, and they rode hunched in the saddle, their knees under their chins; they brandished short bows, which might have been little sticks; they carry swords somewhere in the tangle of woollen cloaks, but they do not draw them until they charge. They looked like a crowd of camp-followers, who would not for a moment dispute the field with the mailed lancers of Romania.

When they saw us preparing to charge this gang of ruffians gave a most imposing yell of defiance; these savages also make use of a novel instrument to hearten them in the field. On the march they carry metal cooking-pots; in battle the mouth of each pot is covered with tight-stretched sheepskin; the cook puts it on his saddle and beats on it with padded sticks, until it makes a thundering, thudding roar which sets the blood pulsing. Everywhere in the Turkish throng we heard the hollow thunder of these 'kettledrums' (as they are called), as though all the innumerable ponies of the plains of Magog were bearing down for the ravaging of Christendom. Whitefoot flinched at the sound, and I confess my heart fluttered. But the Romans had heard it before, and it left them unmoved.

Our high-pitched trumpets cut through the din, calling us to halt. Of course, we meant to get to close quarters, but I suppose the Emperor hoped that if these barbarians saw us apparently falter they might charge themselves. But in spite of the noise they made, and the aimless way their little ponies scurried about, the Turks were under the control of their leaders. Both sides remained halted, two hundred yards apart, each waiting for the other to move. It was the greatest battle of this age, and the fate of all Asia hung on it; both Emperor and Sultan were overawed by their appalling responsibility.

I had of course worked my way to the front rank of the colour-guard, under the battle-flag of Europe; now Bryennius shouted above the clamour, ordering me to fall back. 'Bows to the front young Roger,' he called. 'You may ride beside the standard-bearer. I appoint you his sword-arm, to defend the flag with your life.'

Among Franks I would have been compelled, for honour's sake, to disobey an order which took me to the rear just before the charge. But I was surrounded by professional soldiers, who always took post in the rear rank if they had any choice in the matter, and they would not understand the noble impulse which underlies western insubordination. Besides, the place he offered me was in fact very honourable.

Then all down the line our trumpets squealed for the Charge.

Roman bands are perpetually drilled to advance or retire in one line, and the Schools in the centre delayed until the order reached the wings. Three miles of horsemen cantered forward together. The Turks remained halted, and a hope flashed through my mind that the Sultan had lost his head and forgotten to give orders. If they stood to receive our charge nothing could save them. But as we quickened into a gallop a cloud of arrows rose to meet us. A short bow means a short arrow, and these puny twigs will not penetrate mail, or pierce a horse to vital spot; but the infidels shoot them high, with a falling trajectory, to lodge in the quarters or shoulders of the beast; then he is lamed, and his rider must pull up.

The arrow-shower was unpleasant, but I held my shield high, the skirts of my mail covered my calves, and only my feet were exposed; my horse might be lamed, but my own life was in no danger. Everyone around me galloped forward, and I set my teeth and rode in my place.

As I couched my lance, the whole Turkish army whipped round and fled before us, easily keeping their distance. But some riders stood high in their stirrups, twisting their bodies, and in this posture shot over the tails of their ponies. Then our trumpets sounded the Halt, and as I raised my lance upright I looked round to see if any harm had come to our army.

A sprinkling of Romans rode injured horses to the rear, but I saw no dead or wounded men. Then I saw a pony lying before our line. I had forgotten that our men also carried bows. Naturally they charged sword in hand, but the moment we halted Roman arrows sped towards the infidels. The Roman bow is longer and more powerful than the Turkish, and inflicts a more deadly wound; but it is more cumbersome, and a mounted man can only shoot over his horse's ears.

It was very hot, and a dense pillar of dust hung over the battlefield. I could hardly see our right wing, and the disgusting film on my lips made me very thirsty. But my companions seemed cheerful; they were veterans of many encounters with nomad horse-archers, which had always ended in victory.

For some minutes we exchanged arrows, both sides halted. Then the Turks withdrew out of range, but obviously in obedience to a command, not as men who are beginning to flee. While we ordered our ranks pack-mules brought arrows from the second line to replenish our quivers. Then the trumpets sounded Walk March, and as we closed the range our front ranks shot again. I glanced at the sun, and called to my lord Bryennius:

'Sir, if we are to chase these Turks over the rim of the world at this speed, it will be a very long battle.'

He answered cheerfully: 'None of your bull-headed Frankish charges! This is a disciplined army. Remember, they must stand to hold the Sultan's camp.'

As we advanced the infidels withdrew, keeping always just within long range. We moved at a steady walk, always in line; but the Turks scurried about, waiting at a stand until we had nearly reached them, and then galloping swiftly for a bowshot until they halted again; and this not as one man, like the Romans, but in a continual rolling retreat, as those nearest spurred their ponies to reveal behind them others with bent bows. We seemed always on the point of catching them, but we never did. Yet their ponies remained fresh; the short scurries let them stretch their legs, and those poor-spirited nags are always willing to stand; while our fiery chargers took more out of themselves, straining and rearing to get at their foes, than if we had given them their heads in a brisk charge. Presently I recalled that the centre division, the School of the Guards, were steel-clad lancers, unable to reply to the arrows of the infidel. The Emperor was undoubtedly a trained soldier of great patience; he fought by the official hand-book of tactics, unwilling to order a second charge until the enemy stood to receive it.

Presently the yellow dust-cloud grew darker; then Whitefoot gave a buck which shifted me in the saddle. Looking down, I saw the scars of many fires, and understood that he had trodden on a hot ember. I called: 'See, my lord Bryennius. We are among the cooking-fires of that immovable Turkish camp. Will the infidels never stand?'

He answered crossly, snapping over his shoulder: 'Every Roman noticed that ten minutes ago. But the Emperor leads us, and we must obey his orders. Keep in line.'

We were making not more than two miles an hour, edging forward as the Turks continually wheeled and galloped, always threatening to stand yet always retiring. We were tired and thirsty and cross, and when I adjusted my helm the steel noseguard burned my hand. But we continued, hour after hour, until we must have covered twelve miles. Then suddenly all the trumpets screamed, everyone bellowed with excitement and relief, and the whole army spurred against the foe.

Of all the warriors in the world only drilled Romans could have jumped in an instant from a languid walk to a fiery charge, every man in the line. The Turks were caught unawares, and we crashed into their foremost ranks before they could escape.

I saw Bryennius split a skull with one blow of his mace. But I was in the fourth rank, by the great battle-flag, and though Whitefoot struggled to reach the front the Romans kept such close order that I could not find a gap. The Turks fled. Those little ponies, bearing woollen-clad archers, always outdistance big chargers burdened with armoured swordsmen. There was no obstacle to check the infidels, nothing but the level empty valley stretching away to the boundless plains of Magog. Soon the whole hostile army had galloped out of reach. Then again the trumpets sounded, and we halted to dress our ranks.

Our thirsty horses had done enough; there were still several hours of daylight, but I was not surprised when the order came to turn about and retire at a walk. We had been cheated of the decisive battle we had marched so far to seek, but on the whole we had done well enough. The Turks dared not meet us; next summer they would fear to raid Romania. As I wheeled

Whitefoot I looked forward to the cool tent of Nicephorus Bryennius.

But a retreat in the presence of the enemy is more difficult than an advance. As we turned the infidels closed in; and now if a horse was disabled the rider would fall into their hands, instead of retiring safely to the second line.

As we crouched in our saddles, flinching at the hostile arrows, Bryennius shouted to his trumpeter, bellowing in his ear above the triumphant roar of the kettledrums. Hitherto our orders had come from the Emperor; this worried intervention by a subordinate commander brought back my earlier fears. But when I heard the signal I hastened to comply with it. For we were to quicken our retreat since the Schools of the Guard had turned too soon, breaking our line by moving off before the order could reach the wings. We could all see that things would become very unpleasant if our formation dissolved.

When we were once more in line we were ordered to walk. The steady veterans obeyed the signal; but I could sense, from their impatience and bad temper, that I was not alone in thinking the battle was beginning to go wrong. Just then a dismounted trooper ran up and begged to be taken on my crupper; there was neither oath nor kinship between us, so I told him to find a horse with a lighter burden, and threatened to cut him down when he persisted. In that surging throng a dismounted man had no hope of escape, but Whitefoot could not carry double.

The Turks pressed closer. Some galloped round our flanks and engaged the second line at long range; but while that second line kept station it did not matter if we were surrounded, since each band would have the foe on one side only.

Suddenly a Roman band turned about and charged by itself. The Turks fell back and we halted while our men returned to the main body. That made things easier, and all down the three miles of battlefront the same tactics were repeated. But it was a difficult manoeuvre; our soldiers had to listen very carefully to make sure the order was intended for their particular band, and there was a great temptation to gallop to the rear when our comrades galloped past us after the charge. All the boring drill which these troopers endure every day was now proving its worth; the mighty army of Romanus Diogenes was as easy to manoeuvre in complicated patterns as a choir of monks in a procession.

Our second line seemed more distant; perhaps Andronicus had not noticed that we were retreating more slowly.

At every quarter of a mile some band delivered a partial charge to clear the archers from our rear; each time a different band was chosen, but Bryennius remained with the main body. I suppose if his great battle-flag had moved to the attack the whole wing would have followed. I had no opportunity to strike a blow against the infidel.

Each band in the Roman army has its own trumpet-call, which is sounded before the main message; in theory every man ought to know whether a particular order concerns him, but in practice, with trumpets blowing on all sides amid the confusion of battle, mistakes were made. A few men charged without orders, but many more disregarded the commands addressed to them. That kind of fighting makes shirking very easy, and I have already explained that a professional army of paid men is tender to shirkers. Each successive charge seemed to be delivered by a smaller force.

Presently, while I faced the foe at a halt, watching a band wheel between the hostile lines, I heard the rumble of kettledrums behind me. Bryennius turned with a broad smile, shouting through the din:

'We've done it, young Roger! Now you see what a drilled army can accomplish! We've tempted the rascals, and they've ridden right into the trap! Andronicus has only to charge and those fools will be caught between the two lines. Face about and knock them over as they flee!'

But when I faced about all I saw was a crowd of Turks shooting their silly little arrows in our direction. The mass of scampering ponies blocked my view, but I thought I could make out the regular array of Roman standards moving slowly to the rear.

'I suppose Andronicus is obeying the last order that reached him,' said Bryennius in a worried tone. 'Why doesn't the Emperor recall him? He's missing the chance of a lifetime.'

To this day no one knows why the second line abandoned us, just when the Turks were between the two halves of the army; Andronicus said afterwards that he was obeying orders, and that later, when things grew desperate, he thought it his duty to draw off what soldiers he could save. But in my opinion treason is the only explanation; he was determined that his cousin Michael should reign as sole Emperor, and he did not care what became of the army if his end was achieved.

For a few minutes we remained at a stand, our ranks facing both ways. Then we heard trumpets blowing the Charge. 'I suppose that means charge forward, the way we advanced this morning,' Bryennius said aloud. 'After this campaign I shall invent a call for Charge to the Rear as well as Charge to the Front. We need it while we fight these Turks.'

Some men wilfully misinterpreted the order, and made off towards our camp. But we saw the tall Labarum advance, and Bryennius led most of us after it. Our ranks had grown ragged, and I was able to push Whitefoot into the front line. As I couched my lance I hardly bothered to choose a worthy antagonist, for all day Romans had been charging and Turks getting out of their way. But this time the infidels rode to meet us, waving their silly little swords.

I have heard, from a Roman renegade, the Turkish version of the battle. The Sultan knew that eventually he must meet the Christian charge, or return to the hungry pastures of Magog; he had delayed as long as possible, to weary our horses; but now the time was propitious three hours after noon on a Friday, when all the infidels in the world call on Mahound to help them in their warfare against God's Church. He threw away his gilded bow, and the nobles of his guard copied his example; all down the line the infidels charged sword in hand.

Such a charge, when drilled and armoured sergeants meet a cloud of woollen-clad skirmishers, could have only one ending. At last I drove my lance into flesh and blood. But our horses were exhausted; soon Whitefoot stumbled to a tired walk, and I dropped the lance to draw my sword. When I had it out there was no foe within reach, and Bryennius was yelling to his trumpeter, and to any who could hear him, to turn about and meet the attack which bore down from our rear.

We had lost all formation. But these drilled soldiers rallied to the standard, and quickly we formed a shapeless cluster, facing outwards, while arrows poured in from all sides. By now nearly half our men were dismounted, though they drew their bows on foot.

But in the centre things were much worse. The Schools and the nobles round the Sultan clashed together very stubbornly, while more Turks charged into the rear of the Emperor's mesnie. We could see the Labarum, surrounded by the lesser standards of the Schools; but the mass of infidel archers hid its defenders.

Bryennius rode among his men, trying to get them to reform. 'Now, boys,' I heard him call, 'at last we have a mark to charge at. Form line facing right, and we shall catch those presumptuous fools who came in behind the Emperor. One good charge, and the battle's won. Remember, if our horses are tired so are theirs.'

But that wasn't true. Those little ponies carry a light weight, and each Turk has dozens of them; many infidels had mounted second horses during the fight. They scurried about, as fresh as in the morning.

I formed on our new front; Whitefoot was going short since he had trodden on the ember, and it was hard to keep him up to his bit. But there was one charge left in him, if I rammed the spurs well home; and one charge would be enough to decide the struggle in the centre.

Then far to the right a great mass of horsemen streamed up the valley towards the Christian camp. The standard-bearer beside me cried out in dismay: 'Our Lady of Blachernae save us! There go the Themes of Asia! If the right of the line has broken we Europeans may get out without disgrace. There's a pass yonder, leading west.'

But of course a standard-bearer is chosen for his steadiness, and though he wished to flee he held his ground.

We were a long time forming our new front, for the Turks in our rear could shoot into our unshielded right shoulders, and the men moved reluctantly. When at last we were arrayed the throng before us was thicker than ever, for the flight of the right wing had released a great host of Turks. The trumpets blew and Bryennius cantered forward, the flag and its escort behind him; but I did not hear the expected thunder of hoofs, and looking round I saw the main body still halted.

A Frankish knight would have charged alone, and perhaps when it came to the point his men might have followed. But Bryennius was a trained officer, not a paladin. He pulled up, rating his men at the top of his voice. But I knew the fighting was over. Those men would not charge again until rest and food had restored their courage.

Bryennius had another try. He summoned the colour-guard and all the officers within reach, and set off at a slow trot, looking over his shoulder to see who would follow. Naturally I did; in this valley I was the only Frank, and I felt that the honour of Normandy was in my keeping; besides, we would probably be killed whether we charged or fled, and on Judgement Day I don't want my resurrected body to show the mark of an arrow in the back. But the troops did not stir, and after a few yards we halted, rather sheepishly. Bryennius addressed his officers:

'Gentlemen, you see how it is. If the Emperor would sound the Retreat he could still cut his way to our camp; though he might be no better off when he got there. My duty is to save the Army of Europe. Tomorrow they may be the only troops under our standards. At the halt, about turn. We shall ride west, and cut our way to that notch in the hills. We may find water the other side, and dismounted archers can hold the crest while the horses drink. Then we shall retire, in the best order we can, and get in touch with the co-Emperor in the city. You will bear witness that I fought while my men would follow.'

The Turks, glad to see us go, did not bar the way; we climbed a difficult pass, leaving in the fatal valley of Manzikert the Emperor, and the Labarum, and Our Lady of Blachernae, and the Schools of the Guard; all trophies for the infidel.

CHAPTER SIX

Anarchy

During the days of retreat our discipline vanished. Bryennius wished to garrison the frontier Themes whose troops had perished in the lost battle; but his men were eager to go home, and made it clear that if they were ordered to halt they would just ride on independently. This longing for the familiar fields of Europe quashed a plan which occurred to every senior officer; that Nicephorus Bryennius, who led the only surviving wing of the regular army, should march on the city to seize the Purple. I heard it proposed at many open-air bivouacs of our baggageless march, only to be dismissed as impracticable. No one considered it treacherous; the Emperor of Romania is commander in chief of the only army which is perpetually at war in defence of Christendom; it may be the duty of a good soldier to snatch the office from the hands of an incompetent. But he cannot do it unless troops will follow him.

We rode west as hard as our worn-out horses would carry us. No quarter-masters had gone ahead to order rations, and we lived by plunder; such a host, too tired and frightened to spread out, does as much damage to the countryside as a raid by the infidel. But the peasants did not hide their grain; what we did not eat the Turks would burn.

I was the only Frank with the army. I lived as an officer, because Bryennius liked me and the Romans are vague about the difference between a knight and the son of a blacksmith. I inquired everywhere for news of the Franks, but to rustics all foreigners are alike; we may have crossed their line of retreat, but of course they would be described as Turks. I wondered whether perhaps they had all been killed under the walls of Chliat.

In October, after more than six weeks' marching, we reached Ancyra, headquarters of the metropolitan Theme of Bucellarion. We expected to find it ungarrisoned, for every trooper of the Theme had ridden with the Schools who died round the Labarum. But the gates were closed, and the suburbs had been levelled. Bryennius said with satisfaction, 'A trained soldier has taken charge. Perhaps more fugitives than we could see got away from Manzikert. I propose, gentlemen, that we put ourselves at the disposal of whoever rules in the city, even if it is that scoundrel Andronicus Ducas. That's the best way to get a quick passage to our homes in Europe.'

A clerk of the provincial Treasury hailed us from an embrasure above the gate: 'Ancyra obeys the Autocrator Michael Ducas, but our garrison are barbarians who can't understand a word we say. If you are loyal soldiers of Romania I shall try to make them open the gate.'

Suddenly I recognised a face peering from an arrow-slit. 'Peter, ahoy,' I called in French, 'is my lord Roussel in the town? Here is your comrade Roger fitzOdo, who will interpret if you have no other linguist.'

The clerk leaped aside, as though kicked on the bottom; then my own dear lord pushed his flaming red head through the embrasure, and shouted cheerfully:

'Roger, ahoy. If you need rescuing from your companions wave your hand and we shall charge. But if they are truly friends of yours bring them right in. Supper will be ready in an hour.'

I rode proudly through the main gate, smiling in a patronising way at the hungry Romans who would be fed because I said so.

Ancyra has a very strong castle, but Messer Roussel did not invite the Romans within it. The troopers bivouacked in the portico of the main square, and the leaders supped with my lord in the provincial Treasury, which showed signs of recent pillage.

I was so busy I could hardly eat. First every Frank tried to tell me his adventures during the retreat, then I was called to translate at the high table. Out of half a dozen linguists attached to the band not one was left. I never found out exactly what had befallen them; I think they had been abandoned, either dead or alive, when every mount was needed to carry Frankish women and children; linguists of the Dromos could not keep up on foot when their mules had been stolen.

As a result, for the last six weeks Messer Roussel had been entirely in the dark, not knowing who ruled in the city or whether there was a Roman army in the field; he had seized the strong citadel of Ancyra, meaning to hold it against all comers until things cleared up; the puzzled townsmen fed him and allowed him to guard their walls, because these barbarians were at least Christian. There was a lot of explaining to be done.

Bryennius and my lord explored the situation while I translated, and by bedtime we had a picture of the condition of Romania which was probably more coherent than the reality.

At the first tidings of disaster the young co-Emperor Michael had proclaimed himself sole Autocrator; he was no warrior, but he administered the Treasury with the assistance of a clever but unpopular eunuch, one Nicephoritzes, whom he had appointed Logothete of the Dromos. Andronicus Ducas had deserted his lord in the field, hoping to become supreme in the state; but his noble followers scattered to defend their own castles, and he reached the city with only a small escort. The Emperor Michael had promptly appointed as Domestic and commander in chief Isaac, head of the late Imperial house of Comnenus; so the Ducates, though the Emperor bore their name, found themselves still in opposition.

So much for the city, which was all that interested the Romans. My lord wished to learn the news of Asia, which politicians disregard, since they think that whoever holds the city must in the end rule all Romania. But the condition of Asia was indescribable; in the first place, Romanus Diogenes had not after all been killed in Manzikert; he had been dragged, wounded from under his dead horse; he was making an excellent recovery as a prisoner of the Sultan, and his partisans were collecting the ransom which would set him free; then presumably he would march against Michael Ducas, who had declared him dethroned for culpable incompetence. This approaching civil war gave every provincial governor the opportunity to sell himself to the highest bidder. The Duke of Antioch, Philaretus, had already proclaimed himself an adherent of Romanus, and kept the frontier-dues of Syria for his own purse. But Europe obeyed the city, and the general opinion was that Michael would keep his throne.

The oddest thing of all was that the Turks made no use of their victory. The Sultan regarded the Roman war as a tiresome interruption of his campaign against the rival Caliph of Egypt; he was preparing to march south when news reached him of a revolt at the eastern end of his vast dominions, and he led his whole force eastwards instead; small bands of Turks were raiding the frontier; but so far not a single walled town had been attacked.

The Roman officers were cheered by this unexpected respite; though there was no longer an Army of Asia, and when the Turks did march west, as they would in a year or two, they would find no obstacle beyond the walls of the cities. The obvious remedy was to hire mercenaries; but there was no money. The provinces would send no tribute to the city until either Michael or Romanus was deposed and blinded. As Bryennius said bitterly, the Emperor Romanus had done great harm by seeking a decisive battle so far to the east; but he had done even worse in allowing himself to be taken alive where so many brave men died. No one could attend to the Turkish menace until he was out of the way.

It was not the kind of reunion which is celebrated by heavy drinking, and soon the Roman officers retired; I of course remained with Messer Roussel, and he called me into the council which was held as soon as the Franks were alone.

'I don't see my way,' he began, addressing his knights and a few of the more influential sergeants. 'But whatever we do we must stick together. I shall be guided by your advice. I swore fealty to Romanus, but they say he has done homage to the King of the Turks; so that is cancelled, for no Christian may serve an infidel overlord. We have drawn no pay since August, and we need not expect any. We are masterless men. The safest plan would be to ride to the sea and take ship for Apulia. Or we can wait in this castle for something to turn up.'

Messer Robert de Hal replied for the band; he was a brave knight, of a noble family in Brabant; but like so many Brabançons he thought only of plunder. 'This is a rich land, and its defenders are dead. All my life I have sought such a land. Let us stay, and tallage the merchants. The churches are full of holy pictures sheathed in silver; yet it is the paint which is pleasing to God; the pictures will be all the more holy when that silver is safe in our wallets.'

'Don't sack churches,' I said at once. I had been only my lord's page, but now I was the expert on Roman affairs. 'The citizens will stone us if we commit sacrilege, and it brings bad luck anyway. But Romanus and Michael are about to fight, and we are the stoutest warriors in this land. They must bid for our services. My lord, let us stay here in Ancyra. If we take what we want without paying for it we shall not need money; but no Emperor can object when his defenders, unpaid during the crisis, live at free quarters until things settle down. Don't seize gold, silver or jewels; that's stealing, all over the world. But wine and meat and oats for the horses are legitimate requisitioning in time of war. The merchants won't like it, but we can hang them up by their thumbs if they argue; and all the time we are faithful servants of Romania, defending this great Theme against the infidel.'

'That's well put, young Roger,' my lord said kindly. 'If we can stay here until they get used to us they may prefer an honest Norman ruler to the Emperor and his tax-gatherers. It began like that in Italy. The towns hired Norman pilgrims to defend them, and now the fitzTancreds are lords of the land.'

On the next day the Army of Europe rode out; Bryennius saw that the Frankopole was preparing to seize Ancyra for himself, and he would have liked to remain; he was a patriot, who hated to see Romania diminished. But his men would not linger, for news of the disaster had reached the Danube and the Patzinaks were already riding over Haemus. We settled down to live in the citadel as our cousins live in Calabria and Apulia and Sicily and England, and so many other foreign lands which pay tallage to Norman protectors.

We discovered that the town possessed a council of leading merchants. Through them we levied all the food and wine and clothing we needed, quite peaceably and without using force. This was our due as lords of the citadel. The remaining clerk of the Treasury, who had spoken to me from the wall, tried to keep account of these tallages, saying they would be deducted from our pay when eventually we got it. One day he was picked up in the street with his head bashed in; perhaps he had fallen from an upper window.

At the beginning of Advent I was sent on a mission. My lord found an accountant who knew the formal handwriting of the Treasury, and told me in French what to dictate in Greek. It was a request to the civil governor of Constantinople, who is called the Eparch, to allow me to escort my lady Matilda from her convent; there has always been a regulation forbidding strangers to dwell in the city unless they have definite business, and we had heard they were beginning to enforce it, now that so many refugees flocked in from the unguarded frontiers. My lord gave me another letter, addressed to the Dromos; this said we had lost our linguists and could do with one, if there was a speaker of Italian available. But this second message was only to be presented on the day we departed; we did not wish to remind the Domestic of our existence for fear he might order us to leave our comfortable quarters. My lord as Vestiarius had a most imposing seal with his name on it in Greek; when the letters were engrossed on good parchment, with this seal affixed, they looked like official despatches; that would help me to pass any guards who might be holding the ferries of the Bosphorus. But of course they were not official despatches. The last thing we wanted was an order from the Emperor.

I took an escort of a dozen sergeants; the journey of two hundred and fifty miles took a fortnight, and I felt very grand, carrying the letters of a great lord with a clump of lances behind me. Why not? My father was a smith, but the grandfather of the King of England was a tanner.

The Theme of Bucellarion lay ungarrisoned, but prosperous and peaceful. No one imagined the Turks could get so far, though there was no army to keep them out. In Optimaton, which lies on the eastern shore of the Bosphorus, we found pickets at crossroads and bridges, and troops in the walled towns; the regular Schools of the Theme had been destroyed at Manzikert, and these were Alan mercenaries from the Caucasus, ignorant barbarians who took no part in Roman politics. The Emperor Michael could not defend his frontier from the infidel, but he had scraped up enough money to guard his capital against Romanus Diogenes. The savages were impressed by the official seal, and let us through without demur.

The city seemed as prosperous as ever. A real native of New Rome does not believe in his heart that anything of importance can happen beyond the walls of his sacred city, and regards all provincials as rustics who may as well be raided by Turks as not; the defeat at Manzikert was felt as a shocking disgrace to Roman arms, but not as a disaster which might affect their lives. At my inn the only complaint I heard was that government salaries were beginning to fall into arrears, since the provinces neglected to send tribute.

In the morning I called, alone, at the main gate of the convent where my lady had been living since we marched in the spring. No men were allowed beyond the gatehouse, but that was a comfortable room, with glass windows and a broad cushioned bench against the wall. So many Roman widows, or other ladies who are not wanted at home, live in these convents without vow or vocation that their gatehouses are among the gayest places in the city. I had not sent word in advance, and I waited a long time; but when at last my lady entered she was in excellent health and spirits.

'Welcome, young Roger,' she said very graciously, 'I suppose my lord needs me at once, after leaving me stuck here without news for the better part of a year? But I should not complain. I must have picked up subversive ideas from these Roman ladies, whose guardians write frequently. It's a silly thing to say, but I wish my lord could write. If the Strategus Bryennius had not called in on his way through the city I should still not have known that the Franks avoided the battle and got safely away.'

'Here is in fact a letter from my lord,' I answered loftily. 'It is addressed to the Eparch of the city, so don't let the eunuch dirty it when he reads it to you. It says you must come at once, and bring the children. When can you start?'

'I have been here ten months, so it will take me a couple of hours to pack. Not many soldiers could do it in the time, but I am an older soldier than most. Did my lord send money? The convent will expect an offering, and there should be keepsakes for my friends.'

I had no money, for we had not been paid since mid-summer. We had lived at free quarters in Ancyra long enough to forget that in other parts of Romania people were always giving and receiving coined silver. But my lady was resourceful.

'I shall lay my gold belt on the altar,' she said, 'and Our Lady on the icon-screen can have my pearl necklace. There are rings and brooches for my friends among the nuns. I shall come to my lord as poor as when he wed me. He must plunder more jewels from the infidel. The wife of a captain of mercenaries must look rich, or people will think her husband never wins his battles. Though it's true you were on the losing side at Manzikert, or perhaps I should say a day's march from the fighting.'

She seemed angry, and I did my best to explain. 'My lady,' I said humbly, 'it was not our fault we missed the battle. Our orders went astray. As a matter of fact I was there, and I can assure you that among more than a hundred thousand horse eight hundred Franks would have made no difference. We had a very bad time on the retreat, and it is only because my lord is a brave leader that he can now invite you to his strong town. By the way, don't tell the nuns exactly where we are going. It would suit us very well to be forgotten in the confusion.'

'Oho, that's different,' said my lady quite cheerfully. 'You did not explain that my lord ruled a rich town. I thought since he had no money he must be camped in a wood, whistling for his next meal. Are there ladies' apartments in this town, wherever it is?'

I reassured her on that point, and she went off to supervise the packing. Before nightfall we made a start, and slept at Chrysopolis, on the other shore of the Bosphorus.

I suppose I am very stupid, but it was not until next day that I realised my lady spoke fluent Greek. She had picked it up as an infant learns to talk, merely by sitting among the nuns; she made the most ridiculous grammatical mistakes, but she was never at a loss for a word, and every Roman understood her. Whether or not the Dromos paid any attention to my letter I was in fact bringing another linguist to my lord. At first I was rather cast down to think that another Frank shared the qualification which made me so valuable, but I soon recognised that a woman could not be a rival. She could not talk to strange officers, or carry letters to the city; she might interpret at social gatherings, but that was on the whole a good thing; it would give me more leisure for serious drinking.

It was because she understood Greek that my lady had been so bitter about our part in the great battle; it was said in the city that the Franks had refused to fight; there may have been some genuine confusion with the Turkish mercenaries who deserted, but probably the whole thing was a slander put about by Andronicus Ducas to excuse his own misconduct. The story has even crept into some otherwise truthful chronicles. But you will see at once that it must be absurd. Whatever their other failings, mailed Franks have never feared to charge bowmen on little ponies. When my lady learned the truth she became very friendly.

On our ride to Ancyra she talked mostly about the city. 'Romania is a lovely place,' she said, 'and I never wish to leave it. You can't imagine how pleasant it is to have these women's apartments always in the background. When I felt tired, or had a headache, I could sit on a cushion while a eunuch sang to me, and nobody cared what I looked like. Then, when I felt like company, I had only to walk through the curtain and there were crowds of handsome young men waiting to teach me Greek.'

'Were you content to sit all day on a cushion?'

'Don't be a hidebound Frank, young Roger. Because Romans live in comfort that doesn't mean they are soft. They have a fascinating game, played on horseback with long sticks and a ball; women don't often take part, but I tried once or twice. Unfortunately my horse always turned over when my stick got entangled in his forelegs; and there is a silly rule against hitting your opponent on the head. But young nobles play it in the Hippodrome, and it's pretty to watch.'

'Weren't you bored by the cobblestones of the city?'

'On the contrary, I hunted regularly, and in very good company. The Princess Mary of Alania is being brought up in the city until she is old enough to marry the Emperor. She is very beautiful, and passionately fond of hunting. The Emperor is a ninny who reads books, and of course they won't let her go hunting with men. When she heard there was in the city another female barbarian who could ride she invited me to hunt with her; we made the eunuchs and waiting-ladies gallop till they were half-dead. Nobody called us unladylike. Roman ladies don't ride for pleasure, but they live and let live; they don't see why you shouldn't if it amuses you. Romania is the land for a woman. All summer I have felt as free as a man.'

'If we keep quiet, and the Emperor sits over his books, you may become Countess of Ancyra.'

'That would be wonderful. But I don't expect it. If Romanus

and Michael fight up and down the land someone will notice that Ancyra has a new lord.'

Probably they knew it all the time; the clerks of the Treasury know everything that happens in Romania, for they are constantly reading papers which reach them every week from all the corners of the land. But they never openly admit that a situation is beyond control; if there is nothing to be done they do nothing; often, for Romania has more than her share of luck, the situation presently becomes controllable.

So it was in this case. We reached Ancyra safely, and Messer Roussel kept Christmas in his hall with the lady Matilda and his children beside him. In the spring we watched our peasants plough their fields and sow corn, no man making us afraid. In high summer came news that Romanus Diogenes had been released from captivity. With Turkish aid he occupied the eastern Themes; but his old enemy Andronicus Ducas marched against him, and after a complicated campaign the ex-Emperor was brought prisoner to the city. There Michael, his stepson, blinded him so roughly that he died of it. Eudocia the Empress-mother died in the same summer, but old ladies may die from natural causes, and it is Christian to give her son the benefit of the doubt. By autumn, when we reaped our first harvest, the land was at peace.

All this time the Turks were quiet, because their great Sultan lay dying far away on the plains of Magog; there were fascinating problems of succession and inheritance to keep them busy. But the infidels were as strong as ever, and there was still no Roman army to meet them in the field. It lay unburied at Manzikert.

We kept a second Christmas in the castle of Ancyra, as independent as any pilgrims to Monte Gargano who have won a Lombard town for themselves.

CHAPTER SEVEN

At War with the World

&

One raw winter morning I was roused before dawn. At daybreak I had an appointment to arrange a further supply of wine from the tavern-keepers. Messer Roussel kept Frankish hours, rising early and retiring at dusk; we found the citizens more amenable in the very early morning; I have already explained that normally they sit up very late, by the light of their excellent lamps; their resistance is low after only a few hours of sleep.

When the servants slapped my feet to awaken me I lurched upright, staggered to the buttery for a cup of wine, and was ready for business as by degrees I woke up. On my way I looked in on the guard by the barbican. They had nothing to report except beastly weather with more snow coming; the pickets who were supposed to patrol the town walls had not sent in their dawn messenger; probably they were all curled up in a tower out of the wind; that was slack, but we had no news of a hostile army.

The market-place of Ancyra is the usual colonnaded square that you find in all Roman towns; it is very gloomy, for the sun had not yet risen. As I turned into the portico two men jumped from behind a column; one held a knife to my ribs while the other put a very dirty hand on my mouth. I stood quiet while they robbed me, and then allowed them to lead me where they would. Since they had not stabbed me at once they would probably take a ransom.

But they were not the footpads I imagined (though Romania

before the Turks came was remarkably free from outlaws). They hustled me through empty streets to the south gate. The townsmen were supposed to post a guard on their gates from sunset to sunrise, and I thought my end had come; the sentries would try to rescue me, and I would be stabbed in the scuffle. Instead, both leaves of the gate stood open, and Roman troops were filing through. A young officer sat on a mounting-block inside the gate, with his staff beside him.

'Good, you caught one,' he said casually as I was hauled before him. 'Perhaps the oaf can take a letter to the castle. The bother is that no barbarian can read.'

Things were looking up. Romans are strict about the inviolability of envoys; if they used me as a messenger I ought to be safe.

'My lord,' I said humbly, 'I can speak the Greek tongue, the language of Holy Scripture. I cannot read, but I could arrange a conference with your linguists.'

The young lord looked up with a frown; I told him quickly that I was a Norman, who had learned the language in the Theme of Langobardia. Romans hate renegades, and if they catch a citizen who has thrown in his lot with the barbarians they blind him without mercy. But they consider foreigners capable of any wickedness, and make allowances; once they knew I was Italian they became quite affable.

'I have heard the Strategus Bryennius speak of you,' said the young lord. 'I am Alexius Comnenus, brother of the Domestic. The Vestiarius Roussel has used you as an envoy in the past, and you can take him a friendly message. Make it clear that we come in peace. My brother sent me to summon the Frankopole to his standard. We arrived after dark; of course the citizens opened their gate to the Roman army, and I thought my men would be warmer inside. We shall breakfast in the market-place, and until noon I shall await the Frankopole. Impress on him two things: I have brought money to pay his band, and if he isn't there by noon I shall call on him in the castle.'

This was said in a very friendly way. The lord Alexius was a handsome young knight, with the frame of a warrior. Comne, whence the Comneni take their name, is a village of Thrace, but they boast Armenian descent; he had the hooked nose and grim mouth of an Armenian noble, but his expression was softened by a very engaging smile; he had an extraordinary knack of putting strangers at their ease. I felt I had met someone who would like to be my friend, though he could be a formidable enemy.

In the castle my news caused great confusion. Most of the band were for holding what we regarded as our fief, and clamoured to be led to a bloody joust in the market-place. I begged my lord to try nothing of the sort. I had seen Roman bows in action, and knew our horses would be shot down by dismounted archers from the rooftops before we could strike a blow. There was not much food in the citadel, and now that it was day we caught glimpses, through driving snow, of mighty siege-engines outside the town gates. My lord was disappointed with the citizens of Ancyra. He had thought they would never open their gates without consulting him. But a Roman is so proud of being Roman that in a crisis he always rallies to the ruler of the city. We had lost the town, we were not provisioned for a siege, and no one knew what those machines could do to our walls if they were hauled into position. There was also that enticing offer of arrears of pay.

My lady clinched the matter. She spoke out as though she were a warrior; but she looked so fierce that no one told her to shut up and leave politics to men. Her point was that Romans were very good people to live with, and these particular Romans said they had money. My account of the young Alexius also helped. I swore, with my hand on a holy image, that he was a gentleman of honour, who would not murder his opponents in a conference. As it happens I was right, but I still don't know what made me so certain. Alexius is that kind of man.

My lord went down to the market-place. He wore mail and brought an escort, but the meeting passed off peacefully. Nothing was said about the surrender of Ancyra; the theory, to which every Roman adhered with a straight face, was that the Frankopole had merely lodged in it, awaiting orders, after his gallant and successful retreat from Chliat. Now he had been ordered to join the Domestic, and as soon as his accounts were adjusted he would march.

The money was really there, as Alexius had promised; every mailed and mounted man received thirty gold pieces in full settlement of arrears. This made trouble in the band, which I think the Romans had foreseen and intended. Some warriors, when they saw such a great sum actually in their hands, clamoured to go home to Normandy. Alexius made no difficulties, and when we marched they set off for the city with a strong escort of Roman troopers to stop them plundering on the way. The Frankopole was left with three hundred mailed followers; with such a small force Messer Roussel would not be tempted by ambition.

Once we had agreed to march Alexius treated us as faithful allies. That very night there was one of those late-sitting Roman councils which make Franks so sleepy. It was held, tactfully, in the Treasury building, for the Romans did not enter the castle. My lady insisted on being present, saying she wished to practise her Greek before returning to the city. This was news to my lord. But Messer Roussel was an indulgent husband, and he only stipulated that his sons were to be brought up as Franks, and beaten if they tried to copy freakish Roman customs; the girl might do as she chose; it would be quite a good thing to marry her to a respectable Roman.

In council Alexius was very frank about the state of Romania. There was no army in the field, but his brother, the Domestic of the Schools, had collected about three thousand horse, stragglers from Manzikert and Alan mercenaries, and with this force he would try to protect the open country from Turkish raids. At the beginning of winter, an unexpected season, the Turks had ridden west; their new Sultan had no wish to lead a campaign against Romania; his followers came of their own accord, because there was no one to stop them. They rode in small parties, and fled before armed Romans. But they brought their sheep; they treated fertile Romania like the uninhabited plain of Magog, and where they were undisturbed they cut down trees and vineyards to improve the grazing; of course they killed any peasant they met, but they did not seek out victims. They were not formidable in battle, but wherever they rode the land became waste.

It seemed that we were in for the most tiresome kind of campaign, chasing swift raiders who would not stand and fight; and Alexius said there must be no plundering on our part, for it was vital to preserve what cultivation was left.

Three days later we bade farewell to the lady Matilda, who was taking her children and a heavy bag of gold to her beloved convent in the city. Then we marched to join the Domestic and the three thousand horse who were all the remaining strength of Romania.

We rode up the valley of the Halys. The army was assembling at Caesarea, which needed protection because its walls had recently been overthrown by earthquake. Charsiana and the mountains of Taurus were now the eastern march of Romania; all beyond had been silently abandoned after Manzikert, though Philaretus still ruled Antioch as an independent sovereign. I was astonished at the change in the countryside. Everywhere were ruined fences and ditches blind with weed; the stone farmhouses lay empty; the fruit trees had been felled, and there was not a plough to be seen. It was strange to leave a town, crowded with refugees and already hungry but quite undamaged, to ride through this desert where all traces of humanity were disappearing under the brambles; then in the evening we would reach another walled and unsacked town.

We met no Turks, but we were constantly aware of them. As we rode down the valley we heard from behind every crest the thud of their kettledrums. We saw fresh tracks and steaming horse-droppings, but when we gave chase they outrode us.

The Turks had not sacked Caesarea. But when the walls were

breached by earthquake many burgesses fled, and the Domestic's men had eaten most of the available supplies. It was an uncomfortable bivouac. To make matters worse we were soon on bad terms with our employer. The Domestic was head of the house of Comnenus, whom the Emperor relied on as a counter-balance to his Ducas kinsmen; he had been married to Irene the Alan, a cousin of the Empress, and he might hope to be named Emperor in the future. He was twenty years old, and already a great man. But he had none of his brother's charm, and grandeur had made him pompous. He was a Roman of the Romans, despising all barbarians.

He was angry with Alexius for overlooking our plunder of Ancyra; his view was that what we had taken should be deducted from our pay. Now he decided we must earn our money; every day we were sent out to track down infidel plunderers. We never caught them, but of course when pursued they fled without doing much harm. It was hard work, and the Domestic made it worse by sending with us Roman officers who reported if we did any plundering ourselves.

A Roman soldier respects private property absolutely; he is well paid and well fed, and he knows that if he picks an apple he may earn a flogging. Franks cannot approach this standard. We did not burn houses, or take the whole contents of a barn; but we helped ourselves to anything small and useful we found lying about, and shared the food of the peasants without waiting for an invitation. It is hardly plunder if you do not kill. The Domestic could not see it in this light, and was always complaining to the Frankopole.

Then Robert de Hal went too far. I have already mentioned him as a Brabançon who was more of a robber than the average Norman. He found in a well a bundle of church plate, evidently hidden to save it from the infidel. He put it on his saddle and when we returned to Caesarea inquired openly for an honest silversmith, intending to sell his booty; but two Roman troopers jumped on his back (he had disarmed), and hanged him from the main gate.

His wife was in Brabant, but he had in the camp a concubine, called Gertie the Forsworn because she was always willing to testify to the innocence of any friend in trouble with the law. She came before my lord, wailing and tearing her hair; it was said she was well practised in these appeals for mercy, though on this occasion it was vengeance she sought. At least she raised a great clamour, and a couple of hundred angry Franks collected outside my lord's lodging.

My lord also was angry. By the laws of all Christendom sacrilege is punished with death; but everyone is broadminded about the thefts of a hired mercenary, and anyway it was not for a Roman officer to do justice on a Frank. It was my lord's privilege as Frankopole to keep discipline among his followers, and if the Romans wanted their plate he could have arranged to get it back peacefully. No one was sorry for Robert, but the manner of his death was an insult.

When I joined the crowd Gertie had already subsided into hysterics. Men were slipping away to arm, and it looked as though in a few minutes we should have a pitched battle in the dark. But my lord was still undecided and he called me to confer with him in private. I barred the door of his lodging, and squatted on the floor with the half-dozen knights who had already assembled.

'Well, which is it to be,' said Messer Roussel in great anger, 'make war on Romania or ride to the coast and take ship for Italy? I don't mind which you decide, so long as we stick together. But I won't serve the Domestic another day. Robert de Hal is all the better for his hanging, but he had no trial, and it might have been any of us. Make up your minds, or the sergeants will fight without us.'

A young knight spoke at once. 'The hills are full of Turks, and we can stick a horse's tail on a pole. If they see us riding under their ensign they might join us, even though we can't talk to them.'

'I don't mind making war on Christians,' said another, 'but to use infidel allies brings bad luck.'

'Well then, what about going home?'

'And leave the land which has given me thirty pieces of gold?'

They all began to argue. They could not bear to ride out of reach of that wonderful Treasury. But we had all fought the infidel in Sicily before we came to Romania; an alliance with Turks against Christians was more than we could stomach.

'Why not chase the Domestic out of Caesarea, and then tell them we are willing to serve another commander?' said a very stupid old knight. 'Isaac Comnenus is a young lord, newly promoted. King Michael must have dozens of others to choose from.'

'Don't call him King, it's an insult,' I put in automatically. For so long had I been trying to prevent unintentional insults that I forgot we were now enemies to the Emperor.

'I'm not sure three hundred of us can chase three thousand Romans,' said my lord. 'The second idea, offering to serve under another Domestic, is merely silly. Remember the fate of Messer Crispin. I would eat something that disagreed with me.'

We were all talking at once, undecided what to do. Then a veteran sergeant pushed his way in, and shouted: 'My lord, the boys are armed. They are getting mounted, and if you don't lead them they will charge by themselves. I can't get anyone to stay behind and guard the women; I've ordered it, and they laugh at me. For God's sake take over, or the Romans will murder our families while we joust in the market-place.'

My lord picked up his shield. 'I won't fight for Romania, and I won't fight against Christendom, I won't go home, either. Tell you what. We'll go together to the eastern march, and fight the Turks for our own profit. We'll keep what we win, against Christian or infidel. Will you follow me, gentlemen?'

We cheered as we poured out after him, and helped with the flat of our swords to get the excited sergeants into some sort of order. They obeyed my lord when they understood what was proposed, and then began the hard work of preparing for a forced march in the dark. It was now two hours after midnight, and raining hard. Luckily our animals were picketed nearby, and the Romans did not interfere; all they did was to form under arms in the market-place. We were bivouacked in the eastern end of the town, whose ruinous walls were no obstacle; we could march as soon as we were ready.

Just before dawn a party of volunteers charged the main gate, and rescued the body of Robert de Hal. They left two Romans hanging in exchange, and we began our march in good spirits. We buried our comrade at the first ruined church; when we looked for his concubine to be chief mourner we found she had stayed behind, and someone recalled hearing her say that the city was the place where whores prospered. She should have thought of that before she roused us to mutiny. We made about twelve miles before halting to graze the animals, and our rearguard reported no pursuit. We camped on open ground, with very little food.

We followed the river-valley, because the road led that way and all the country was strange to us. It was eerie to ride thus through an unknown land, with foes behind and the infidel ahead; we had no guides and no quarter-masters, and no idea what we would see from the next hilltop. We were a litt'e island of western Christendom in the war-torn east, a moving island whose shores were the points of our lances; it was easy to keep the men closed up, but difficult to find volunteers to go foraging.

I was suddenly a very important person. I was the only linguist in the band, and I rode under the banner of St Michael of Monte Gargano which was our standard; two sergeants were detailed as my bodyguard if it came to a general action. But in fact we had no fighting. Day and night we heard Turkish kettledrums and infidel scouts watched from every hill. But they did not attack. I think this was because we were obviously on the move; they only wanted to be rid of us.

Our worst hardship was hunger, for the land was incredibly wasted; you young gentlemen have raided Maine and the Vexin if you are true Norman warriors; you know what a foe can do as he rides in haste. But knights who have conquered a country cease burning and killing; they need ploughs to work for them once they have gained possession. The Turks are different. All they want is pasture for their sheep, and for that they prefer a desert of unfenced grass. They had been in these parts all winter, and we saw no cultivation. For a week we ate foundered pack-horses and the few biscuits we had brought from Caesarea. Then the road led us to Sebaste, and our troubles were for the moment ended.

From a hill we saw the town, with ploughed fields stretching for two miles from the walls. It is the headquarters of a Theme, and since it is near the frontier a small garrison had been left when the main army marched to Manzikert; after the disaster this had been reinforced by a burgess militia. The Turks rode round, leaving it undamaged. As we approached in order of battle we were relieved to see a small party come out to parley. I went forward to interpret.

The citizens had seen from our banner that we were Christians, but we puzzled them. I told their spokesman with deliberate vagueness that we had recently been mercenaries of the Emperor, but were now looking for another employer. Romans are quick to understand a hint; their leader addressed Messer Roussel. 'Welcome to Sebaste. We are of course faithful Romans, but the Emperor has left us undefended. We can pay your band from our own treasury, since with the roads so disturbed we cannot send our tribute to the city. Would your lordship undertake the defence of our Theme? We have heard good accounts of your rule in Ancyra.'

Oddly enough, there had been widespread reports of our mild administration. Different lands have different customs; we had lived very much better than the lords of any western fief, but we had not taken money, only food and wine and anything else we wanted; this was very much less than the tribute Ancyra normally paid to the city.

Thus we found another home. In Sebaste is a great castle, as in most of these frontier towns, and it was at our disposal. About half the two hundred Roman soldiers in garrison agreed to serve us, and we allowed the others to depart unhindered. There was food in the granaries, for the neighbouring fields had not been ravaged. This was because the men of Sebaste knew how to cope with Turks; an Armenian who had traded with the nomads told the burgesses what to do. It appeared that the infidels would not stay where their sheep were in danger. A Turk reckons his wealth in sheep; if he has none he is of no account, though his pony may be laden with gold. The Armenian told us not to wear out our horses in pursuit, but to search for the sheep, which would be hidden in some steep valley. The first time we tracked down a flock the infidels actually stood to defend them, and we delivered a real western charge; of course we killed most of the foe. After that they gave Sebaste a wide berth.

I have never talked so much in my life as in the spring of 1073. I was the only man in the Theme who could translate a serious conversation, though by now most of us had picked up enough Greek to make love or go shopping. It is astonishing that no Roman ever seems to learn Italian. In Sebaste were merchants who spoke Armenian and Syriac, some who knew Arabic and the Alan languages of the Caucasus, at least one who spoke Turkish; but not a soul who had even a smattering of Latin or Romance. Since my lord was, by deliberate policy, very accessible to his vassals, I spent every evening at the council board.

In this way I learned all the news. The Romans were accustomed to civil war, and if a Theme is in revolt that doesn't stop merchants and private messengers, who have ways of dodging pickets on the road. The men of Sebaste knew all that passed in the city. At first we hoped the Emperor would take our defection peacefully; it is the kind of thing that happens in Romania, and there is even a title for men in Messer Roussel's position: Curopalates, which means vassal-chief. Philaretus of Antioch had been granted it, and now he permitted trade with the city, though of course he sent no tribute. But we learned during Lent that the Domestic was marching against us; the Emperor considered us more dangerous than the Turks.

We cleaned out the ditch and took hostages from the burgesses, in preparation for a siege. Then we heard that the Turks had done our work for us. Isaac Comnenus fell into an ambush and was taken. It may seem odd that the infidels so often captured Roman leaders, first the Emperor Romanus and then the Domestic; but it is no reflection on Roman courage. The truth is that Turkish arrows seldom kill a mailed warrior, and their victims are first unhorsed and then stabbed as they lie shaken among the hoofs. Now the barbarians were beginning to find out that it paid to spare a well-dressed officer; Isaac was soon ransomed. I was glad to learn that his brother Alexius, who had been so tactful at Ancyra, had been left in charge of the baggage; he got away safely with no blot on his reputation. Rumour said he would be the next Domestic, since the Emperor needed the house of Comnenus and Isaac had proved unlucky.

We were now in undisturbed possession of our fief, and my lord began to set it in order, introducing the decent customs of the west.

CHAPTER EIGHT

The Bridge of Zompi

℃

Many of the townsmen of Sebaste are Armenians or strangers from the Caucasus, where dwell a medley of little nations known collectively as Alans. The Romans hold that their Emperor should be supreme over all Christians, an idea which seems absurd to Franks but is more plausible in Asia, and yet they also hold that a man who cannot speak Greek is unworthy of office; you should remember, when you get out there, that other nations are jealous of the real Romans, and would be happy under Frankish rulers. When Messer Roussel decreed that lawsuits should be tried by a large jury, in the language of the defendant, the townsmen became enthusiastic supporters of his rule.

For the town of Sebaste that summer was a golden age. Last year's harvest had been gathered in spite of the Turks, and hunger would not show itself until the autumn – meanwhile our Frankish dues were very much less than the tribute they used to pay to the Treasury, and my lord compelled his followers to live peaceably. We were nervous at being so far from home, and knew that our only safety lay in sticking together; Messer Roussel was obeyed.

Armenian traders can find a way through any number of warring armies. Some of them bought from the neighbouring Turks, raw savages who could be bribed cheaply, peaceful passage for a caravan; a long train of camels arrived from Baghdad, bringing sugar from Arabia, trinkets from India, and leatherwork from Mesopotamia. They were led north, over the mountains, to the next Theme of Armeniakon; the idea was to march by way of Amasia to the coast of Sinope; if the goods eventually reached the Bosphorus by sea no one could be certain how they had come. The passage of this caravan doubled the extent of our fief. The strong walls of Amasia were guarded only by its own inhabitants, and when they discovered that Sebaste had a protector who had opened a route to the east they sent a deputation begging to be allowed to join us. The men of Sinope were also very pleased and excited, but every port on that coast must keep on good terms with the customs-house on the Bosphorus; they let us know we might send more goods the same way, but dared not disturb the small squadron which held their harbour in the name of the Emperor.

Now my lord ruled a mighty County, two hundred miles long, which in the old days had supported an army of twenty thousand regular horse. It had been ravaged by Turks, but still gave a very good living to three hundred Franks.

The Turks were a nuisance, but not a menace. They rode in small bands, each under a leader who was jealous of other leaders, and they sought grazing rather than tribute. They considered us more formidable than the wreck of the Roman army, and they usually crossed the Halys to march westward as quickly as possible. Our state seemed to have a bright future, though the Emperor in his great city was still our enemy.

He had changed his advisers. Michael no longer feared that his kin would set him aside, and he had appointed as Domestic, his cousin Andronicus, the traitor of Manzikert; his uncle, John Ducas, had been given the great title of Caesar, and father and son were raising troops for the reconquest of Armeniakon. Soon after Pentecost they crossed into Asia, and we rode to meet them on our boundary, the Halys.

When we reached the river our old comrades, the men of Ancyra, sent a deputation to say the Caesar was still in Optimaton, a long way to the west; would we occupy their citadel, and free them from tribute? Messer Roussel decided to advance. This was Italy over again; there the towns had called in stray Norman pilgrims to protect them, and now there was a Norman state, recognised by every Christian ruler. In a few years my lord would be King of Asia, and we his counts and barons; the band was elated, ready to overthrow any army in the world.

Once over the Halys the next line must be the river Sangarius, though that meant a long and risky advance. By St John's Day we had reached the right bank, and learned that the Caesar was in the neighbourhood. We had excellent information, for though the peasants were surly the burgesses who accompanied our train were clever at getting the truth from them; a Roman who lives in a walled town regards ploughmen as animals without human rights. We moved up the river opposite the Caesar, until after a few days we halted at the eastern end of a stone bridge; it stood in open country, but was called the Bridge of Zompi, after the nearest town.

I expect there are Norman mercenaries in India, and the plains of Magog, and any other part of the world where steel wins gold. When my lord became famous, stray Franks had ridden in to join us, until our band contained five hundred mailed sergeants and thirty knights. We drew up in order of battle at our end of the bridge.

The Caesar had lined the western bank, and we could count his numbers. He had four thousand horse, arrayed in the usual Roman formation, a centre, two wings, and a reserve. We could ride down any number of mounted archers, and the odds did not dismay us; but the thousand men who formed the enemy's right wing were Franks; we could see their unmistakable shields. That made a difference; there was no reason why five hundred Franks should beat a thousand, especially when neither side had a just cause.

All day both sides watched each other across the steep gorge of the Sangarius. We might have stayed there for days, or been compelled to retreat when food ran short, if the burgesses of Ancyra had not fixed things. Their eyes would be in danger if we lost, and Romans are very good at fixing.

That evening a Roman of Ancyra hustled me off to translate to my lord. He was very pleased with himself. 'Tell the Frankopole he will win tomorrow's battle,' he began. 'The Caesar will cross the bridge, and I know his order of march. His Franks will lead the advance. I slipped over the river and had a talk with one of their women, a whore from Ancyra whom I knew in the old days. I pointed out that the curse of this country is the tribute we pay to the Emperor. Why should mercenaries fight for a few pieces of gold when by joining the other side they can have all they want, and still leave us richer than if we remained loyal to the city? Tomorrow the Franks will cross the bridge, but when they reach this side they will join your banner.'

It was a dirty business, but it's the sort of thing you get used to out east. I persuaded my lord that the burgess was telling the truth, and he was convinced when he heard the name of the Frankish leader. The Roman said he was called Papas, which is not a western name; but we remembered old Ralph de Mauron, who had talked of coming with us three years ago; everyone called him Pop, and he was the biggest rogue in Italy; if the Devil hadn't got him yet he was just the man to change sides on the battlefield. We passed the word to be ready to fight next morning, but to be on the lookout for unexpected allies.

That settled the battle of Zompi. Pop had his men under good control, and he played his ugly part skilfully; he cavorted about until the centre and left wing were also on our side of the river, and then joined us. The Roman reserve made off without fighting; it was led by the Strategus Botaniates who had seen the rout at Manzikert; he felt it his duty to save the last body of drilled troopers who still followed the Labarum. That left two thousand Romans on our side of the stream, their only retreat the narrow bridge; we were fifteen hundred strong, and expected them to surrender immediately.

But I suppose the Caesar wanted to show that a Ducas can fight harder than a Comnenus; when we charged they threw away their bows and fought very bravely with swords and maces.

My lord sent me to the rear, for I was his only trustworthy linguist in a world of treachery; I tried to watch the battle from a hilltop, but that sort of close combat, when both sides have charged to a standstill and are hacking over their horses' ears, is very difficult to follow. It continued a long time, to the credit of the Romans, but the victory of mailed Franks over men with linen-clad limbs was never in doubt. One party of Romans nearly got away; they made a gallant charge, then suddenly turned about and rejoined their main body; I learned afterwards that they had been led by young Andronicus, who turned back at the last minute to rescue his father. But he left it too late; the Caesar was already in our hands, unhorsed and bruised but not wounded; Andronicus lost his helm, and was then very gravely wounded in the head. His standard-bearer lowered the great battle-flag of the Domestic, and the Romans surrendered in a body. They had fought gallantly, and our men, who had suffered few casualties, were not in a bloodthirsty mood; quarter was given even to common soldiers who could pay no ransom.

That evening our victorious warriors feasted, but as was only fair I had to work very hard. Our supporters from Ancyra were supposed to sort the prisoners, putting to one side gentlemen who could pay ransom, and offering the common soldiers the choice of serving Messer Roussel or going home in their shirts. But you can never trust a Roman to be honest with a Frank, and the men of Ancyra had friends or relations among the captives; I had to interview hundreds of prisoners, and I was only just in time to prevent the troopers learning that they would go free unblinded; if that had become generally known of course no one would have admitted he was rich enough to offer ransom.

It was midnight when I was ready to report to my lord. I found him sober enough to give orders, though of course our victory called for celebration; most of his knights were round the same fire, and the drinking-party easily became a council of war.

I explained that we could not begin to collect ransom until we had settled the fate of the common troopers. 'If you let them go most of the rich will escape with them. If you mutilate them, or sell them to the infidel, you will anger the men of Ancyra and Amasia and Sebaste, who can still be most useful. If you keep them hanging about we must feed them, and the Turks have left little food in this land. Please give me orders at once.'

'No, Messer Roger,' my lord answered smiling; it was the first time I had been addressed by that gentleman's title, and my heart warmed to my generous leader. 'No, Messer Roger, I shall give no orders until I have heard your advice. No Frank really understands a Roman, but you know more about them than the rest of us. Eh, do you agree, Messer Ralph?'

That made me notice the old rogue lying on the other side of the fire, in the greasy leather tunic he wore under his mail; for his baggage had been plundered by the camp-followers of both sides, as he thoroughly deserved. But he was still the nominal leader of a thousand men; my lord treated him with deference, though it was doubtful how long his men would obey a captain they despised.

Old Pop answered lazily: 'Do as you think right, Messer Roussel. Just remember that all Romans are treacherous intriguers, and the only way to keep your eyes is to betray them before they betray you. Promise them anything convenient. If you break your promise they will admire you the more.'

My lord spoke in a noncommittal tone: 'It's a bore if no one believes you when you take oath on the Cross. I shall try to think of some bargain I can actually keep.'

'We could do with reinforcements,' said a knight. 'If we allow these captives to join our banner they might fight for us honestly. Though Pop set them a bad example,' he added in a low voice.

I had been working hard and was sober, though everyone else was a little drunk. I thought it wise to get down to business before Pop tried to restore his dignity in some ridiculous quarrel.

'These men would be glad to join our banner. Because of their language we must put them under their own officers, in a separate unit, and that makes it easy for them to change sides again. But they could be trusted to fight the Turks, while we hold our western border.'

'That's not much of a life,' said my lord, 'holding this long river line against superior numbers. We've won a great victory, and the boys want to relax. They won't relish hard riding with no plunder to reward them, while their native auxiliaries kill Turks whose waistbands are stuffed with gold. But I'm not fit to take important decisions; this wine has a kick, in spite of the tar in it. Keep the captives alive. We can talk it over in the morning.'

I was dismissed to snatch what sleep I could, while all the friendly Roman burgesses tried, in private interviews, to buy the freedom of some cousin in the defeated army. Life would have been smoother if my lord could have made up his mind about our future, but our success had been so astonishing that was not easy. We had routed the last army of Romania, but now we had to govern men who were more skilled in politics than any Frank. When you see a hostile banner all you have to do is overthrow it; victory can be too complete.

For a week we remained by the Bridge of Zompi. The Turks kept out of our way, for we were now a very famous army, and most of the wounded died, as wounded do, which made things easier; but the Caesar was unwounded, and his son Andronicus seemed likely to recover, though Romans and Franks have different ideas about the treatment of a head wound; his father would not let him eat the strengthening beef and wine I provided. The other improvement in our position was that old Pop went bathing in the river, caught colic, and died within two days; there were the usual rumours of poison, but in this case I think they were unfounded; he was disliked, but our men didn't know the country well enough to get hold of poison, and to the Romans he was just a typical Frank; for I am sorry to say they consider us all very treacherous. Pop was an old man who had led a rackety life; the cold water killed him, after wine had undermined his defences. Nobody mourned, not even his concubines, and his men joined our band as individuals. Messer Roussel was undisputed lord of the three Themes of Bucellarion, Sebaste and Armeniakon, held by the strongest army in Asia. So long as the neighbourhood could feed us we lived a pleasant idle life. But nobody knew what would happen next.

CHAPTER NINE

High Politics

Wat actually happened came as a surprise, though we might have foreseen it. But masterless mercenaries far from home take a girl friend and then change her for another, forgetting the wives they have left in some safe place. When our scouts sighted a body of Roman horse on the other side of the river we expected an embassy, but did not guess whom the Emperor would send as ambassador. Our scouts were of course Roman auxiliaries, and they reported to me; I seemed to do everything in that army except fighting. I was about to inform my lord that envoys were on the way when another scout came in, very excited because he had got near enough to the strangers to make out that their chief was a woman riding a warhorse, accompanied by three children on ponies. I went straight and interrupted Messer Roussel, though he was fitting a new saddle to his best horse, a job he took very seriously; and indeed it is important.

'My lord,' I said, 'a lady and three children are two miles beyond the river, and since the lady rides a warhorse and even the little girl has a good pony they cannot be Romans come to ransom an officer. In this land of litters only the lady Matilda would ride a warhorse on a peaceful errand. Shall I inform your steward?'

My lord was rather shaken. In the last six months we had completely forgotten the lady Matilda; at first Messer Roussel lived by himself, but when the big caravan got safely to Sinope a merchant made him a present of six young girls from the

126

Causacus; he would have a stormy evening if my lady found them washing his shirts.

'St Michael aid me!' he said in some confusion. 'It must indeed be the lady Matilda. Tell the steward to prepare for her honourable reception. Hustle off my hand-maids by the next mule-train to Sebaste; explain to Goodman Theophilus that I am grateful for his kindness but the girls don't understand the care of Frankish arms. And drop a hint that they are not to be mentioned. If any man sings that song about the drake and his six ducks he shall ride picket until his bottom grows to the saddle. Get hold of two respectable married Italian women to attend my lady; and make sure they are not only married, but living with the right husbands. Is my shirt reasonably clean?'

When my lady reached the river the whole camp had been prepared for her, by men who worked as frantically as though to repel a sudden assault. The captives had been set to cleaning our lines, and the women were collected in two separate enclosures, wives and the faithful concubines who had followed their men from Sicily in one, in the other local whores, guarded by sentries who had orders to keep out my lord's children. A dismounted but fully armed guard was mustered by the bridge, where Messer Roussel waited in his silk tunic, his uniform as Vestiarius. His knights stood by him, and since Messer Roger fitzOdo now ranked as a knight I witnessed the meeting.

My lady looked very fit, and tougher than ever. At the western end of the bridge she dismissed her escort, who at once rode off towards the Bosphorus; she and her children, with a collection of mules and servants, charged over the river and reined up in a cloud of dust. She jumped from her horse and darted into my lord's embrace.

'Ah, my hero,' she exclaimed, 'so this is where you beat the whole army of Romania. I salute you on the battlefield, which my old friend Bryennius will render immortal when he writes his memoirs. But though I came because of the love I bear you, the Emperor would not have given me escort and baggage-mules if I had not also brought a message from him. May I deliver it now, in the presence of your council?'

'Of course, my dear,' my lord answered. 'I have no secrets from these knights, and I shall be glad of your advice.'

'Well, little Michael is beat. When they told him of Zompi he hit his head against the wall and cried that he was a Jonah who should be cast into the sea. All he wants is to get you back in his service. I've brought the children and the maids, and my possessions, and a great treasure besides, a free-will offering from the Emperor. All I promised in return was to ask you to re-enlist under the Labarum. He will make you Hetairiarch, commander of all the foreign mercenaries; and if you give back Bucellarion and Sebaste you may keep Armeniakon as your private fief. Will you do it? You will be fighting in defence of Christendom, and our children will be Roman nobles.'

'Until I eat something unwholesome,' said my lord without hesitation. 'No, my dear, I am very well as I am, lord of three Themes and leader of the best army in Asia. I shall fight for Balliol, and St Michael of Monte Gargano; then our children will be more than Roman nobles; they will be princes by the Grace of God.'

'Very sensible, my little red fox,' answered Matilda, beaming. 'I promised to deliver young Michael's offer, and you will admit I spoke it fairly, as though I believed in it. But I'm glad you refuse. What I didn't say was that Michael probably won't be Emperor much longer. They loathe him in the city, and my friend Bryennius thinks he will soon be overthrown. Things are going very well; there's no need to change them.'

'By your leave, my lady,' I put in firmly, 'things are going very well at the moment, but the situation changes whether we change it or not. We are sitting on a stinking battlefield, with no plans either for advance or retreat; and we must make up our minds what to do with these captives.'

'How like you, young Roger,' said my lady with a frown. 'You're always planning for the future. You should be a monk, not a mercenary. While you have a sword and the strength to use it, why make plans? We shall all die on a dungheap and go to Hell after; that's what happens to mercenaries. Don't croak while for once we are prosperous.'

I was annoyed. In the old days my lady thought of the future, and encouraged me to do the same; now she was so excited at meeting the lord she loved (and who thought so highly of her that it took six slave-girls to fill her place) that she could not be bothered to plan, and snubbed those who did. I bowed stiffly, and went off to see the captives get their dinner; the cooks usually stole it unless I was present.

Later my lady visited the prisoners' enclosure. Now she spoke Greek she could not keep away from the society of noble Romans; they are, I agree, more amusing to talk to than even the best-born Frankish warrior, who is usually in a permanent daze from all the heavy blows which have glanced off his helm. She was very friendly with those she liked; she had liked me when I was a penniless young page, and one of the reasons that brought her was to make friends with me again.

'I am sorry, Messer Roger, that I took you up so shortly,' she said graciously. 'We ought to make plans for the future, I know very well; but in this queer country is foresight any good to us? When my lord rode in anger from Caesarea did any of you foresee that in four months he would be lord of three Themes? What can we do? We never know what goes on in the mind of a Roman. The only sure plan is to sit here until we have eaten up the country, and then move on.'

'Like the Turks, only worse, because they at least move on swiftly.' I answered bitterly. But it was foolish to remain on bad terms with the wife of my leader. 'I am only a promoted page, not born to the honour of knighthood. I don't really know what we ought to be doing. But I think we ought to do something, and I hoped that you, my lady, would have thought of a plan. Do you suppose the Emperor's offer was genuine?'

We spoke in Greek, because we had just been questioning the captives in that language. Nearby stood a Roman, the Protovestiarius Basil Malases, who was unwounded although he had fought well enough; he was rich and of noble birth, but he had undertaken the nursing of young Andronicus and often came with me on my rounds to see that the poorer prisoners got enough to eat. (Roman officers care little for the hired soldiers, paid by the Emperor, who are put under their command; you must remember that all these people draw wages, even the nobles; and there are no oaths of fealty to make the leaders serve their inferiors.) Basil overheard what we said, and joined in uninvited:

'I have a plan for you, lady,' he said very politely. 'We have all heard that our gallant captor refused rich offers from the tyrant Michael, preferring to guard the three Themes to whom he is bound by mutual loyalty. That was the act of a hero, but it leaves Romania divided. I have a scheme whereby the country will be united under a better Emperor, the gallant Frankopole will be suitably rewarded, and the Turks will be driven back to their plains. May I explain it to the Frankopole in private?'

My lady smiled. 'Noble sir, you may indeed speak to my lord in private, if you give your word not to escape when you are let out of this cage. But since he is ignorant of your beautiful tongue either I or Messer Roger here must translate for you. Will you give us an outline of your plan here and now?'

Basil addressed my lady, doing his best to ignore me; but I listened all the same, so that later I could check her version with my own recollection.

'Noble lady, my mother is a Ducaina, and I was brought up as the companion of young Andronicus, who is now so sorely wounded. Michael is a Ducas, but he has turned against his kin, seduced by those bloody Comneni. Our house is oppressed, and my first thought was that the lord Roussel would make a better Emperor. The best soldier is the best ruler. But nowadays the Romans of the city would not submit to a barbarian. However, you have among your captives the head of the house of Ducas, the Emperor's uncle. He is unwounded, though he did his duty; and in Asia he has many adherents. If he was made Basileus he could appoint the lord Roussel Domestic and Hetairiarch, commander of all the armies of Romania. The Emperor John would rule the city, and the Frankopole would protect the frontiers. Then the Turks would flee, and Romania would flourish.'

'And you would go home without paying a ransom,' I said with contempt. I knew the Romans well enough to understand that they would not obey even one of their greatest nobles if he came to power by the strength of barbarian lances.

I despised Malases for plotting to betray his Emperor. He was one of those men with great energy and a quick brain, but no code of conduct at all, who are the curse of the eastern world. I was convinced that his chief object was to get free without paying ransom. It is hard for a Frank to be fair to a warrior who has been captured unwounded, though even honourable Romans see this matter differently; they hold that to fight on when all is lost is equivalent to the mortal sin of suicide, and regard a bloody battle as a misfortune, whichever side wins it; they say that men, who have the gift of reason to show them when they are beaten, lower themselves to the level of lions and leopards if they refuse to acknowledge it. But Malases was altogether too quick to make friends with his foes. A few years later he died suddenly; I imagine someone poisoned him for being too clever.

Yet my lady was attracted by the idea. She had fallen in love with the city, and would support any plan that might get her back there as a friend. She was all for taking the scoundrel to my lord, but I did not value his promise not to escape and stopped it by running to fetch Messer Roussel to the prisoners instead. He sent for others of his advisers, and it ended in an informal council then and there, among a crowd of interested Roman captives.

I cannot complain. My opinion was asked, and I advised against the idea; but everyone else was in favour, and in the end I bowed to the majority. Orders were given to prepare to march westwards, and then someone remembered that John Ducas must play an important part, and it would be as well to hear his views. In the evening he was summoned to another council, held privately in my lord's tent.

The Caesar had been taken unwounded, like Malases, though with more excuse. He had fought gallantly until pinned under his dead horse, a misfortune which may come to any knight. In captivity his behaviour was honourable; he had offered a ransom, but not a big one, and he resolutely refused the usual promise never again to bear arms against his captors. Even now he would not give his word not to escape during the council, and came to the tent in fetters. His courage made a good impression; with such a soldier to lead us we might really become rulers of all Romania.

But you must bear in mind that even the bravest Romans are also intelligent; they have none of the western feeling that honour and stupidity go together. The Caesar saw that the scheme made him our master, and began to lay down conditions. This was a shock to most of the council, though I had foreseen it from the beginning. (The manner of the council was this: the lady Matilda and I put into Greek what was said by Messer Roussel, both talking at once and disagreeing over the correct phrase; but we did not interpret the Caesar's replies, for by now most of our knights could follow a speech in Greek. So the discussion went more quickly than three years ago, when everything had to be said in both tongues.)

The Caesar spoke up, using simple phrases that all might understand: 'You make me Basileus. I am crowned in the city. I order the Franks to go away. What happens?'

'Of course we don't go,' said Matilda indignantly. 'You must swear never to dismiss my lord. Or else we make another Emperor.'

'Then I am not really Emperor at all. Why don't you fight for the Frankopole, without bringing me into it?'

'Because Romans will not accept a barbarian ruler,' I said. 'You know that. Don't pretend to be stupid.'

'Look, Caesar,' said my lord roughly, shouting at the top of his voice while my lady and I screamed slightly different translations. 'Look here. I can hang you. Or I can make you Emperor, if you swear what we ask of you. I've a damned good mind to let you dangle by your thumbs while you decide. Which shall it be?'

'Of course I will swear anything you like. I am your captive, and you have just threatened me with death. No theologian in the world would consider binding oaths taken under such duress.'

'Oh, what's the use. Never argue with a Roman,' I said to my lord. 'Tell the Caesar he is free; put him on a horse and escort him to the bridge. Then ask him if he will join us as an ally and an equal. If he rides away we still have his son. We can put the ransom for young Andronicus so high it ruins the house of Ducas.'

In the end we came to terms with the Caesar. They were his terms, as I had known from the beginning they would be; but his interests were to a certain extent ours, and he graciously consented to exchange his fetters for a crown if we did everything he asked. Only in one matter did we bargain with success. He was very attached to Andronicus. He was convinced that our treatment of the wounded man would kill him; and we didn't much mind if it did, for we despised the traitor who had turned the check at Manzikert into disaster. When eventually we allowed the invalid to go free his two young sons were delivered as hostages for his ransom. On our westward march our leader was John Ducas, and his grandsons, the heirs of his ancient and noble family, were our prisoners; an odd arrangement, but the politics of Romania are odd.

About the Feast of St James we advanced on the city. It was a pleasant campaign. Optimaton had not yet been ravaged, and the harvest was nearly ripe. With the reinforcements which old Ralph de Mauron had brought, and other stray Franks who rode in, there were now two thousand seven hundred mailed horsemen under the banner of St Michael. To our great delight John Ducas proved to be more than a figurehead whose presence turned banditry into respectable civil war; he was actually popular in the countryside, in fact nearly as popular as he thought he was, a rare quality in politicians; many of the local nobility joined us, until the Caesareans, the Romans who were willing to fight for John against Michael, were three thousand strong. After a pleasant march through a prosperous country-side we reached Chrysopolis, the Golden Town that looks across the Bosphorus to the dome of Holy Wisdom.

Michael had lost all his dominions in Asia; what was not destroyed by the Turks was held by the Caesar; and the unimportant Themes of Europe usually follow the lead of the east. For a week we sat in Chrysopolis, waiting for Michael to take sanctuary, to save his life if he could not save his throne. His army did not cross over to fight us; in fact no one made any effort to drive us away. But we had to move all the same. For the eunuch Nicephoritzes called in some Turks to attack us in the rear; a base treachery to Christendom which we had not expected even from that sinister figure.

We heard on all sides that Nicephoritzes was the real ruler of Romania, while Michael amused himself with the respectable pastimes of theology and literature. His proper name was Nicephorus, but there are fashions in baptismal names, and he shared it with half the prominent men of the Empire, Bryennius and Botaniates and many others; just as most of my contemporaries in the west are called either William or Robert; Nicephoritzes was the contemptuous diminutive by which he was known. His office was that of Legothete of the Dromos, who in theory is nothing more than the clerk in charge of couriers; but that meant that he interviewed the Emperor every morning, and a minister who sees the Emperor every day can easily become more powerful than dignified officials who report in writing. The Romans are accustomed to imperial favourites; at least Nicephoritzes was a trained official, not a cook or a dancer. It was not really his fault that he was unpopular; ever since Manzikert the Treasury had been in desperate straits; he had to raise money by tallaging the inhabitants of the city, who have got it into their heads that they should live scot-free on the tribute of the provinces. They disliked him for that, and of course no proper man likes taking orders from a eunuch, even though the theory of Imperial administration ranks them above husbands and fathers. We expected a rising as soon as the local fishermen saw the standard of Ducas in Chrysopolis.

But Nicephoritzes was clever; he put it about that provincials were trying to impose their will on the sacred capital of the world; once he had aroused their pride the Romans rallied to defend their supremacy. They are not warriors, but they had only to shut their gates; the city is so strongly fortified that it has never fallen to assault. Meanwhile the loyal fleet patrolled the Bosphorus and we dared not embark on the fishing-boats of the Asiatic shore. Once more the city had shown herself more powerful than the provinces.

Chrysopolis is a flourishing place, and we enjoyed our stay. We put the Caesar in the biggest mansion we could find, and his supporters formed a court with the appropriate ritual; the only bother was that he had not been crowned, because Holy Wisdom, the church of coronation, was in Michael's hands; John refused to have the rite performed in the local church, fearing it would be regarded as an admission that he had abandoned hope of entering the city. There is a lesser ritual for an Emperor-elect, not nearly so impressive. Meanwhile we lived in pleasant luxury, and began to overwork the willing horse in financial matters; until the most faithful retainers of the Caesar realised that even a bad Emperor with a rapacious minister came out cheaper than two claimants to the throne.

Some of us took to Roman life more easily than others. Messer Roussel ate with his fingers in the Frankish mode, and went to bed with the sun as though he were still dependent on dim Italian candles. But my lady was more Roman than the Romans. She discovered that the wife of the Hetairiarch is entitled to a special robe of gorgeous green silk; she wore it always, though it was not designed for ladies who ride a warhorse, astride, at full gallop, as the normal way of getting from the palace to the bath. She had made for her a special blunt eating-prong, since those who are not brought up to use that instrument from childhood are in danger of digging the points into their cheeks. She tried to get the pedagogue of the young Ducas hostages, a eunuch named Leontacius, to teach the alphabet to her own children; my lord stopped that, considering such knowledge degrading to the offspring of noble parents. My lady had her revenge by buying a Roman lady's-maid, who painted her face in the conventional colours. The effect was startling; I have never seen a Roman lady with such a falcon's beak of a nose, or such a weather-beaten neck where the paint ended. Even some of our knights began to put white powder on their noses; the bravest Romans do not consider that effeminate; my lord checked it by giving orders that no Frank might adopt Roman ways until he had taught a Roman gentleman to joust. The Romans dread disfigurement, and will not joust for fear of broken noses or swollen ears. Altogether we had a great deal of harmless fun in the mixed Roman and Frankish court at Chrysopolis.

We had assumed that Nicephoritzes also would be short of money. But the partisans of Ducas owned fine palaces in the city. The eunuch held a big auction of rebel property, and sent the money to a band of Turks who were ravaging Anatolikon; their leader was one Artouch, who fought for his own hand but was not actually in rebellion against the Sultan, and therefore could hire reinforcements from the east. Word reached us that he was marching north on the left bank of the Sangarius, then that he had swerved westward to threaten the rich town of Nicomedia.

We decided, reluctantly, that we must defend Nicomedia. Our weakness was that we were not bandits fighting for spoil; once we had forced John Ducas to call himself Emperor we were compelled to protect his supporters. We had all the cares of a conscientious ruler, and while Michael held the city we lacked the consolation of a key to the Treasury. Our sergeants were very angry when they were ordered to march away, their backs to the great city whose domes they could discern across the water. As we rode out someone set fire to Chrysopolis; it wasn't me, but I joined in the sack which followed. We left it a smouldering ruin, and naturally a great many Caesareans went home in disgust. The sack was justified by the laws of war, for what we did not take would be Michael's; but politically it was a mistake.

Basil Malases deserted at this point. He had great influence with the Caesar, for Romans admire a clever man even if he is untrustworthy. His flight depressed the partisans of Ducas, but we Franks were rather encouraged by it; somehow we thought an army which contained a man like that could not expect good fortune in battle.

CHAPTER TEN

Mount Sophon

B ecause of the sack of Chrysopolis the Caesar feared to lead us within the walls of Nicomedia. But for the moment we were rich, and there were no complaints when we occupied a camp in the foothills of Mount Sophon, overlooking the town. It was a large fortified bailey, where in the old days the Emperors mustered their men for campaigns in Asia; there were excellent entrenchments, and a plentiful water supply; even the latrines, in a special quarter of the camp, emptied into a stone conduit which carried the filth right away to the bottom of the hill. We commanded the main road to Nicomedia, and could ravage its suburbs and farms; so the burgesses, though they disliked us, sent in plentiful supplies. The weather was very hot, for it was now about the Feast of Transfiguration, and for Franks the open-air life was really more enjoyable than being cooped within the walls of a town.

But there was no disguising that we had lost popular support. Romans take these rebellions very lightly; there is nearly always one going somewhere, but the populace do not expect it to affect their lives. Great nobles may wager their eyes to win power, and nobody thinks worse of them; but they are not expected to devastate the countryside during their operations. Our sack of Chrysopolis was a breach of the customs of civil war; now every Roman who was not too firmly committed to the Caesar to draw back saw us as unprincipled barbarians, little better than Turks. My lord grew alarmed for the safety of his family.

The camp was comfortable and strongly fortified, but too large for our numbers to hold against a serious siege. Luckily there was in the neighbourhood a small castle named Metabole; there my lady and her children were installed with a small guard. We had collected a very rich treasure, from Chrysopolis and the estates of the Comneni; this was not to be divided until the end of the campaign, and meanwhile it also was stored in the castle.

The Turks approached slowly, ravaging as they came; but there was no point in marching against them, for they could always outride us if they were unwilling to give battle. We decided to await them where we were. But the Caesar was worried. He had retreated, and that is normally fatal to a pretender. He decided that to hearten his followers he must have himself crowned. A coronation by the Archbishop of Nicomedia lacked the prestige of the real ceremony in Holy Wisdom, but it was better than nothing; on the Feast of the Assumption a rather depressing ceremony took place. I was there, and I enjoyed the singing and the splendour of the vestments; afterwards there was a great breakfast, with plenty of wine; but the whole thing emphasised that our advance against the city had ended in failure. No recruits came in, and the Caesar's Roman forces grew less every day.

Next morning our camp was in turmoil. During the coronation discipline had naturally been relaxed, and it is always very difficult to make a freeborn Frankish sergeant stay on watch unless the enemy are actually in sight. The pedagogue Leontacius had seized his opportunity; at dusk he had taken the Ducas children to the latrine, as always at their bedtime. But he had gone to the far end, where the conduit led over the ditch, and thus escaped with his charges. A sentry should have been there, but it was an unpopular post on account of the stench; of course he had been drinking in the guardroom, though he denied it, saying the learned Roman had caused the children to vanish by enchantment. That is a maddening excuse which may always be true, though I did not believe it in this particular case. But my lord did not punish him, for a captain of mercenaries is ruined if his men consider him too severe. I am glad to say the slothful sentry died in battle soon after. But perhaps the spell lingered, hampering his eyesight; nobody knows what Roman magic can really accomplish.

Anyway, the grandsons of our new Emperor had been smuggled away to take refuge with Michael; which showed what their pedagogue thought of our chances. Leontacius himself was captured; he was a fat old beast, incapable of marching, and he must have given the children to local peasants. I questioned him that evening, but I learned nothing. He had been beaten by those who caught him, which is always a mistake, though natural in the circumstances; his legs were already broken and he was too dazed to respond to the torture. Two days later he died; a very brave creature, especially when you remember he was a eunuch; but he went into the business with his eyes open, knowing the penalty of failure. No one would make treaties if hostages got into the habit of running away.

We could all see that the attempted revolution had ended in failure. The old followers of Ralph de Mauron suggested we should sack Nicomedia before the Turks arrived, and then go home with our plunder. But Messer Roussel had sworn fealty and thought it dishonourable to desert his lord; besides, the Caesar still had a small bodyguard of regular Roman soldiers and enough partisans in the countryside to bring in more information than Frankish scouts could gather. My lord was ashamed to be a brigand; while John Ducas rode with us we were respectable mercenaries, engaged in civil war. But I think my lady also influenced him. She had no desire to return to Italy; and she was enjoying a very good time in the castle of Metabole. There she had the best of both worlds, commanding the garrison like a western chatelaine, and at the same time painting her face, bathing in hot steam, and giving supper-parties to the smart young gentlemen of Nicomedia. She had collected a really good choir for her chapel, though her own rich western voice did not harmonise with the piping of eunuchs.

In the end the council agreed that we should stay where we were, give Artouch a beating when he arrived, and continue to live in luxury on the taxes of Asia.

Five days after the coronation we had word that the Turks were approaching. We were eager for battle. We had ridden down every band of infidels who had dared to stand against us, and though at Manzikert they had destroyed a great army that was because Andronicus Ducas betrayed his lord. It was likely these men would not face us when it came to the point; perhaps they had taken Michael's money only to gain unopposed entry to the Theme of Optimaton; they might even join the Caesar, and then we could have another try at capturing the city. But my lord, who did not forget his family so long as he saw them frequently, wisely insisted that all our noncombatants should remain in the shelter of Metabole.

It was two months since our last fight, the Battle of Zompi, and our horses were rested and fit; our mail was in good condition, and the recruits from Pop's band knew their neighbours and their places in the ranks. The Caesar, who marched with us under a makeshift imitation of the Labarum, brought only a lifeguard of fifty Ducas kinsmen; but we were more than two thousand five hundred mailed Frankish horse, and in a way it was an advantage that we did not have to alter our tactics to fit in with a crowd of Roman archers. We had scattered the infidel on many a Sicilian battlefield, and there was no army in the world which could sustain our charge.

We bivouacked in the plain, within sound of Turkish kettledrums, and at dawn our scouts reported the foe marching to meet us. This was better than we had hoped, a head-on collision between trained warhorses and Turkish ponies. My lord marshalled us in two lines, about two bowshots apart. Since in fact none of us carried bows the Turks could get in between; but then they would be crushed by the charge of the second line. I took my place with the other knights in the centre of the first rank, near the banner of St Michael. The Caesar with his little troop rode in the second line, a neat solution of the problem of precedence. For according to Roman ideas the place of the commander in chief is in the rear, not several lengths ahead of his most eminent followers.

As the Turks came over a rise in the rolling plain my first impression was that there were a great many of them. How many I cannot say, for they rode in loose order, always changing places; but they must have outnumbered us by two to one. In the midst rode their leader, kettledrums banging away all round him. But what really annoyed me was that behind his horsetail banners, in a place of little dignity, a shaggy barbarian carried the standard of Anatolikon. The Emperor Michael, or rather the eunuch Nicephoritzes who ruled in his name, had granted this great fief to the infidels on condition they rid him of the Frankish army. It was an insult to rank us as worse pests than the Turks; and of course a betrayal of Christendom as well. When I explained to my comrades the significance of that desecrated cross every knight spurred his horse, and Messer Roussel had to gallop hard to keep his place in the front of the charging mass.

As you may have noticed, I had done less fighting than most knights of my rank, and in that wild onset I concentrated on the management of my shield, crouching low and bracing myself for the shock. I was riding against a drummer, and I thought what a satisfying clang there would be when those brazen vessels hit the ground, mixed up with the legs of a broken-backed pony. Nothing could stand against my lance, the weight of my steel-clad body and a heavy warhorse concentrated behind the point. Fighting seemed very easy.

At the last moment, when we were only a few lengths away, the Turks whipped round and galloped before us, shooting over their horses' tails. That brought a disturbing memory of Manzikert, where a more sedate advance had been countered by the same tactics. But surely no rider who turned in the saddle to shoot behind could keep ahead of galloping knights; we must just squeeze a little more speed out of our horses. But we got no closer, and when a horse came down with an arrow in his leg the rider was cast among the hoofs, where even good mail would not save him. At the end of four miles our horses were beginning to falter, and Messer Roussel waved his lance sideways as a signal to stop. Those near him obeyed, but we were not drilled Romans. When the banner of St Michael came to a halt that was good enough for me, and my horse was only too willing to stand and get his breath. But some proud knights wanted to be further forward than anyone else. They continued to gallop; then the Turks suddenly halted in their turn (I never heard them pass orders; they seemed to move all together, as a flock of starlings wheels). Our heroes galloped straight into the mass, but instead of breaking the infidels clustered round them like hounds round a boar; when each knot dispersed a Christian lay on the ground.

We had lost more than a dozen good men, and were thoroughly sobered. But none of us doubted the outcome. For more than a year there had been Turks in the field, and always they had fled rather than face our charge. Now all we had to do was to form up and start galloping again; when we had pressed them a little longer they would scatter, even if we could not catch them.

Then we heard war-cries behind us. I glanced over my shoulder to see our second line with their backs to us, preparing to charge a mass of Turks who had hidden in a fold of the ground and come in on our rear. My lord saw it also, and shouted for us to turn about and ride after our supporters, lest the army be divided.

Our second line was made up of about a thousand Frankish sergeants, beside the Caesar and his little bodyguard; fifty Romans should not have much influence over a thousand Franks, but in fact this second line was easier to handle than the first. Only biddable and level-headed sergeants fall in with the reserve; the uncontrollable paladins who never heed an order naturally ride in the front rank of the first line. The second line

143

performed their about-turn in very fair array, and charged all together; what is more, the Turks rode to meet them, and they actually got home. They overthrew many, and in a moment the survivors were galloping hard to get away, even beating their ponies with the little whips they carry because they are too barbarous to wear spurs.

This was comforting as far as it went; the second line had knocked over a number of Turks, and the rest tended to disperse as they fled at top speed. But meanwhile we in the front line were facing all ways at once, for the infidels whom we had charged had now come back to long arrow-range. Apart from the difficulty of explaining an arrow in the buttocks we could not bring ourselves to turn our backs on a foe who advanced against us. The front line was too disordered to move in any direction.

The Caesar was a trained Roman officer, who kept his head in the excitement of victory. He quickly halted the second line, and brought it back at a smart trot. The usual two bowshots away I heard his trumpets sound the Halt. But then things began to go wrong; some of his sergeants were brave, and seeing the main body of the foe before them pressed on to the encounter; others were nervous, anxious to get as close to their comrades as possible. The second line continued its advance, and the Caesar brought up his flag and his bodyguard when he saw he would be isolated if he obeyed his own orders. The whole army, more than two thousand excited warhorses, was clubbed in a dense mass. Arrows began to arrive from every direction. The fact is that Roman officers are a menace to a Frankish army, for they set tasks to the troops which they are not trained to perform.

'I never thought Turks would come back to the fight after we had charged them,' my lord said anxiously. 'Roger, tell the Caesar we must get sorted out before we do any more. There's a little hill over there. Let him bring up his flag, and we will ride to it in one body.'

The Caesar objected. 'When you fight Turks don't take high

ground. It makes it easier for them to shoot the horses. That ravine on the left would be better, where there are bushes to give cover.'

'Who's in command of this army?' grunted Messer Roussel. 'Everyone always rallies on high ground.' He pushed his horse through the throng, and we steamed, in no sort of order to the steep little hill he had fixed on.

It was a round dome, not high but with steep sides. The Turks made way for us, still shooting at long range, and we reached it unhindered. Of course we knew exactly what to do when we got there, for this is the Frankish manner of fighting; the lesser sergeants, and the fifty or sixty men who had already lost their horses, formed a ring round the base, while the knights grouped themselves at the summit, ready to charge in any direction. The Turks, who think that whenever their enemies make a move it is to draw them into ambush, withdrew out of range.

'There, what did I tell you,' said my lord with satisfaction. 'Up here we can reform at leisure, and deliver a charge which will finally scatter those Turks. I've never seen them so obstinate. Why don't they ride home to look after their confounded sheep?'

When the Caesar looked up inquiringly I translated my lord's remark. 'Tell the Frankopole,' he answered, 'that the situation is more serious than he thinks. These infidels are not the furtive raiders of two years ago. They have seen an Emperor in chains, and ridden in triumph from the Euphrates to the Sangarius. Our horses will soon need water; we are ten miles from any sort of fortification where we can dismount in safety. Nicephoritzes has promised an enormous sum for my head, and Artouch may earn it.'

Messer Roussel had picked up enough Greek to understand; he frowned and turned sharply away. But as if to prove the Caesar right the infidels at this moment began to advance in a great half-moon. They had concluded there was no Roman ambush hidden in the plain, and the battle was going as they liked it.

It was midday, and blindingly hot. Our mail glowed in the sun, and the horses, their eyes sunk deep and the poverty-line beginning to show behind the girths, kept on turning their heads to nibble our feet, trying to remind us that it was time to give them water. We were hungry, hot and tired.

My lord considered. 'Come on, gentlemen,' he said briskly. 'This is a very tedious fight, and it has not gone as I planned it. I propose we call it a draw, and end it as quick as we can. When I give the word we shall charge back on our tracks, and keep moving until we reach the camp on Mount Sophon. Ride well closed up, and watch our old footmarks, or we may go astray.' Mount Sophon was only ten miles away, but the heat had brought out a yellow haze all round the horizon; the sun shone through a tunnel in this haze on to a parched featureless plain.

A retreat was the wisest course; but very few of our men had been wounded, our charge had pushed back the foe, and it took a cool head to recognise our awkward position. Several knights protested. My lord had no patience with vainglorious chivalry, and if it had been only a question of the disgrace of turning our backs on the infidel he would not have listened; but someone raised a more practical objection. 'There's my cousin, Messer Eudes,' a young knight shouted. 'He's unhorsed. If you tell me to leave him among the infidels here's my defiance, you cowardly old fox.' He actually began to pull at a glove, as though to challenge my lord on the field.

'Then take him up behind you, Messer Ranulf. We shall not desert our comrades. But the Romans, who know the Turks well, say we should get back to camp before our horses collapse.' At once there was a stir in our ranks, as dismounted men sought out friends who would do them a favour. The Turks saw something was happening, and withdrew with their usual caution.

But they could see all we did on that hilltop, and horses carrying double would not frighten the most cautious infidel.

They again formed a half-moon on our line of retreat awaiting our charge.

Even a big western warhorse is heavily burdened by a man in full mail, and when he carries two he can hardly trot. The enemy easily kept their distance, still pouring in arrows. More horses were disabled, and each time someone had to stop to pick up the man.

When we had gone less than a mile a quarter of our horses were down and a band of infidels actually charged our rear, killing three sergeants before they were wiped out. Messer Roussel suddenly seized the banner of St Michael and drove the pole into the baked and crumbling earth.

'Halt, gentlemen,' he called. 'We shall wait for darkness before continuing our march. Let the dismounted stand in front, to protect the horses with their shields.'

'Heroes, form a shield-ring!' shouted an eccentric old sergeant, who may have had a touch of the sun. To well-brought-up young gentlemen who learn the old poems in praise of their ancestors it is a familiar cry; but it was strange to hear it on a modern battlefield. Yet we were in a strange world, where the foe shot arrows from a distance and would not charge honestly; other, more sensible men took up the archaic call, and my lord hoisted a leg over his crupper and slid to the ground. He whacked his weary horse with the flat of his sword, and shouted that all might hear: 'Uncle Odo is a wise leader. Why not hold out on foot until dark? It's only ten miles to safety, and we can keep moving all the time. By all means, heroes form the shield-ring!'

The Romans thought we were mad, but in the crisis of a battle such madness is catching. The Caesar also dismounted; his horse was clothed from ears to fetlock in the purple housing that marks an Emperor, under a very heavy saddle of gilded leather; it was already so exhausted it was not much use to him. Normally an Emperor takes several spare horses into battle, but John Ducas had only enough to mount his bodyguard. His followers swung out of the saddle at his command; they were brave men, for their light corselets did not cover their limbs, and on foot they were still a mark for Turkish arrows.

We Franks, on the other hand, were practically invulnerable. Our mail covered everything except ankles and face, and we had our great shields as well. Our warhorses were valuable; to abandon them was a serious financial loss, and a galling admission that the Turks had got the better of us; but we saw that in this queer battle, where the infidels would not fight fairly, we were better without them.

Perhaps not quite all of us; a band of more than two thousand mercenaries is bound to contain men who panic in a crisis, though they are not really cowards or they would not have chosen to live by the sword. A foolish young knight called on St Michael and galloped hard for Mount Sophon, and perhaps thirty more asses followed him. The Turks let them through, and then pelted after, shouting hunting-cries as though chasing deer. The fugitives were shot down one by one, and stabbed as they lay on the ground; it was all over in five minutes, but it gave us time to form a solid cluster, our shields overlapping; as our ancestors fought three hundred years ago, before the paladins of Charlemagne taught them to ride to battle.

In that formation it was impossible to march. We were ten miles from the camp, and there were seven hours of daylight and Turkish arrows before we could begin the journey; we were obviously in for a very exhausting day.

At first it was no worse than tiring. Our shields were proof against arrows, and so was the mail behind them; it would be very bad luck if anyone was hurt by a chance wound in hand or ankle. I set the point of my shield in the ground and rested my arms on top, to take some of the weight off my feet, swollen and tender in the heat. The next few hours would be very tedious, as Messer Roussel had said; but we did not appear to be in danger.

Seeing their arrows did no harm, the Turks changed their tactics. Little bands continually threatened to charge, so that we had to carry our shields and keep on our toes; we might not rest, though we were very hot and thirsty. Some infidels even dared to ride home. The light Turkish sword is very handy, and the savages themselves, wrapped in loose sheepskins, are as active as cats; they don't sit their ponies like warriors, but clamber all over them, using the carcass of the beast as a shield; when they rode in, their sword-points darted like snakes, and they were back out of reach before we could bring down our heavy weapons to cleave them from crown to waist; but so long as we remained alert neither side damaged the other. Thus the battle stood for three long hours.

We were blinded with sweat, and very thirsty. My sword was too heavy to lift, and I could hardly manage my shield; my knees trembled, and what I feared most of all was that I would faint. Then ponies would trample me to bits. I have always hoped that when my time comes there will be something for my friends to bury, and such a death seemed more horrible than the straightforward crack on the head which is the end of most warriors. But there was a temptation to sink down and wait for it, if only to rest until the hoofs trampled me. Then a big troop of Turks charged all together, behind a horse-tail banner, breaking the shield-ring. In a moment we reformed, and our heavy swords beat them back; but now we could see a pile of our own dead lying before us. There were still four hours of daylight.

Our stubbornness exasperated the infidels. Tired men run risks they would avoid if they were fresh, and the foe were tired though they rode while we stood. The next band who charged came straight for my place in the ranks, and one man suddenly wriggled up to stand on his saddle (a trick many Turks can perform, and not so difficult as it looks) and jumped down on top of me. He landed on my shoulders, and for a moment I stood tottering, my face buried in stinking sheepskin, while he fumbled with my hauberk to find entry for his little sword. Then a jet of blood blinded me, and I sank to my knees as he tumbled off, his neck nearly severed by a sweep of my lord's great sword. I had not known that my lord stood behind me, and I felt more confident as I tugged at his belt to regain my feet.

But instead of clambering up I pulled him over, and we lay panting into each other's faces; until two loyal men dropped their shields to haul him upright, and as an afterthought me also. Then I knew we were finished. If Messer Roussel de Balliol, the best knight in Romania, was so weakened by heat and thirst that he could not stand unaided, there was no hope. I fumbled with the fastenings of my hauberk; if I could undo it my throat would be exposed, and Turks always go for the throat; I would be killed at one blow, without the long agony that comes to a mailed knight when he is knocked over and trampled to death.

My lord saw what I was at. 'Now then, young Roger, suicide is a mortal sin,' he croaked. 'Only three hours to sundown, and then we go home. If you need a rest I'll take your place. But I ought to stay by my banner, so let me know when you feel better.'

'Let me die and get it over,' I answered.

'Nonsense. They will leave us when darkness falls, and then we can march to safety. They're just as thirsty as we are.'

In fact the Turks had drawn back. But then we saw they were passing round waterskins, and that made our thirst harder to bear. They knew we could not get away, and they were in no hurry.

There was an eddy in our close-packed sweating ranks, and the Caesar pushed his way to my lord. He was fresher than any Frank, for he was accustomed to the burning sun of Romania, and his corselet was much lighter than our mail.

'Lord Frankopole,' he said quietly, not wishing the men to overhear, 'it is time to yield. The Turks may give quarter, and anyway it is disgusting to see Christians fighting hopelessly like wild beasts. If they cut our throats we shall at least die with a prayer on our lips, instead of with anger and despair in our souls. If I cast down the Labarum will you lower the banner of St Michael?'

'I can stand and hold a sword,' my lord whispered in answer. 'My grandchildren will sing of this battle. Go away and kill Turks.' He spoke in French, but there was no need for me to translate.

The Caesar caught me by the shoulder. 'You understand me. Persuade that mad Frank to surrender now, during this lull when no one is fighting. It's our only chance of quarter.'

I wanted to live; but I could not bring myself to say so. I answered roughly: 'You may think it fitting. You will live content in the city, while we are known as dastards in all the lands of the Franks.'

'I hope I shall live content,' he answered quietly, 'though it will be in the dark. Surely if *I* counsel surrender you must see it is the only course.'

I had forgotten the fate of a defeated pretender. John Ducas really did hate useless bloodshed.

But Franks don't surrender to infidels. I turned back to face the foe. They had finished drinking; now they charged all together with a thunder of kettledrums.

In the next hour there were three general charges, and three times we beat them back. If only they had jousted like that in the morning we would have won easily. But we were too exhausted, when at last there was flesh for our swords to bite on. Our mail turned their blows, but they knocked us bodily off our feet; when the third charge was repelled there were not more than five hundred men round the banner of St Michael; the rest lay on the ground, trampled or stabbed.

The Turks once more watched from a distance. The last charge had been nothing more than hard pushing, with both sides too weary to strike. Night was not far off, but darkness would not help us now; we could no longer walk. I had lost my sword and I leaned, doubled up, on my shield, with only a little eating-knife for weapon; I couldn't have broken an egg with it anyway, for my trembling arms would not obey me.

Then a single man rode out from the Turkish array. Six feet off he halted and called in Greek: 'The Lord Artouch offers you life. Embrace the True Faith and you may ride with his band; or if stubborn in superstition you will be sold at a fair price.'

'That means ransom,' the Caesar called to my lord. 'I shall take the offer, whatever you barbarians decide.' With half a dozen followers he staggered out of the shield-ring; his Labarum fell to the ground, and I don't know what became of it.

The Turks pressed forward, thinking we had accepted their terms; and when it came to the point we did. A filthy rider, smelling of old rams, jumped off his pony and seized my shield; I might have stabbed him; instead I lowered my head to get out of the shield-traps. In a moment three or four of them were tugging at my mail; they were rough, but not deliberately cruel, and when they left me I lay sobbing on the ground, naked and a slave, but longing for life.

I have no excuse. I was standing with steel in my hand. But after twelve hours without water under the August sun of Asia the bravest knight thinks more of life than of honour. I was not alone in my shame. As I pulled myself together and looked round I saw my lord close by; he was completely naked, but quite self-possessed; altogether four hundred Franks accepted dishonourable quarter that evening.

CHAPTER ELEVEN

Matilda the Deliverer

A frightening thing about the Turks is that they are completely merciless but not actively cruel. In camp they go about with smiling faces and lend a hand to any captive who is in difficulties filling a strange water-skin or saddling a restless horse; then one will come with a spare bowstring and strangle some prisoner who is no longer worth keeping, showing no particular emotion, just doing one of the endless round of petty jobs that fill the life of a nomad. They have no feelings, one way or the other, about human beings who are not fellow-tribesmen or at least fellow-Turks; any more than a housewife has feelings of charity or remorse when she feeds her pullets or kills them for the table.

That night they gave us water, and blankets from a pile of stinking felt; they saw we could not march, so since to them one place is as good as another they pitched their tents on the battlefield. Then a fatigue-party examined the prisoners, and strangled about a score who were seriously wounded and unlikely to recover. (They have a superstition about shedding blood in camp, thinking it brings civil war; and strangling does not make a mess.) I was too exhausted to feel fear, and after the disgrace of surrender it did not seem to matter whether I were strangled or not; I slept soundly, and when I woke at dawn I was too hungry to worry about anything except whether I would be fed before my end came.

Our conquerors were warriors on campaign, and their sheep had been left in some valley to the eastward. But even on a swift march they take a great herd of animals, mares and cows and camels, to provide the milk which is their principal food. As soon as the sun rose they all went to milking, many sucking breakfast straight from the udder; but some remembered their responsibilities, and dumped among the naked prisoners leather bags of sour milk. Others approached with leather halters, and I thought how typical it was of savage lack of forethought to give us a meal just before execution. But the halters were not for strangling; they were fastened round our legs as ponies are hobbled to graze, and the linguist told us we might wander about the camp until evening, when the council would decide our fate. He added that we would be wise to make ourselves useful if we wanted any supper.

We were not guarded, and the hobbles allowed quite long steps, but no one tried to escape. We wore nothing but a blanket folded round the loins, and we all knew that a Frank would be skinned alive if he did not find shade during the heat of the day; besides, Turkish pickets could ride us down. We wandered among the tents, looking for shelter in return for help with the household chores. Each tent held a group of Turkish women, slit-eyed dumpy figures who were quite unabashed in the company of naked captives; when the barbarians march light they leave their pretty Roman and Arab concubines with the sheep, but the honourable wives, of their own tribe, accompany their husbands to war; in battle they manage the herd of spare ponies which is one reason why nomads out-distance their enemies, and some of them shoot well enough to be useful in the rear ranks. Most of my comrades were set to beating heaps of tangled wool to make felt, or scouring crockery; but I was lucky enough to find a smith hammering out arrow-heads from a pile of broken Roman corselets. I picked up a spare hammer, and he soon saw I knew as much about it as he did (he was very incompetent). This was harder work than washing milk-jugs, but I was glad to get it; even if there was a hitch over my ransom my life should be safe; the most improvident barbarians would consider an arrowsmith worth a drink of milk and a place by the fire.

In the evening we were given a scanty meal; then we were bound and sat down in a row. One at a time we were hauled off to see the council; but those who went first did not come back, a sensible precaution to prevent us backing up a lie told by a comrade.

When my turn came I was hustled to a round dome of black felt as big as a small church. A great fire burned before it, and my escort pushed me very close; I was a little scorched, but I know now that this was not a torment to weaken me, but a precaution against treachery. These barbarians believe their sacred fires can discover evildoers; if I had been planning to assassinate Artouch it would have turned my skin black. Then I was pushed down on my knees in the middle of the tent, facing a row of cushions on which squatted the leader and half a dozen of his counsellors.

These tents of the nomads are not constructed like western pavilions; instead of being upheld by a multitude of poles they are stiffened at the sides with wickerwork, leaving the centre clear. Since they have no other homes they hang on the walls any fine carpets or weapons they may have plundered, and often the whole interior is lined with silk. The Turks put splendour before comfort, and in their queer barbarian way they can be impressive.

The linguist was a renegade who addressed me in Greek, which was all right with me but must have been awkward for some of my comrades; the other hindrance was that he didn't know very much Turkish, to judge by the discussion among the council whenever he tried to communicate with them. But the savages could speak no Christian tongue, and I suppose they were used to blundering interpreters and constant misunderstandings. Anyway, the ideas the linguist was trying to convey were fairly simple.

He began by asking if I would renounce salvation and worship Mahound; if I consented they would give me arms, and

I might ride with them as soon as the slight wound which such treason entailed had healed over. I had feared that a refusal would mean martyrdom, which I dreaded, though every Christian must face it if it cannot be avoided. Luckily I realised from his tone that he was repeating a form which meant nothing. Not long ago the Turks were idolaters of the type who willingly embrace a civilised religion because they think it smart to belong to an organised church; unfortunately the infidels met them first, and quickly converted them; but they are not fanatical, and this preamble is hurried over at the beginning of all interviews with Christian captives. They would be rather annoyed if a rich man sold his soul to save a ransom, though they might keep the bargain unless he was very rich indeed.

When I answered, as politely as I could, that I was a baptised Christian and a gentleman of honour, he at once dropped the subject and came to business. 'Forty pieces of gold is a fair price for a slave,' he said. 'If you can raise it within a week you may go free. Or if you think you might produce the money one day, but not now, you may cut a tally for it. But I warn you not to lie. If you can't offer ransom the wisest course is to be frank about it. Perhaps my lord Artouch will send a convoy to the slave-market in Baghdad, and I shall do my best to get you into it. But the odds are you will be strangled to save the bother of guarding you. Now make up your mind and don't keep us waiting.'

Although he was a renegade who had sold his soul to escape from slavery he was not the worst type, who hate Christians because they feel ashamed in their presence; he seemed anxious that as many as possible of us should pay up and go free; of course he probably got a commission, but it was better than the envy of a damned soul for sinners with a chance of salvation.

I answered frankly: 'Until yesterday I was a knight, and in our camp on Mount Sophon I have a little bag of silver, besides my share of the plunder which has not yet been divided. Or rather I had these things. Who has them now I cannot say, or whether they will be delivered if I demand them. But if they offer ransom for my lord Roussel or any of his knights they will probably offer it for me. That is all I can promise.'

'Very well. I shall put you with the men who have money if their kin will pay. That means no work and better food, but of course if your women don't pay quickly you will be mutilated to help them make up their minds. Perhaps the poor soldiers will have an easier end.'

I was dragged out and tied to another knight, but not too cruelly, for we could sit on the ground if we got down gently. As the evening wore on more of our comrades joined us, but many of the lesser sergeants were never seen again.

I have said very little about my feelings; partly because they were very depressing and you can guess them without being told; but partly because for long stretches of time I had no feelings in particular. When you are constantly in danger of death and cannot do anything about it your mind grows numb. That evening I thought of supper, and after I had gulped down a cup of sour milk I thought of breakfast (we were very hungry); but Death, Judgement, Heaven and Hell, which should have been the objects of my constant attention, slipped out of my head unless I made a deliberate effort. I even managed to sleep, when the comrade tied to my back took the weight; later I supported him while he slept.

We could not have long survived this treatment; Turks are too negligent, and themselves too tough, to give captives the food and rest necessary to support life. They cannot be bothered with slaves, which is why their raids are so wasteful of life. But next morning our ordeal was ended. While we were being unbound for breakfast we heard shouts at the edge of the camp, and a drum began to beat the alarm; it was quickly silenced, and someone came running to fetch the renegade in charge of us. As he hurried away he called out: 'Cheer up, lads. The envoys have arrived to discuss your ransom.' He was not a bad creature, though of course doomed to Hell.

Then there was a scurry of hoof-beats, and round a tent came my lady Matilda, riding her warhorse at the hand-gallop which was the slowest pace she would adopt even in a crowd of camels and camp-followers. She wore her green silk dress, slit to the middle for comfort in the saddle, with crimson Roman riding-boots showing underneath. On her head was her silver-gilt Roman crown, and a mass of necklaces and bracelets jangled all over her. Her hair was dyed an improbable red, and her face painted more vividly than I had ever seen it. In the crowd of more than two hundred naked men she picked out my lord without hesitation; she jumped from her horse and ran into his arms, then turned to address us as we swarmed round her.

'You poor things, don't be shy. I've borne three children and I know what a man looks like. Now then. I'm going to Artouch about the ransoms; though I insisted on coming here first to make sure you were still alive. How many are you?'

'Two hundred and eleven at supper,' my lord answered; he kept track of his followers as a leader should. 'There were nearly four hundred taken,' he added. 'You might ask what became of the others, though I don't think we shall see them again.'

'Holy Michael! That's more than eight thousand gold pieces, at forty pieces a man. But we'll raise it somehow. By the way, boys, I suppose I have authority to dispose of all property in Metabole? I shall do it anyway, but I should like your consent.'

'Do what you think best, my dear. But you're not going to Artouch alone, without exchanging hostages? There's nothing to stop him putting you in with us and demanding another ransom.'

'What, put me in with two hundred strong men with no clothes on? I might not offer ransom to get away. Seriously, my lord, there's no point in taking precautions as though we were dealing with a treacherous Norman. Artouch is a savage, and if we ask for hostages it will only put ideas into his thick head. Besides, there's no time. You must be freed today, or you'll die. I shall get straight down to business. Oh, I had better take a linguist. I can gossip in Greek, but I'm shaky about figures. Roger, will you help me? Here, you can't negotiate with your legs hobbled like a cow on a common. Let me get at them.'

She snatched a knife from the belt of a Turk who had strolled up to stare at the painted foreigner, and with a hearty swipe cut my legs free. She smiled as she handed back the knife: 'Here, sir, and thanks for your assistance. No, you can't have my finger-ring as well.' The barbarian was rocking on his heels, as a horseman will who is unused to standing; as he tried to grab the ring she gave him a push that made him sit down. I felt frightened, but he grinned all over his face as he rose, and actually held her stirrup while she mounted. Turks are tough with one another, and never bear malice.

All the idlers in camp had collected outside the tent of their leader. The crowd was so dense that even Matilda must ride at a walk, and I limped beside her on my bare feet. The sentry tried to push her in the direction of the sacred fire, but as she slid from her horse she thrust the reins in his hands and brushed past him. 'No fires, thank you,' she said with an artificial society smile. 'I suppose you need them to get into training for Hell; but Christians find it quite warm already.'

My lady often chatted in Italian when she found herself in a crowd of foreigners; she said it was only good manners to assume they could understand the language of gentlemen, and that even if they didn't they would be flattered by the compliment. Now the Turks stared in fascinated awe at her brightly painted lips; they had never imagined anything like the lady Matilda, and they thoroughly enjoyed the unexpected entertainment; luckily they had decided at the outset that she was amusing, not dangerous.

Artouch was not prepared for negotiations so early in the day, and there was a delay while his counsellors were summoned. He made his own decisions, but his council must be in attendance to bear witness that the ransom he received was divided fairly among his warriors. My lady filled in the time by walking round his tent, examining the trophies which hung there.

'Really these tents are very splendid. But don't they ever sit down? What, they squat on those cushions? If they fold up whenever they want a rest no wonder they ride in that silly way, with a bent knee. I suppose it hurts them to straighten their legs. He's got some nice trophies. Oh dear, there's the banner of St Michael. Well, he took it in fair fight, and none of my friends will see it here. I might try to buy it, but if I make an offer they'll think it a precious relic, and we might squabble over the price. Better not, or they may call off the whole deal. Good Heavens, does he wash in a silver font? Still, that's better than never washing at all. Ah, here he is. Quite a handsome man, if you forget those ridiculous bandy legs.'

All Turks are bowlegged, the natural result of riding before they can walk; and their baggy trousers make their legs seem short and more crooked than they are. But even on his short legs Artouch was nearly as tall as my lady, and squatting on his cushion he looked as big as any champion.

Matilda often tried to adopt the tone of Roman light conversation, and somehow she never got it quite right. But her chatter had one good effect; I was no longer a dispirited captive; I began to see the Turks through her eyes, not as mighty warriors but as ridiculous barbarians; they might have beaten us once, with the help of hot weather and a muddle about tactics, but we were as good as they if not better.

As soon as the counsellors were arranged on their cushions Artouch grunted at the renegade to open proceedings. The Roman immediately put on a surly expression, and shouted: 'You want to buy slaves? The price is forty gold pieces a man, as usual. Have you brought the money with you?'

'That's a fair price, and I'll pay it. I'm glad your master is a man of business, though of course since I am a lady born I'm not good at reckoning large sums of money.' The insult missed its mark; neither Romans nor Turks consider it low to haggle about money. 'But before we begin I wish to inquire after some other friends of mine. What has become of the Caesar, and the kinsmen of his bodyguard?'

'The Emperor ransomed his own kin; they have already left for the city. We did think at one time,' the rascal said with a smile, 'of putting them up to auction. More than one party seemed eager to buy. They must be very much beloved. But the Emperor made such a handsome offer, a thousand gold pieces for John and two hundred for each of his companions, that we knew no one else could match it.'

'Oh well, I've done my best. I didn't really expect I could help them. Now about my comrades. This is a straightforward matter of business, and it can be settled in a day if we trust one another. But if we argue about who pays over how much and when, and hostages for good faith, and all the other objections that can be raised, it will take as long as buying two hundred horses. Have you ever seen a Frank buying a warhorse?'

The linguist laughed, and tried to explain the joke to his master. Romania is full of good horses, and the Romans buy and sell them as carelessly as though they were oxen; it is always considered very comical when a Frank insists on trying one, and thinking over the matter for a few weeks, and having it examined by all his friends, before he will pay down his money.

Artouch now took a hand. He knew the Greek for 'forty gold pieces', which is the first phrase a Turk learns; forty is as high as most of them can count. He beckoned me to him, spluttered the Greek words, and pushed me back to my lady; then he did it all over again. His meaning was clear. The captives would be ransomed one at a time, for cash down. That simplified matters enormously; there would be no great heap of treasure to be guarded, and no problem of which should be handed over first.

But my lady had not finished. Quite at her ease, she assumed the tone of haughty superiority a landowner uses to a money-grubbing merchant.

'I want more than just their bodies. In this heat they can't travel naked and barefoot. I won't ask for weapons and horses, because I don't suppose such things are for sale. But my friends must have shirts and shoes, and if there are any donkeys in camp I'll offer a fair price for them. Oh, and before we begin: I can't pay the whole sum in nomismata from the mint in the city. You take gold by weight, of course, but how do you reckon the pound of silver?'

The eyes of the renegade lit up. All Romans love bargaining, and so far the negotiations had gone too smoothly for him to show his skill; he pointed out that in Baghdad one pound of gold bought twenty pounds of silver, and that shirts were precious to nomads who had no skill in weaving. My lady was not to be cheated, and it seemed we might be arguing all day.

But Artouch was bored. Also he was fascinated by Matilda; he could not take his eyes off her painted lips, and I saw him peer narrowly at the roots of her hair. Suddenly he jumped up, threw his whip at the linguist, and strode close to my lady. He pinched her cheek, and examined his fingers. Then he stuttered and spluttered, and jerked out a few Greek words he had picked up from his concubines: 'You give present, me give present.'

'Is this a dishonourable proposal?' said my lady with a giggle.

Artouch held the linguist by the ear and talked earnestly into his face; then he pushed the man over to my lady, and stood beaming while his terms were explained.

'My great leader says he trusts you. If your nose were smaller he would have kept you in his tent. He will ride with you to your castle and the slaves shall ride also. He will give them clothing; that will be a present. But you must give presents in return. He wants that gown, and your face-paint, and all your jewels, and the maids who dress you. He says that when he sees a concubine wearing your gown and your paint he will be reminded of your courage and then his children will be even braver than otherwise they would be. That's his message, madam, but I should like to add on my own that if you exchange presents with him he will be bound in honour never to attack you. It's a splendid bargain.'

The linguist was a scoundrel who thought only of a pleasant life in this world; when Artouch admired my lady's courage he at once became polite and ingratiating.

Turks are inconsequent creatures who seldom know in the morning what they will be doing by midday. Plans come to them suddenly, and then, like children, they cannot rest until they have carried them out. If their leader had ordered them to break camp they would at once have rounded up the camels; now, since he proposed that the captives should be delivered in Metabole they raced to saddle their ponies. As each man armed and mounted he rode to the muster, until six thousand warriors were assembled. My lady watched in growing perturbation. Suddenly she caught the linguist by the arm (everyone who wished to speak through that despised creature always caught hold of him; he must have been sore by evening).

'The garrison of Metabole are frightened men,' she said urgently. 'If an army approaches they may flee to the hills. Two hundred captives are to be ransomed, and an escort of two hundred warriors should suffice.'

'That's all right, my lady,' said the renegade, sneering. 'Two hundred horsemen will drive the slaves. The rest of the horde will ride north to make a sheep pasture. That is a thing you Franks have never seen. You will find it interesting.'

Just then our comrades made their appearance. Each man sat bareback on one of the commonest and roughest of the spare Turkish ponies, his feet tied below the belly; the animals wore no bridles, and a score of infidels rode as herders, driving them with whips. It was the most humiliating manner of riding that could be devised, but Artouch had kept his word. The slaves were mounted for the journey.

I had hoped that in the bustle I might ride home in Matilda's train; but then the Turks would have lost the forty pieces of gold that were my price. They remembered in time, and put me on a pony. To make up for the easy morning I had enjoyed as my lady's linguist I was sat on it facing the tail, which was considered very amusing. Luckily someone tied a sheepskin round my shoulders, for otherwise the sun would have blistered my naked body. Then we set forth on our ten-mile ride, the herdsmen whooping behind, and trying to get their whiplashes under our ponies' tails to make them buck. In fact we had a very rough time. But you must not regard this as torture; it was more in the nature of a practical joke, and when one of our mistreated ponies lashed out and broke a driver's leg the other Turks thought it just as funny as anything that happened to us. These nomads are very childlike, in the worst sense of the word.

My lady knew how far she could go; Artouch had taken a fancy to her, but that gave her no influence over his followers. She did not protest at our treatment, and even joined in the laughter; but she rode beside Messer Roussel and slipped a stirrup-leather round his pony's neck; my lord came home led by his wife, which is undignified enough; but he was not driven by laughing infidels like a stray goat.

Artouch and his escort of two hundred warriors rode with us. The main horde had gone ahead in the direction of Nicomedia. After about six miles we caught up with them, where they had halted to 'make a pasture'; I suppose this was deliberate policy, to impress us with their might. It was certainly very unpleasant to watch.

First we met small parties by deserted farmsteads. Some had dismounted to fell the trees which cluster round every Roman farm, others were knocking holes in the rubble walls; when they have made two small holes they pass through a leather rope, then they all catch hold of the ends and urge their ponies to pull; they are clever at choosing the spot, and by pulling out quite a small piece they cause the whole building to collapse. The work of countless generations of husbandmen was being utterly undone before our eyes. Farther on the main body had encircled a hilltop; in the midst of the circle was a collection of stray animals and stubborn peasants who had clung to the ruins of their farms; the Turks waited until we were close enough to get a good view, and then shot every living creature to death. By next spring the whole countryside would be a desert of grass, like the plains of Magog where their ancestors grazed their sheep.

By mid-afternoon we were outside the closed gates of Metabole. My lady approached alone, and after some hesitation the gatekeepers opened. Then everything went without a hitch. Shortly afterwards she came out on foot, dressed in a plain gown of brown wool; her four maids went before her, each bearing a copper tray with her jewels and the ingredients of her complexion; their faces were attractively painted, and they wore silk. You may think that my lady did wrong to deliver her personal attendants to the infidel; but they were eager to go. They were slaves from the Caucasus, where slavery is regarded as a method of getting on in the world; under a Christian owner they might be pampered, but we are too proud of our pedigrees to marry them; the infidels, who hardly know marriage as we understand it, have no objection to making the prettiest face among their concubines the ruler of her colleagues; in Artouch's household they might end as queens. As to religion, at home they worship fairies; while they belonged to Messer Roussel they were nominal Christians, but they would cheerfully embrace any other faith that seemed profitable. It was a kindness to give them to a rich master.

My lady herself carried a tray with forty gold pieces arranged in piles. Artouch was very affable, and permitted my lord to be the first captive redeemed. Then a stream of women came out, each bearing the ransom for her man; very soon the gold coins were finished, but my lady wisely insisted that we should be generous with the equivalent in silver or jewels, and Artouch accepted them at first glance. I had no wife or concubine, so I was one of the last to be released; but there was enough for all, and my lady did not forget me. That night we ate meat and wine, wearing Christian shirts and chausses as we crowded the courtyard of Metabole.

CHAPTER TWELVE

Matilda the Leader

B ut we were in a very bad way. The thirty sergeants who held the castle were still fully armed; in the baggage were spare swords and lances, enough to give every man a bit of steel; but there was no mail, and not enough shields to go round. No one trained to fight in mail can fight without it; or if he tries he is soon killed, forgetting to guard himself. Worst of all was the sense of disgrace; we no longer thought of ourselves as warriors. This may seem an exaggeration. In the west good knights are always being captured and released for ransom; but they are either seized as they lie under their horses, or at worst they yield when a castle is battered; and their captors are fellow-Christians, who happen to have taken the other side in some unimportant squabble. We had surrendered in the open field, of our own free will. To hearten us, my lady made a speech:

'This is a very mournful occasion. Last week there were nearly three thousand mailed Franks on Mount Sophon; now there are two hundred in this little castle, without mail or arms. But you are still the guardians of a mass of women and children, your own or those left by the comrades who fell beside you. They must be saved. We must get out of here as quick as we can, for there is nothing to eat where Artouch makes his pastures. Where shall we go?'

There was no answer. No one cared.

'Very well. If you have no opinions of your own you must listen to me. We can seek the Emperor's mercy. He's a fellow-

Christian, and he might give us ships. What do you think of that?'

Messer Roussel looked up. 'That won't do. He would blind me. But we might make for the coast and steal ships for ourselves.'

'No, my lord,' Matilda said firmly. 'You might steal one ship, or perhaps two. But that would mean leaving behind three thousand women and children. Remember, it was the women who rescued you from captivity. We might have fled to the city with your plunder. We were faithful, and you must be faithful to us.'

'Well, what can we do?' someone asked. 'We can't fight without mail, and we know no other trade. We must run away somewhere. Why not to Italy?'

'There is a way out,' Matilda continued. 'It isn't safe, but if safety is what you desire I can't think why you became mercenaries in the first place. One part of the world would be glad to see us. In Armeniakon and Sebaste there is food and a friendly population. Amasia has forges and smiths, who can make you fresh mail. It's four hundred miles by a dangerous road. But when we get there we can begin all over again.'

Those were the magic words which persuaded us. We would have undertaken any task for the chance of a fresh start; we hated and despised ourselves as we were. But even after we had accepted the idea we would never have started if Matilda had not taken us in hand. All that evening she went about and spoke to men individually, flattering each by assuming that he would do his duty, even if his comrades failed. We went to sleep with fresh hope, and in the morning began our preparation.

Metabole had been provisioned for a siege, so if we started at once we should have food to carry us through the worst of the barren stretch which Artouch was preparing for his sheep. Apart from that food we had nothing to carry, neither arms nor treasure; which was just as well, since we had no transport.

At first we were hampered by the very large proportion of followers to able-bodied men (alas, we could not call them armed men). But that difficulty solved itself when the women learned our intention. We had been three years in Romania, which is longer than most mercenaries keep the same mate; many concubines were native Romans, and when they knew that our plunder was gone and there was a hard march in prospect they deserted of their own accord, taking refuge in Nicomedia or chancing a lonely journey to the Bosphorus. Apart from those women who still had living protectors we were left with only a handful of Italians, who clung to any Frankish community in the alien east.

There were a few baggage-animals, enough to carry the small children; the rest must walk, and search on foot for food. We were unused to walking, but we had no mail to bear us down. The project was possible, and Matilda's energy drove us to attempt it.

Messer Roussel did not recover from his surrender. What makes a Frankish knight formidable in the charge is his conviction that he is invincible, and my lord had lost that. He was still courteous and good-tempered; but he seldom gave orders and never compelled us to carry them out. My lady was our captain. She allotted the few donkeys and pack-ponies, distributed the available weapons, and divided her force into scouts, foragers, and a main guard. When on the fourth day we set out, thirty armed sergeants, two hundred warriors in their shirts, and about four hundred women and children, she led the main body, with a little picture of the warrior-saint Theodore tied to her staff; she had found it in the castle, and it consoled us in some degree for the loss of our banner.

The plan was to make ten miles every day, to cover the four hundred miles to Amasia before the cold weather. That doesn't sound very hard marching, but we were cumbered with children on foot and we might have to detour to avoid Turkish bands. A great road runs from Nicomedia to Amasia, in fact the most important road from Europe to what used to be the eastern frontier. We could not miss the way.

We set out about the Feast of St Giles, with a week's biscuit and bacon to last us for a six-weeks' journey. The outset of a march is always cheerful, even such a desperate journey as this, and I sang as I strode down the great road. Naturally, since I knew the language, I had been assigned to the scouts; I had a good staff, with a sling on the end, and a handful of pebbles in my bosom; homeless dogs escaped from ravaged farms were beginning to attack men.

Already the whole pattern of the land was changing. You have all seen wasted fields, but even in the most harried parts of Sicily the ploughmen hide in the woods and try to make a fresh start next year; land that has not been weeded or cleared for more than two years looks quite different; thorns grew everywhere, and blocked ditches had turned patches of level ground to swamp; the whole country was well on the way to becoming the sheep pasture the nomads desired.

We hastened along the great road, for such a desert, where grass already peeped between the flagstones, seemed safe for unarmed travellers; not even the smoke of a distant cooking-fire marked the sky, or a fresh hoofprint the dust. With a stone from my sling I knocked over one of a covey of partridges dusting in the road; it was a young bird, and perhaps I was the first man it had seen. It was hardly worth while to scout ahead, and I was striding along with my eyes on the ground when I heard a patter of hoofs behind me, and my lady rode up on a little donkey.

'Don't fall asleep, Messer Roger,' she said as she reined in beside me. 'This country looks deserted, but there may be outlaws in the swamp. I want to find a walled village, well off the road, where we can rest for the night without keeping half the men on guard. There should be plenty of ruined villages to choose from.'

'Yes, my lady, we shall be safer off the road, but it may not be easy to persuade our people to climb a hill at the end of the march. Will they obey if my lord commands it?'

'My lord won't give orders. He doesn't care what happens to him, which is all right if he feels that way. But he doesn't care what happens to the decent Franks whom he brought to Asia, and that is neglect of the first duty of a leader. Don't spread it about, but if anyone is in command I am.'

'We could not have a braver leader, my lady. Your courage saved us from captivity. I shall willingly obey you.'

'Stuff and nonsense. It wasn't my courage, but your skill in plunder. I only offered Artouch the spoil of Chrysopolis; if he had been unwilling to sell I don't know what would have happened.'

'You might have returned to Italy a rich widow. In fact you might have done that anyway. Since we are alone, and you graciously address me as an equal, will you take it without offence if I ask why you bothered to ransom us?'

That was a searching question; ladies always ransom their lords, but then gallant knights always fight to the death rather than yield to infidels. Messer Roussel had broken the rules, and I was genuinely anxious to know why Matilda had not. Her character puzzled me. She took my impudence in good part, and answered with a smile:

'My first thought when I heard the news was that now I might go home and rule a Lombard city as it should be ruled. Why didn't I? I can't tell you. The habit of responsibility is hard to break. Here were Franks without a leader, and they looked to me for orders. If the future is hopeless it is a great relief to do what obviously needs doing. Risking my life in the Turkish camp took my mind off my worries. When you were freed we had to go somewhere, and Amasia is as good as the next place. Tonight I must find shelter and fuel, and tomorrow I must get the laggards on the road. These are all self-evident necessities, which must be done by me if they are to be done at all. Presently we shall meet some difficulty where I can't see an obvious way out, and that will be the end. But until then we shall march, as sailors stick to the steering-oar while the ship fills with water. I don't know why, but it is the honourable way to meet disaster.'

'Then you don't think we shall be welcome in Amasia?'

'Oh yes, we shall be welcome, but how long can we hold it?

The infidels have beaten us in the field, when all our men were mounted and clad in western mail. One of these days they will get into Amasia in spite of our swords. But that's no reason for giving in now.'

'I understand, my lady. The Romans take the same view. They believe the city will eventually fall.'

'Precisely. But it doesn't stop them inviting their friends to gay supper-parties. When the end comes I am sure they will die gallantly in the breach, and of course it may not come for centuries. Theirs is a good life, and the knowledge that it must end in defeat makes it all the better.'

'What a pity we didn't stick to the Emperor's service. We might be holding Nicomedia under the Labarum, instead of wandering as outlaws in this desert.'

'They would have made our life impossible, sooner or later. Romans don't like Franks. If I had been in Caesarea when they hanged Robert de Hal I would have done my best to smooth things over, and perhaps my lord would have continued in his obedience. But then they would have done something even more unpleasant, to force a break. You realise it was all part of a plot? Oh, those devious Roman politics that no Frank can understand! A Comnenus was Domestic, and the Ducates would do anything to disgrace him. They have succeeded, and no one will ever trust Isaac Comnenus with another army. But the Ducates are beaten too. Holy Michael, I wonder if Basil Malases was acting for the Comneni when he persuaded us to set up the Caesar?'

'I never thought of that, my lady, though it sounds plausible now you point it out. Since Franks are the best warriors in the world I thought we had only to charge our enemies, and we would die rich and respected. But the east is too complicated for our thick heads.'

'Well, there it is. I love the city, and it's closed to me for ever. But I am in charge of six hundred Franks, and that will keep me too busy for idle repining. There's a walled village on that hilltop, and it must be deserted since the fields lie untilled. Lead off to the right.'

So we continued for a week, across the Sangarius and then through the wasted Theme of Bucellarion. The great road was in excellent condition, though for more than a year no travellers had used it. We marched swiftly, for men on foot, and must have covered a hundred miles while our food lasted.

Then our troubles began. The great road still stretched before us, smooth and level, running straight through the empty plain. But in that plain nothing lived. On the eighth day we pressed forward, hoping to find peasants or at least deer or wild cattle which we might kill with bows; but there was nothing, and that evening we camped fireless and hungry. In the morning we killed a few donkeys, enough to carry us through one more march. But that was the last resource. Before starting my lady called a council of leading knights.

Messer Roussel squatted in the place of honour, as though presiding over the meeting; but he held his head in his hands and said nothing useful, merely muttering that we were all near death, and deserved it for yielding to the infidel. 'We should have died sword in hand,' he declared. 'That surrender will make us infamous to the end of time, and all we gained by it was two more weeks of a very miserable existence.'

My lady would have none of it. 'It was nothing disgraceful,' she said stoutly. 'You were all dismounted and more than three-quarters had been killed. What would be really shameful would be to lose heart now, when we have escaped from our enemies. The business of this council is to find food, not to curse God and die; even Job didn't do that when it came to the point, though he had lost his wife and children while you still have yours. Now here is my plan. The Turks have ravaged all this plain, which was only to be expected. But they are horsemen; with all the world to choose from they naturally stick to open country. Over there in the north lies a range of hills. It's broken and rough, and I bet the infidels never bothered to ravage it.

We shall march there at once, and work east along the ridges. Any objections? Right. Then we start in ten minutes.'

No one else spoke, even to express agreement. But so it was decided, because Matilda alone knew her own mind.

When I picked up my staff and began to trudge northward my lady walked beside me, as though it was the most natural thing in the world for an unarmed woman to scout through hostile country. Her donkey had been slaughtered for food, and she had given her little image of St Theodore to comfort a dying woman.

She spoke to me crossly. 'You might do something to help, young Roger. You sat silent in council and left the work to me. If they hadn't all been thoroughly discouraged they would have refused to march, out of sheer manly pride and dislike of following female advice. Next time I have a good idea I shall tell you beforehand, and you will propose it. You are supposed to be a man; at least you have more spirit than my wretched husband.'

'Why bother, my lady? Why not go on alone? You will get through, I am certain, and then you may end your days in a Roman household.'

'Yes, in a Roman household. But in what capacity? Do you think I look forward to life in a kitchen? Of course any sensible householder would realise that I am cut out by nature to be a groom. But even Romans are hidebound about what is man's work, and what woman's.'

'Shall we be enslaved by fellow-Christians? Is that the best we can hope for?'

'If we straggle, that is what will become of us. But if we look like an army someone may hire us to fight. I have thought of pressing on alone, and it may come to it if you all sit about and do nothing when you ought to be marching; but then I must leave my children. I've had all the bother of rearing them, without help from my lord or anyone else, and I don't want to abandon them just when they are old enough to be amusing companions. I hate babies, always crying to be fed and dragging you home from the hunt; but even little Osbert is now doing his share; he shows more courage than most of those dreary dispirited grown-ups round him.'

I suddenly realised what Matilda had to bear; we had only ourselves to look after, though that was a burden which had proved too heavy for some of us; she planned for the whole party, setting an example of courage and activity; yet at the end of the day, when we sat down exhausted, she had to clean three rowdy children, and find something for them to eat. Without thinking I spoke my admiration, forgetting the courteous forms of address.

'My dear, you should have been a warrior.'

'What's the use, little Roger,' she said with a sniff of contempt. 'My father was a warrior, until he died in the breach with three Norman swords in his guts. I'm a woman, and that's all there is to it. But you understand horses. You know that a mare inherits the mettle of her sire. Did it ever cross your mind that women have the courage of men? For three hundred years my forebears were lords in Benevento. With the average luck that everyone expects I would have married some noble Lombard and helped him to rule his town, guarding the walls while he raided his enemies. But the Weasel broke in and my old life was ended. It was luck, and none of my contriving, that what came next was honourable marriage, instead of rape by the whole army. That encouraged me, and I picked up as many of the pieces as I could. I set to work to make Messer Roussel de Balliol a great man. Like all you bloody Normans, he's brave while he sits a good horse with a good sword in his hand. And he's a jolly companion, so it was never difficult to keep his band up to strength. But if I hadn't taken charge he would still be following that landless Roger fitzTancred. I was the one who saw that for a mercenary a change of lords is the way to promotion. Then we had this wonderful chance, to get away from that gang of Norman land-pirates; to a country where women may take part in great affairs; a country where they are not interested in barbarian pedigrees, and our grandchildren might be Roman nobles. After all, three generations ago the

Comneni were Thracian peasants, unless they were Armenian bandits, which is their own story. If only we could have kept out of politics! But Romanus Diogenes got himself beaten, and then every magnate in Romania began to intrigue for his own hand. Well, I must begin again. In Armenia there are petty chieftains who have come to terms with the infidel; they pay tribute, but otherwise they rule undisturbed, as my father ruled undisturbed after paying tribute to the Catapan. Among those mountains there is a chance for my children to live free, and I'll take it if I have to drive my lord with a stick when he sits down in despair.'

There was nothing I could say in answer. We trudged silently for the rest of the morning. My lady occasionally looked curiously at me, and I think she regretted her frankness. But I had been a page, and pages are trained to discretion.

At midday we halted, though rather from habit than for any better reason, for we had nothing to eat. When we resumed our march the way led uphill. The range ran clearly east and west; it was heavily wooded, and in spite of the haze I could make out threads of smoke on the skyline. This was not the sort of country Turks would choose to raid, when all the plains of Asia lay open and undefended. A few sergeants grumbled at having to climb a steep hill, going north, when we knew our refuge lay to the east with a good road leading to it. We might have dispersed then and there, for Messer Roussel was too listless to assert his authority; but luckily a woman, searching for a strayed donkey, climbed a ridge and found the beast feeding in a pocket of ripe barley. Men who grew barley might give us food. We pressed on in better spirits.

That night we slept in a village of the mountaineers, friendly people who had paid tribute to the Emperor; but no tax-gatherers had come among them since the disaster of Manzikert, and they had grain to spare. They used a language of their own, and claimed to be the Galatians whom St Paul converted; but one of their elders spoke Greek and told us we might reach Amasia by following the range to the eastward.

Asia is a land of wide plains, which until the Turks came were closely cultivated by Roman peasants; but as soon as you get into the hills you find communities of a different race. These live apart, not inter-marrying with the Romans, and whenever you talk to their Greek-speaking elders they tell you at once that there was a time when their ancestors ruled the whole land. It is not a bit like Italy, where the peasants are all of the same race and language; here you can walk up a steep hill, leaving some densely inhabited town of the Romans, and in three miles you are among a people with strange traditions, another language, and even a different way of practising religion.

So it was with these Galatians. Looking down from their heights they could see the road, the great road which until recently had been crowded with the retinues of Roman officials; until the Turks came they had hardly heard, for many generations, of any ruler except the Equal of the Apostles; the Empire surrounded them for hundreds of miles on every side. But they never considered themselves to be part of it. They paid tribute, unless the sum demanded was so great that it was cheaper to abandon their fields and start again in some other valley; occasionally, when their young men robbed the rich villages of the plain, soldiers would come and burn their huts; sometimes a serious dispute would be judged in the lawcourts of the alien officials. But they kept to themselves, talking over in the evening the great days when their ancestors ruled the lowland; they heard Mass once a week, but never confessed or communicated; there was good and bad luck bound up with various boulders and high peaks, and that sufficed, when it was properly controlled, to bring the right weather for their harvests. All this I learned that first evening, talking with the headman of the village. It gave me a new picture of Romania, which I had previously regarded as a community of Christian Romans. Now I saw it resembled a great vessel of gilded bronze; the gilding was the Roman cities, the bands of the Themes and the educated officials; but the strong metal which gave shape to the structure was composed of alien mountaineers; over most of

Asia the gilding was wearing very thin, and the metal was ready to be melted and cast into another shape.

(That is called a figure of speech, and I am very proud of it. But even an illiterate laybrother picks up these tricks after hearing a great many sermons.)

The villagers were quite pleased that the Army of Romania had perished at Manzikert; iron and salt were scarce, since they dared not descend to the plains to trade, but for the last two years they had not been taxed, and the Turks did not bother to climb up and plunder them. They welcomed us, not because we were fellow-Christians in peril from the infidel, but because we were fugitives from the wrath of the Emperor. They promised to guide us eastward in the morning, handing us over to another Galatian village at the end of the march.

I was very tired, but the Greek-speaking headman had taken a fancy to me, and I sat by his fire while he told me all about his people, and eventually, when he had finished the wine-jar, recited an epic in his own language. When I heard it I sat up and minded my manners; if he knew by heart a long poem about the deeds of his ancestors he must be a gentleman of good birth. That is the test of breeding all the world over.

Next day I staggered along, very sleepy and tired, by a narrow path which followed the tree-line below the naked crests, and which in consequence wound round the valleys till we had to walk four miles to gain one; but it was beaten smooth by the passage of many feet, and the women found it easier than the paved road in the baking heat of the plain. The headman told me it was the escape route they all used when tax-gatherers called; but he did not come with us, and our guides spoke only their own dialect; we could not discover how far it was to our next halting-place, but that did not matter, since mountaineers can never measure a journey so that it can be understood by plains-bred horsemen.

At the midday halt Matilda sought me out. I was sitting among our guides, grinning and making friendly signs, because I was now a professional linguist who must do his best even with an unknown language. My lady beamed at the mountaineers, and made friends by admiring the carving on a bone knife-hilt; then she leaned across and spoke to me, casually, not to arouse their interest.

'I want to discuss the future, Roger, and this is the best place for a conference. We don't look as though we are talking secrets, yet no one can understand us. Do you think these people will really help us to Amasia? They gain nothing by it. Suppose they sell us to the Turks?'

'No, my lady,' I answered. The point had occurred to me and I had given it careful thought. 'If they didn't like us they might have driven us away last night, when we were too weary to resist. They can't *sell* us to the Turks, because the Turks wouldn't pay. They might deliver us to the infidel, but only to score off strangers. The Turks would seize the guides as well, if they want slaves, but usually they don't. We must assume our guides are honest. In fact they seem very pleasant people. Why should we march farther? In these hills we are safe from raiding horse. Let us stay, and swear fealty to their rulers. I would live content as a Galatian mountaineer.'

'Oh dear, Roger, do you also feel that?' said Matilda with a sigh. 'My lord wants to stay, and I have been trying to argue him out of it. Can you see my sons sowing their own barley, and climbing a tree to escape from their enemies? By St Michael and all the Host of Heaven, Ralph and Osbert shall ride to battle, and eat bread that others have reaped; or they shall die in the attempt. Just because you were beaten once you have given up hope of winning fortune by the sword. Am I the only warrior in the band?'

'It isn't only, Matilda, that we were beaten. It's the knowledge that the Turks will probably beat us next time. In the camp on Mount Sophon I thought myself a knight, but it's a difficult and dangerous trade. I shall be happy to plough my own fields.'

She looked at me queerly. I understood; for nine years I had called her 'my lady' and stood until I was granted permission to sit. Here we squatted together in the greenwood, and because I thought of her as Matilda, a fellow fugitive in a band of frightened outlaws, the name had slipped out by mistake.

'Little Roger Smith,' she said after a pause, 'you are of base blood, for all that your father made pilgrimage to St Michael. I shall tell you a secret. It will be very hard to restore my lord's courage. I had been thinking of leaving him, to join some braver Frank. Now I see there are no brave Franks in this band. I shall march on with Messer Roussel, whether you and your base comrades stay here or not. We shall rule in Amasia, or some other castle, until a stronger takes it from us; then we shall die by the sword, as my father died in the town he ruled. Goodbye, peasant.'

As she strode away the guides looked up in amazement. They did not understand the quarrel, and it was the compulsion not to behave foolishly before foreigners which kept me sitting with my mouth open, instead of running after my lady to seek pardon. Then the impulse passed, for I realised it was too late. My head was in a whirl. I *am* a peasant, the son of a smith; in a distant land I might win the arms of a knight, but I would never be the equal of Matilda de Balliol, of the Lombard stock of Benevento. Yet she had been proposing to set me up as leader in place of Messer Roussel. Perhaps she was in love with me. I puzzled over the odd situation.

Even in my young days I was never a success with the ladies. I am shorter and darker than most Franks, and constant brain work as a linguist, for which I am not really fitted, gave me a frowning, bad-tempered expression. Besides, the man who really seduces a lady must labour all day to appear frivolous; I was not sufficiently interested to undertake the toil. Before I entered religion I would occasionally sleep with a whore, when I found my mind filled with lust to the exclusion of more profitable thoughts; now fasting and mortification provide a remedy which is really less trouble. But I never won a woman by charm alone; there was always money to be paid in the morning.

I never regarded Matilda as desirable, and I doubt whether the thought occurred to anyone else. That was her own fault.

She was plain, with masculine features and a great beak of a nose; but she had a strong athletic body which might have been attractive if she had employed the ordinary feminine wiles. But she was either neat and clean, and dressed as much like a groom as she could be without incurring ecclesiastical censure for wearing male attire; or she so exaggerated the Roman adornments, painted lips, dyed hair, white powder on nose and red powder on cheeks, that everyone thought she was making fun of a ridiculous foreign custom. Perhaps there was something wrong with her eyes. Even her horsemanship, the one quality in which she outshone every woman I have met, was too good to be an attraction; instead of thinking 'that's a brave little girl controlling such a fierce warhorse', you merely said to yourself 'that rider can manage without help; is there someone prettier who needs a strong hand on the bridle.' In the Turkish camp she had shown greater courage than I had realised at the time; when Artouch asked for her maids and her face-paint, while letting her go, it must have cost her great suffering to treat the affair as an amusing adventure.

Of course I was tempted; she had offered herself to me, I suppose because bitter experience had taught her not to aim too high; she thought that I, ugly and lowborn and not a good jouster, would be flattered to meet her half-way. There was still time for me to make the conquest, if I sought her out and pretended that my slow wits had only now grasped her meaning; I have seen it done often enough, and I could have repeated the usual meaningless declarations of devotion. But that particular temptation was not difficult to resist. I admired Matilda as a hero, but I had not the slightest trace of love for her as a woman; and there were the obligations of honour. Like most laymen, in those days I cared very little about the Ten Commandments; but everyone above the level of the beasts that perish has some sort of code, and mine forbade me to overthrow my leader by seducing his wife. Besides, though I could have got rid of Messer Roussel quite easily, the band might not have obeyed me afterwards.

It is as pleasant to resist an uncongenial temptation as to yield to one that has more charms. I trudged through the woods feeling honourable and knightly, which is a great help to sore feet. When we passed a stretch of open moor I saw Matilda talking earnestly to her husband. Probably under that stimulus he would get back his courage in a day or two.

We were more than a month in the hills of the Galatians, but the journey contained no hardships. The mountaineers had food to spare, and they would just as soon give it to travellers as save it for a rainy day. There were one or two rivers to cross, the only dangerous stages of the march. But the Galatians knew secret fords, or kept a hidden store of goatskin floats near placid reaches. We crossed the rivers by night, after careful scouting. Otherwise we were safe all the time, which had a very good effect on our bodies and minds. We had been in constant danger since we marched from Ancyra; not always serious danger, but a chance of being killed in the next twenty-four hours; nine months of that makes the bravest warrior sleep badly; now we lay down in the evening tired, but confident that we would eat tomorrow's supper.

Messer Roussel improved rapidly. Matilda was his constant companion, and though I suppose in private she told him what to do she ceased to give orders as soon as he was fit to take over. I was glad I had not helped her to get rid of her husband. Matilda was unique; if she had been false to her own standards, with my encouragement, I would have felt as mean as if I had wantonly defaced a beautiful picture.

A few days before All Saints the headman of the village where we halted told me we had finished our journey. Amasia was ten miles away, in the plain. If we wanted to go there we must descend to the great road, for this was the limit of the mountaineers. But there was an empty valley to the north, and he would lend us ploughs and seed-corn. This was the first time the mountaineers had actually invited us to join them. I felt it my duty to pass on what he said; it might cause dissension in the band; but a linguist who does not translate fairly will one day bring worse trouble.

Messer Roussel and his council were squatting on the floor of the large hut which in all these villages is kept for chance strangers. They had difficulty in following the broken Greek of the headman, but when I put his proposal into French several knights wished to accept it. In particular there was an elderly ruffian who had been a monk in Normandy until he was expelled from the cloister for persistent fornication; he had once heard read someone's *History of the World from the Creation to Charlemagne*; he was very proud of it, and often spoke of the lessons of history and the wisdom of accepting the inevitable. Now he made a formal oration, to this effect: Romania was finished, the plains of Asia belonged to the Turks, and the walled towns would presently fall under their sway; but the mountains might remain free, because on the hillside infantry can beat horse; therefore our best plan would be to stay where we were and learn to fight on foot.

It sounded wise and logical as he said it; we felt that if we stayed we would be conforming to the march of events like educated civilised men; it would also be safe and easy. When he finished there was a mutter of agreement. But Messer Roussel jumped to his feet; his left hand moved over his chest as though bearing a shield. 'St Michael and Balliol!' he shouted, 'I am a free man and a Christian. I can choose for myself between Heaven and Hell, and in this life I can choose whether I fight the infidel or hide behind a rock! Ranulf the Monk says Romania is finished. It's only finished if the Romans despair! Thank God I don't know any history. All I know is that down in Amasia there are smiths who will make mail for me, and up here there are peasants who will lend me a plough. We march at dawn, and if the men of Amasia don't open their gates I shall escalade the wall! The warriors will follow me, and the renegade monks can stay here and grow barley. I have never worked for my bread, and I would rather die fighting than begin now.'

This was the old Messer Roussel, the gallant leader of Sicily and Zompi. Matilda had picked up all the pieces. Of course we all marched with him.

CHAPTER THIRTEEN

Amasia Revisited

In Amasia all went smoothly. We learned that the men of Armeniakon had continued to regard themselves as loyal vassals of Messer Roussel; they had been distressed to hear of the disaster of Mount Sophon, and obviously they would no longer feel quite safe under Frankish protection. They would be happy to have us back again, but their spokesman made it clear, in the clever Roman way which tells unpalatable truths without rudeness , that we might no longer tallage our subjects at will; instead the council of magnates, rulers of Amasia, would hire us to defend them. But that was as much as we could expect after we had lost arms, horses and prestige. We gladly accepted these terms; soon after All Souls we were safely lodged in the citadel.

The whole Theme had kept up a version of the Frankish customs we had taught them in the spring. But Romans cannot copy any Frankish institution without giving it a characteristic twist of their own; the magnates who took the lead were not landholders and warriors, but wealthy merchants; and the courts were more frankly biased in favour of the rich than any similar body of oath-bound Normans. We fear the punishment which Heaven visits on perjury, and that keeps even litigants arguing an important suit within reasonable bounds. Romans will risk the wrath of God whenever a large sum of money is at stake; the decisions I heard in the law courts of Amasia made me understand why in normal times even free Romans prefer to have their causes decided by a professional judge.

This injustice made the lower classes disloyal. But of course the lower classes dare not make war on their betters – at least in a walled town where they cannot flee to the waste as outlaws. The peasants were slightly more contented, because the council had come to an arrangement with the nearest Turks which gave them a chance to till some of their fields in peace. These Turkish bands were beginning to settle down in definite territories, if you can call it settling down when they moved their tents with the seasons; but each band now had a regular range of pasture which they would defend against other Turks. Those who roamed the plain near Amasia were led by one Tutach; the council paid him a fixed tribute, and in return he spared their fields. What with tribute to the Turks and pay to their Frankish garrison the council were spending more than their tallages brought in; but they could keep it up for the present by selling plate and jewels, and something might turn up before all their wealth was gone. In those days in Asia no one could plan further than that.

The financial condition of the council, though precarious, had been slightly eased by an unexpected windfall. The Bishop, its president, told us that while we were in the mountains a messenger had arrived from the city. He brought a sack of gold and a letter from the Logothete. This explained that the money was to be spent on strengthening the defences of the town against outlaws; in other words, it was a bribe to persuade them to shut their gates against us. It seemed odd that Michael should try so much harder to finish off a defeated band of Franks than to expel the Turkish infidel; we did no permanent harm, while the Turks inflicted damage that could not be repaired for generations; but the Bishop explained. He pointed out that even Malek Shah the great King of the Turks had never marched on the city; but Messer Roussel had set up a rival Emperor, and his watchfires at Chrysopolis had frightened the Logothete. We were not serious enemies of Romania, but to the Emperor personally we were a greater menace than the infidels.

In fact we had not been a month in our new castle when we heard he was sending an army against us. There were practically no regular Roman troops left in Asia, but that wonderful Treasury can always produce money when it is urgently needed, and he had managed to hire six thousand Alans. They were marching east, led by the Strategus Nicephorus Palaeologus. The reasons for the change of command were intricate. I have already said that all Romans are deeply interested in the politics of the city, and the Amasians were well informed of what passed at court. They told us there had been a shift in the alignment of parties. Hitherto the Emperor had reigned by playing off Comnenus against Ducas; but both these great houses had threatened to combine against Nicephoritzes the Logothete, thinking it more disgraceful to be ruled by a eunuch than by a rival; the Emperor was hard put to it to find a general he could trust.

But these difficulties in the city did not make things easier for us. By now we were armed in mail and mounted on good horses; yet my lord was reluctant to fight six thousand horse with the two hundred Franks who remained to him. There were anxious discussions in the citadel. If there had been a way of retreat we would have fled; but there wasn't. East lay the lands of the infidel, the Alans were approaching from the west, and to north and south the Turks were so thick that two hundred men would be overwhelmed. We heard that Alexius Comnenus had won great fame by a march from Ancyra to the Bosphorus, during which he and his men hid on foot among some rushes and escaped a roving band of Turks; he was Domestic at the time. When we came to Romania, only four years ago, sixty thousand mailed horse followed the Domestic; two years after Manzikert he won fame by hiding in a swamp. It was not until I heard this story, related with pride by a hereditary partisan of the Comneni, that I realised what a change had been brought by the defeat of Romanus Diogenes.

One day we learned that the Roman army was only twenty miles away; we closed the gates of the citadel, since we were too few to hold the town. We had no plans, but we thought that if we negotiated from a strong castle we might get passage to

186

Italy. Then five hundred Alans rode up to the barbican across the river. We were puzzled by the absence of the rest of the army, and feared they might try a surprise assault from the east. But the Alans by the bridge sent in their linguist waving an olive-branch, and when he had delivered his message we drank most of our stores in celebration. For the savages explained that the Emperor was unable to pay them, though Palaeologus kept strict discipline all the same; accordingly, they had left Roman service; some were riding home, some were pillaging at large, but this particular five hundred wanted to know whether Messer Roussel would take them into pay! Such was the discreditable end of the last army the Romans sent down the great road to the east.

We could not pay these Alans, and advised them to go home; they are not very useful as mercenaries; they are brave in single combat, and extremely skilful at getting their horses over broken ground; but they are much too excitable, and too fond of quarrelling among themselves, to be reliable in a set battle. We needed more men, but we hoped that by next year we might enlist some of the town militia, though at present they refused to go beyond their walls.

We talked in terms of next year, for it was now Advent; even the Emperor Michael, though he hated us, would not send another army in the depth of winter. We had found a safe haven, and we did not look further ahead than the spring. No Frank can plan his future in that unpredictable east. It was time for the Christmas feasting.

My lady and I were again good friends. Matilda made the first overture, muttering something about feeling over-wrought on that dangerous march, and I was glad to meet her half-way. She had regained her spirits as soon as she found a competent maid; but now she was more careful with the face-paint, for Amasia was a town of provincial manners; she might have passed anywhere as a rather horsy Roman matron. Ralph, her eldest son, was in his twelfth year; Messer Roussel jousted with him in the meadow by the river, but my lady taught him most of his riding. This absorbing occupation kept her contented.

She was still the real leader of the diminished band. Messer Roussel was a good comrade; he hated to see unhappy faces, and even used what influence he had with the merchants to organise relief for the starving refugees; he was the most popular Frank in Amasia. But while there was a good dinner waiting for him he did not make plans. My lady did, and she was always raising the question of what we should do in the spring.

'On her next birthday Joan will be ten,' I remember her saying as we sat round the fire (there was an arrangement of pipes under the floor of the hall, by which hot air was supposed to circulate from a furnace in the cellar; but it was out of order, and no one knew how to mend it; the floor made a good hearth, though the coloured marble cracked with the heat). 'It's time the girl was betrothed. In Armenia there are Christian lords who would be glad to make alliance with the leader of two hundred horse. We should move east. By the way, why is this Theme called Armeniakon, when the inhabitants are not Armenian?'

'Because it was the fief garrisoned by the bands of Armenia, when they were driven west by the first infidels. All the Roman armies moved in that crisis, and the Themes were named from the troops stationed in them. In the same way Thrakesion is not in Thrace but in Asia.' I was glad to show off my knowledge of Roman institutions; Matilda seldom asked my opinion.

'Oh well, that's not important,' she continued. 'Romans often call things by very odd names. But we must make up our minds whether we stay here, and if not, where we ride next.'

'I still think we should make a deal with the Emperor,' said Ranulf the Monk, who considered our position much too dangerous. 'He is so anxious to be rid of us that he might provide shipping. Then we could sack this place as we marched out, not to arrive in Italy penniless.'

My lord spoke firmly. 'We can't pillage our own employers. No one would hire mercenaries with that record.'

'Besides,' said Matilda, 'we would never reach the coast. The Turks are too strong. If we don't stay here, where we are safe for the moment but there is no future for the children, the only way out is by the Christian mountains of Armenia.'

'Some Armenian princes are moving south,' put in a cheerful young knight who kept an Armenian concubine. 'They hold a chain of little fortresses in the south-east, which practically link up with the Duchy of Antioch. My girl says Antioch is still Christian, though it pays no tribute to anybody.'

'That is getting too near the homeland of the Saracens,' said my lord. 'If we march farther east we shall never see Italy again. But the real trouble is that we don't know how far the infidels have advanced. Are Sebaste and Caesarea still Roman? Perhaps the Bishop can tell us. Ask him, Roger.'

The Bishop of Amasia was a Roman of the city, said to have bought his consecration by open simony; a man of evil life, and unpopular with his flock, but well informed about local conditions. He sat apart, on the other side of the fire. It was one of those days of severe fasting which are so frequent in the eastern church; at such times he would visit the citadel, to enjoy a good dinner without giving scandal.

But he knew nothing of the south-west. Amasia's nearest link with the sea lay to the north, and there were good roads to Sinope and Trebizond; he could tell us that both ports were blockaded on the landward side by the most savage tribe of Turks, the Men of the Black Sheep. We were isolated in a desert of infidel shepherds, and our only link with Christendom was the great road to the Bosphorus. The Bishop summed up: 'This town is lost. Presently it will fall to the Turks, unless we first offer tribute to the Saracens, who are also infidel but rather more civilised. If you want to get out you must ride west. But why not stay at least until you have drunk up our good wine? This is the end of the world, the beginning of the reign of anti-Christ. You must be drunk to face it. I have not been sober since I heard of Manzikert.'

Many Romans took that view.

'In that case we must return to Italy,' said Matilda. 'We can't have our children growing up to pay tribute to infidels. What about making a bargain with the Turks for safe passage on the great road? Didn't they send an envoy a few days ago? What was that about?'

I knew, for I had interviewed the Roman renegade who brought the message. 'Oh, that was a hare-brained scheme which I did not bother to lay before the council,' I replied. 'Tutach of the Six Horsetails is bored with this neighbourhood. He would like to move west, but he isn't strong enough to displace his cousins who live on the blackmail of Ancyra. He proposed an alliance with *us*! He didn't realise that such a proposition was an insult to Christian men.'

'All the same, you should have reported it,' said Matilda severely. 'We don't want to quarrel with Tutach. The council pay him tribute and he does us no harm at present. An envoy of his should get a civil answer.'

'Yes, my lady. I sent a polite acknowledgement, and I meant to tell the council, one of these days.' I had been taking my own line in politics, and now it had been made public it seemed unpopular.

'I kept it dark,' I plunged on, to justify myself, 'because our sergeants might be tempted to close with the offer; and that would be more disgraceful than the surrender at Mount Sophon.'

'What's all this?' said my lord, at last paying attention. He left discussion in council to Matilda, but any mention of Mount Sophon roused him. 'Have you suppressed messages, young Roger? A linguist must pass on everything said to him, even if it is insulting. Besides, there may be something in the idea. Supposing we find that next summer we can't hold this town? Then a temporary arrangement with Tutach would give us a way out to the west. We could take the town council with us, and any other burgesses who were willing to abandon their homes. What do you think, my lord Bishop? Oh, I forget. He doesn't understand French. Ask his opinion, Roger, and give the answer faithfully.'

Bishop Damascenus listened carefully, and I could see he was attracted by the idea. He was not a holy man, and he had only bought his appointment to his provincial See to increase his standing in the city which was his real home; after Manzikert the Patriarch had compelled him to visit his imperilled flock, and for two years he had been stuck in the east while all sorts of vital intrigues were carried on in Holy Wisdom without his participation. 'You can make a treaty with Tutach without waging war on Christendom, if you go about it carefully,' he told me earnestly. 'The Six Horsetails want the tribute of Ancyra, which means forcing Artouch to move on; but they do not propose to attack the towns which still obey Michael. You can march with them as far as Nicomedia, fighting any other infidels you meet on the road. Afterwards you might turn pirate, if you understand the sea; or pillage some rich town and hire ships to carry you to Italy, if you think that is safer. I shall come with you, and so will most of the local magnates. But Turks are slippery people to deal with. You must take valuable hostages for good faith.'

I put all this honestly into French, and most of the council thought it a good idea. Matilda was the only opponent. She said that if all else failed we should break down the walls of the town, drive out the surplus population, and hold the citadel as an isolated castle. But then she had two fixed ideas, that we must have no friendly dealings with the infidel, and that we must hang on to a strong fortress, no matter how dangerous its situation.

When the Bishop saw opinion was in his favour he gave us a further piece of information; he had kept it dark hitherto, which showed he was not to be trusted (if we did not know that already); it was still so secret that we had not heard it from any other Roman.

'You assume that you can keep Christmas here in peace,' he told me, 'but Michael is making another effort to dislodge you.

He has dismissed Palaeologus, and turned once more to the Comneni. Or it may be a plan to make the Comneni look foolish; with Michael you can never be sure. But Isaac Comnenus has been appointed Duke of Antioch, which in practice means envoy to Philaretus who commands there for his own hand; and young Alexius has been ordered to march east. The story goes that the Emperor wouldn't give him an army, or even money to hire mercenaries. But he is a very competent young man. He might try a surprise escalade. Didn't he once turn you out of Ancyra without a sword drawn?'

'That settles it,' Messer Roussel said firmly. 'I shall send envoys to Tutach. We can look at it in this way: As lords of Armeniakon we are arranging with our neighbours for legitimate self-defence. The neighbours happen to be infidels, but we are not making war on Christendom; Michael is attacking an independent Christian state. No one can blame us.'

My lord's plans always sounded right while he expounded them; if you admitted that we were rightful lords of Amasia there could be no objection to the treaty. Only Matilda spoke against it, and she did not disapprove on grounds of morality; her reason for disliking it was fear that Tutach would betray us. Turks have a reputation for faithlessness, but there seemed to be no reason why he should break a bargain which he had himself proposed; the council decided to trust him, after first taking plenty of hostages, and as usual I was chosen to ride to his camp to arrange the meeting. That might be dangerous, and it was none of my seeking; but we had treated his envoy honestly; Tutach might keep the rules in return.

Our plan was at once known all over the town. Romans seem to pick up that sort of news from the air. It affected them, and of course they were interested; but they take such delight in politics that the poorest hawker can tell you of the struggles of Comnenus and Ducas, and how Bryennius scored over Palaeologus at the last batch of army promotions, though he would be no better off personally if the whole Imperial family were blinded tomorrow. I had expected riots when they learned that their protectors intended to march out, but though interested they remained unmoved. They wished us well in our tricky negotiation, but they would be quite happy to see the last of us. This attitude so puzzled me that I called on the Bishop and asked him to explain it.

He was delighted to dazzle a barbarian with the superior wisdom of the Romans. 'Amasia has been a market since Alexander the Great passed this way,' he said in a satisfied voice, settling himself in his cushioned chair; it was early for a Roman, only two hours after sunrise, and he had drunk enough to get over last night but was still on the whole sober. 'First came the Galatians, then a great King called Mithradates, then our ancestors the Romans of Rome fought all up and down the country. Five hundred years ago the Persians swept up to the Bosphorus, and a generation later came the first of the infidels. They came, they pillaged the open country, and then, sometimes after quite a long interval, the great Emperor chased them away. But whenever the Emperor liberated us he found Amasia flourishing, because the Amasians are sensible men who make terms with barbarian invaders. At first, when it looked as though the Turks would have the run of the country for a couple of years at most, we were pleased that lord Roussel should protect us. But the Turks have come to stay, and it is time to make peace with them. If I intended to live here I would have made terms a year ago; but I shall soon go into exile, earning credit in the city as a Christian Confessor; in fact as soon as you make the road safe for my journey. So I left matters to the local merchants, who are not so quick to recognise a new state of affairs as a Roman of the city. When you look at things with an open mind the Turks might be very much worse than they are. They pillage the fields, and kill any peasant they catch; but peasants don't have much of a life anyway, and are better off in Heaven as martyrs. Yet Turks don't bother walled towns. They allow their subjects to remain Christians; in fact they don't encourage renegades, because each is another mouth to share the plunder. Since they like showy and vulgar objects of luxury our craftsmen have plenty of customers, and oddly enough Turks usually pay for their trinkets, though of course they have stolen the money in the first place. One might find worse rulers. The men of Amasia have decided to submit. They are grateful to you Franks for seeing them through the dangerous anarchy of the Turkish arrival, but now Tutach looks on this town as his own, and will defend it against other plunderers. You may go with the goodwill of all Armeniakon.'

That was a reasonable attitude, for men who disregarded the compulsions of honour. It is the fault of the Roman system of government; if you have a small body of soldiers who do nothing but fight, and a much larger part of the population who do nothing but pay taxes, when the regular army is beaten the tax-payers do not attempt to carry on the struggle.

That removed the chief objection to our retreat; you cannot compel men to be free against their will. Our council gave me detailed instructions. I was to offer our help if the Six Horsetails planned to attack Artouch; that would be our revenge for Mount Sophon; otherwise we would pay for safe conduct on the great road, swearing never to come back. But I might not promise the infidels armed help against Christian men.

Once a month the Six Horsetails sent a renegade to collect the blackmail of Amasia. The next time the scoundrel arrived at the barbican I was waiting, unarmed, with the silver on the saddle of my mule. I wore a long Roman gown and a complicated fur hat, the local adaptation of the tall mitres of the city. The idea was that I should look like a clerk or an official, anything except a warrior; then the Turks would treat me as a peaceful envoy, although at the opening of any negotiation, before hostages have been exchanged, the first messenger always runs a considerable risk. I was very frightened; but I was not a trained jouster, and I felt that in our present dangerous position I ought to do what I could for the band. I should know in the first five miles whether the infidels would kill me or treat, and I was in a State of Grace and ready for death.

The renegade was affable. 'So you want to arrange safe

passage for envoys to negotiate with the great Tutach,' he said in a patronising tone. 'Last month I hinted that would be your only way of getting out of Amasia, and you didn't bother to answer. I'm glad your leader has learned sense. I suppose you don't speak Turkish? I shall translate faithfully.' He was relieved to hear I was dependent on his aid; these renegades fear a qualified competitor, and usually arrange an accident if they meet one.

Tutach's camp was about ten miles from Amasia, in a deserted village. The Six Horsetails were not such a strong horde as that which had followed Artouch to Mount Sophon, but their leader was a skilled politician who had often dealt with foreigners, both Roman and Arab. He lodged in the ruins of the church, whose roof had been replaced by the black felt of a barbarian tent. Many tribesmen were camped in the neighbouring houses; in that winter weather they were not so snug as in a stuffy nomad tent, but the renegade pointed with pride to this mark of civilised life. 'My comrades are not really barbarous,' he said as we struggled up the filthy street. 'They are learning to live in houses, and what we want next is a strong town on the Bosphorus. Chrysopolis would do very well. Then I shall show them how to fight on shipboard, and piracy will make us rich. Armeniakon is ruined. We must move to fresh ground.'

I gave a noncommittal grunt. I was an envoy seeking to get on good terms with these infidels, and it would be wrong to remind him now of what would happen if they dismounted and put themselves within reach of the galleys of Romania.

The usual fire burned before Tutach's door, but my escort only made me brush through the smoke; these men were beginning to abandon the ways of their ancestors, and did not really believe I would turn black if I meditated treachery. Then I was led, over a magnificent carpet, in to the desecrated church; though the effect of civilised manners was spoiled when they led in my mule also, as the easiest way of carrying the tribute. The building had been completely gutted, and no trace remained of altar or sacred furniture. This made it easier to do business; I might have lost my temper if I had seen an infidel spit into a chalice. The leader and his council sat on a row of cushions, waiting to share out the blackmail, and I could open the discussion without delay.

I had not come to conclude an agreement with the barbarians. My business was to arrange an exchange of hostages so that my lord might treat in person. That sounds straightforward, and so it is among western leaders who know each other's families. In the west we are also agreed on the sanctity of oaths; not many Franks would commit blatant perjury, without at least blaming the other side for doing it first. But among these savages I was in the dark. All Turks take as many wives as they like, and beget enormous quantities of children; furthermore, each chooses his heir, who need not be the eldest son; and since they all dress in grubby woollens I could not tell by looking at them who was an important magnate.

Tutach professed to be delighted by my proposal, and at once offered six hostages of my choosing. But when I answered that in that case I would choose the six councillors who sat beside him of course the reply was that nothing could be decided without their advice. Then the renegade had the impudence to suggest that our hostages should include the lady Matilda. I told him that was out of the question. Then we wasted a lot of time trying to fix up a meeting in some open space, each side to bring an escort of equal strength. That didn't work because there was no plain, within a day's ride, so level that the Turks could not hide an ambush in it. In the end Tutach grew tired of the argument, and caused his kettledrums to be beaten; his whole force, about two thousand men, assembled in arms, and the renegade told me to walk down the ranks and take my pick; any ten men must come back with me to Amasia, and in return the Frankish embassy would bring the Bishop's chaplain, two members of the town council, and one respectable knight from our band. This was a diplomatic victory; we gave only one of our men, three of our subjects, in return for ten of their warriors. After such generous treatment I could make no more difficulties; I chose at random ten well-mounted Turks, who looked as though they habitually had enough to eat. It was too late to return the same day, and I spent an uncomfortable night on the floor of the church, with the servants of Tutach's household sleeping all round and on top of me; but a stray Frank would not have been safe in any other part of the camp.

Next day I rode home with my hostages. They made no trouble on the road, but they seemed frightened. In the west that would be a bad sign, showing that they knew their lord intended treachery; but with these savages it might be nothing more than the dislike all nomads feel of being shut within stone walls.

In the citadel we held another council, to draw up the details of our proposal. Matilda was still against the whole idea; she wanted us to stay where we were, or retreat towards Armenia if the town could not be held. But that meant giving up all hope of getting back to Italy, and no one supported her. Several wicked knights wanted to join Tutach in attacking the towns of the Propontis; Messer Roussel answered that he would find his way home alone rather than join infidels in attacking Christendom. In the end we decided to help Tutach if Artouch barred his way, and otherwise part company outside the first town we found in Christian hands. To me it did not seem a wise plan, for we did not offer Tutach enough to make him friendly. But the others were so pleased at the thought of turning their horses' heads for Italy that they insisted we must give it a trial.

Of course I rode on the embassy, to translate into Greek what the renegade would then translate into Turkish; the curse of Babel is one of the worst afflictions of sinful men, and it is especially trying to linguists who understand the first time and then hear everything said all over again. Besides our hostages we were a party of only eight negotiators, Messer Roussel, six of his council, and myself. Ranulf the Monk had been appointed hostage from the band; he was not exactly respectable, but he had influence, so that was fair enough; and by putting him in the hands of the Turks we made sure he would not persuade his comrades to break the agreement. We rode unarmed, which I thought a mistake; but my lord said his rowdy and hot-tempered councillors would be more likely to keep the peace if they had no swords to hand. He was convinced we could make a treaty, if only our men would behave themselves. He had not formally handed over the castle of Amasia to a deputy-castellan; it was more or less taken for granted, after our march through the hills, that Matilda commanded in his absence; but some men dislike taking orders from a woman, and it was more tactful to leave the position unfilled. In a crisis all would quickly seek my lady's advice.

The Turks seemed pleased to see us. Like most barbarians, they are very fond of making pompous speeches, the only way in which a clever man among them can display his cleverness. They knew that Christians who ride with a long stirrup are uncomfortable with their legs tucked under them, and they had arranged a row of packsaddles as a bench for us; this was in the roofless church which they used as a hall, facing the row of cushions where sat Tutach and his council. The renegade stood before them, and I stood before the Christians. Tutach spoke in Turkish, it was put into Greek, then I told what he said word for word in French. The reply went the same way, so everything was said three times.

The Turks had two main objects, to drive their rival Artouch from his remunerative position on the Roman border, and then to plunder the shores of the Propontis. We were willing to help them with the first, but not with the second; but they wouldn't take no for an answer, and the argument continued. Some of our knights were tempted, remembering the rich booty we had won from Chrysopolis; the infidels spotted this division of opinion, although I was careful to translate only my lord's view. At length Tutach himself led us to a large tent where an excellent meal of roast mutton was spread on the carpeted floor; there he left us to ourselves, obviously hoping that before negotiations began again my lord would have been persuaded by his own men to join the attack on Romania.

The infidels had provided plenty of wine. They drink great quantities themselves, though their unnatural religion forbids it; but then the only part of their disgusting faith which they really follow is the injunction to wage war on Christendom. But there was no bread and no cabbage, since these are scarce among the nomads. I was hungry, and ate heartily, until I felt some discomfort. The thought of poison entered my mind, only to be dismissed; these savages could never calculate a minimum dose; if our food had been poisoned we would have writhed in agony after the first mouthful. It was just roast meat and red wine, gulped down greedily, which had upset my digestion. I told my lord, saying I would go outside; he nodded agreement, but told me to come back soon, since without a linguist they could not resume the discussion.

Nomads are dirty; but since they live mostly on the floor of their dwellings they usually appoint some place in the open as a latrine. There was a sentry outside our tent; I gave him a friendly grin and indicated my business by a rather coarse gesture. He smiled, pointing to a canvas screen fifty yards away.

I had finished my business and was preparing to depart when someone popped round the screen in a great hurry, knocking into me. 'Sorry,' he muttered in Greek, 'but those seeking the latrine have right of way.' That is a Greek proverb, meaning roughly that urgent business should have precedence; I had heard it often and it made no particular impression. Then suddenly my mind began to function; this stranger wore Turkish dress, but Greek was his native language; I recalled that the renegade had told me there was no one in the band who could take his place.

'One moment, sir,' I said politely. 'I am a Frank and a Christian. If you are held captive perhaps I could arrange your ransom.'

'Damn it all, I've broken my parole,' said the other, but rather in confusion than anger. 'I promised that if they let me out the Franks wouldn't spot I was a Roman. That's why I wear these funny trousers. If you must know I am Theodore Docianus, and

I am not a captive, but a hostage for my cousin Alexius Comnenus. They treat me well; don't mention that you've seen me. My companions are under guard, but the sentry let me out because this blasted dysentery is really too much inside a stuffy tent.'

'Thank you, sir. I shall inform my lord of our meeting, but we will keep it most secret from the Turks. If they found out they might strangle you.'

Theodore shrugged his shoulders. 'They may do that any day. But now we have no army the best service for a brave man is to volunteer as hostage.'

I hurried back, puzzling over this encounter. Alexius was commander in chief of the Roman army; why should he send hostages to the infidels? If he did, why must it be kept secret from Franks? Then I understood. I burst into the tent, shouting: 'We must get away, quickly. Tutach is playing Romans against Franks. Roman hostages are hidden in his camp!'

All jumped to their feet, clamouring in panic. But at that moment the renegade entered. He walked straight up to my lord, and stared insolently. 'Now then, Roussel,' he said sharply, 'you know enough Greek to answer Yes or No. Are you willing to follow the mighty Tutach of the Six Horsetails, or do you still hold to the Christian dogs? If you do, you will visit the Emperor immediately.'

Behind him crowded armed Turks. My lord held out his hands, speaking over his shoulder to his dismayed followers: 'No fighting. I would rather be sent to the Emperor, where I shall see a priest before the end, than die here unshriven. Submit quietly.'

The Turks thought it an excellent joke. They bound us comfortably, without beating us; I think they liked my lord, though of course that did not stop them selling him to the highest bidder. I made one last effort, after I was bound and they could see I was not trying to escape; I pushed forward and whispered to the renegade: 'Remember your hostages. Matilda

200

de Balliol holds them until my lord returns. Are you willing, is Tutach willing, that they should die by torture?'

'Perfectly willing,' the scoundrel answered with a grin. 'You forget that Tutach is young; his sons are still too small to ride in arms. Among the hostages you chose were two of his cousins, as well born as he and rivals for his command. As Martyrs for the Faith they will reflect credit on the family, while at present they are a nuisance. The other eight are decent men, but they may as well die tomorrow as the next day.'

That is the trouble with barbarians; a chief who has two hundred wives is not bound by the family feeling which is the basis of the western system of hostages.

When we were safely bound (but they did not steal our clothes), we were hoisted to the backs of the worst ponies in the herd of the Six Horsetails. Then we were driven by happy whooping Turks to the edge of their camp, and handed over to an escort of Roman troopers. The Roman hostages watched us, openly wearing their Roman gowns; they were very cheerful, for everything had gone their way, but of course they would not be released until Tutach received his blood-money.

As we jogged by, bouncing on those rough ponies, Docianus called to me. 'You will soon be in Christian hands,' he shouted. 'Alexius is merciful, and his quarrel is with your leader only.' I suppose he meant it kindly.

Messer Roussel heard and understood. He addressed us in French: 'Gentlemen, I release you from your fealty, in the presence of these witnesses. They are free men and warriors, competent to bear witness; though they happen to be infidels, and can't understand a word I say. Since I give permission no one may hold you recreant if you enlist under the Labarum.' One should not expect too much of mercenaries; many of the band would have sought another employer anyway. But it was thoughtful of my lord to make things easy for us. I loved him all the more, and decided to serve him while he lived; after the Emperor had judged him I would look after his widow and children.

We rode five miles in the direction of Amasia, until we reached a small Roman encampment, not more than six hundred men; but in the midst was a great tent, with the standards of the Domestics of Asia, Europe, and the Schools planted before it. In the diminished Roman army Alexius Comnenus held these three commands at once.

CHAPTER FOURTEEN

Alexius

T he Romans are humane, and they have the imagination to put themselves in the place of a prisoner, knowing that the worst of his misery is wondering what will happen next. They helped us gently off our ponies, and an officer called: 'Take courage, Franks. You are only hostages for the delivery of Amasia, which the Domestic will arrange immediately.'

Then we were led into the presence of Alexius Comnenus, commander of all the armies of Romania.

He was seated on the magnificent folding stool which is part of the insignia of a Domestic. But he wore the short undress tunic which normally goes under the corselet, and his only attendant was an elderly monk. He smiled pleasantly, and waved a greeting. 'We are not strangers. I met you, gentlemen, at Ancyra last spring. Well, well, fortunes of war. I'm not proud of the way I caught you, but to defend a great Empire without an army I must use tricks my ancestors would have despised. I cannot offer you refreshment. You have just come from a feast in the infidel tents, a feast provided by the unfortunate peasants of Romania; and this little army looks to Amasia for its next meal. Now then, lord Roussel, I have orders to bring you before the Equal of the Apostles to receive judgement from his own lips. You will be fettered and put under guard. An officer will visit you daily, to hear any complaints about rations or quarters; but no one may remove your fetters without a direct order from the Emperor, so don't waste time asking for that. You other gentlemen have nothing to fear. I want to get Amasia without fighting, and if you help me I can arrange for you to enter the Roman army at the usual rate of pay, letting bygones be bygones. Now which of you is the linguist? You must have had one, to speak to those Turks.'

I stepped forward. A captive linguist sometimes has an unpleasant time, for his gaolers may torment him to encourage him to plead for peace and freedom. But it is worth running that risk to know what goes on; anything is better than hanging about in helpless ignorance.

'Oh yes, we met before, when you arranged for the surrender of Ancyra. Tomorrow you shall speak to the castellan of Amasia. I won't let you inside; we are the stronger party, and their envoys should come to us. But you need only tell them the truth. Now it's bedtime. We are all on short rations, but you will have as much food as my men.'

We were chained to tent-poles, but they gave us blankets, and a little biscuit. Alexius is a chivalrous enemy. I thought over my own position, and what I should say to Matilda in the morning. Messer Roussel had come to the end of his career; the Emperor might spare his life, but the best he could hope for was long years in a monastery, blinded and castrated. But he had very bravely foreseen this when he was taken, and I was no longer bound to his service by oath. I was free to serve any lord I might choose; and the lord I wished to serve was my lady Matilda.

Nowadays people always think that if a man and a woman work together, or even see a lot of one another in the course of business, there must be a love affair in the background. It is the fault of those idle Provençals, who hang about their neighbours' castles, composing poetry and playing on musical instruments, instead of spending the summer ravaging the fields of their enemies as a gentleman should. In my young days only serfs fell in love; a lady was sent to the husband chosen by her parents and they both made the best of it. Matilda was one of those old-fashioned ladies. She had been lucky to marry at all, as things fell out; but she served her chance-met husband loyally. She was plain, and could never dress properly. I repeat, I was not in love with her.

But she was a very gallant companion; her horsy ways and delight in manly sports gave her rather an eccentric character, but it was consistent all through; she did not behave quite like other people, but once you understood her you could count on what she would do next. Besides, I had known her for ten years, and the Balliols were my substitute for the home I had lost. All that night I tried to find some way in which, despite the wreck of our fortunes, she and her children could live with dignity and comfort.

In the morning we rode to Amasia. We found the gates closed and the wall manned; but when Messer Roussel was paraded in chains the burgesses opened a wicket and sent out the Bishop to arrange peaceful entry. I did not hear the discussion which followed, but before noon the little army had dismounted in the market-place.

It was time for me to play my part. I had given my word not to escape into the citadel, and Alexius trusted me, as he always trusted those whom he considered honourable; he was very rarely mistaken, and by avoiding a lot of unnecessary precautions he got his business done quickly and smoothly. I climbed the steep track unguarded, with only a Treasury eunuch as witness. The gates of the fortress were closed, and a plume of smoke showed that my comrades were heating pitch to repel an escalade. I was gratified to see dangling from the gatehouse the ten Turkish hostages; they were naked, because it is always a pity to waste warm clothing in winter, but the bodies were unmarked. I recognised the firm command of Matilda. These hostages deserved death, and a great many angry wives would have impaled them, or at least flogged them to pieces; she had killed them swiftly, in a manner which brave warriors can endure with dignity, instead of forcing them to disgrace their last moments by shrieking with pain. To do less would have been weakness, to do more cruelty; she always knew what to do, and did it efficiently.

The garrison, who from their towers could see what went on in the market-place, awaited an envoy. When I was recognised Matilda herself came to an arrow-slit over the gate, and I told her all that had befallen. She made up her mind without hesitation. 'Tell the Roman commander,' she said in a level voice, 'that I shall be in the market-place within an hour. I do not seek hostages for my safe return; I should be within my rights in demanding them, but I want to get things settled. The only condition I make is that before negotiations begin I must see my husband face to face. I don't want to surrender this strong place to buy his freedom, and then receive a corpse as my reward; that trick was old when I was in my cradle.'

'My lady,' I answered, 'you should certainly come down and treat, to save all the Franks in Amasia. But my lord's freedom you cannot buy. Alexius has orders to take him to the city; make up your mind what else to ask for, and consider him as already dead.'

'Nonsense, young Roger. Until I am widowed my first duty is to my husband, and he's got out of worse fixes. But thanks for reminding me that the whole band looks to me for protection. I shall see you in an hour. Tell the Roman commander I speak fluent Greek, and expect a private interview.'

I went back and told Alexius that my lady was ready to treat; but I did not pass on her last message, for her Greek was not really as perfect as she supposed.

While we waited the Domestic chatted pleasantly; he is a charming companion; he may have thought I had more influence than in fact I possessed, but it may have been only that he never neglects the chance of gaining a friend. In marching so far with his small force he had performed a very gallant exploit, but he did not boast of it; all he said was that the Emperor had ordered him to restore Roman authority in Amasia, and of course whatever the Emperor commanded had to be done, even if it was very difficult. Most of the time he was apologising for having captured Messer Roussel by bribery; but he pointed out that all the treachery had been shown by the Turks; he could not refuse what Tutach offered to sell, and all our misfortunes had been caused because we were careless in our selection of Turkish hostages. I think Alexius has the inclinations of a gallant knight; but he is also a patriotic Roman, and now that he has no force behind him he will continue the struggle by any means, fair or foul.

When my lady appeared it was evident that she had occupied the delay in dressing herself as the lord of a strong castle. She wore a Frankish gown, and a big bunch of keys on her right hip was balanced by a heavy broadsword; above her kerchief was a little steel cap, and she rode the best warhorse in Amasia. She brought no attendants, save a Frankish groom to hold her horse.

The official tent of the Domestic had been erected in the market-place; within it Alexius sat on his ceremonial stool, with several officers in attendance. I also was there, and though I was not called on to translate I heard all that passed.

My lady began by complaining that she had stipulated for a private interview; but on this point Alexius was firm. 'You, madam, are an independent sovereign,' he said with a bow, 'and your treaties need no ratification by a superior. But I am a servant of the Emperor, with the added difficulty that some years ago my uncle held the Purple. These gentlemen are not here to spy on you, but on me. If you wish to treat you must put up with their presence.'

'You mean you will not follow the example of the Caesar? Well, I don't blame you; it brought him no luck. But you would make a better Emperor than that silly Michael. I hope for the sake of Romania you have a try at it one day.' My lady smiled politely, as though this was only social gossip; but it was a clever opening, for it made Alexius uncomfortable.

'Well then,' she continued, 'let's get to business. You hold my husband, and at present he is unwounded and in good health, for I have seen him. When you set him free I shall render to you the castle of Amasia, my followers will disperse, and my lord, with not more than ten servants, will ride east to some castle of

Armenia. If that suits you we can begin to arrange hostages for fulfilment.'

'I'm sorry, madam, but I rode here for no other reason than to bring Roussel before the Emperor,' answered Alexius. 'There is not enough gold in the world to buy his freedom.'

'I didn't think there was,' my lady said calmly. 'But there was a chance, and it was my duty to try it. Very well. Messer Roussel remains a prisoner. In that case all you have to do is storm the castle. Of course the Turks may attack while we fight, but you took that into consideration when you refused my offer.'

'My lady, I cannot do anything for the accomplice of John Ducas. But that still leaves room for a treaty. If you yield the citadel I promise that you and your children will be safe.'

'That's no sort of offer, young man, and you know it,' Matilda answered briskly. 'My children and I have never been safe, and we don't wish to be. Noble Franks seek power, not safety. When you assault the citadel I may not be able to hold it, but if we charge your line no Roman soldiers could stop us. There are Armenian castles which will take us in.'

'Then, as you say, madam, the war continues. You may return to your castle, but when the gate closes I shall bring up my engines. You might cut a way through my lines; I know Franks are formidable in the charge. But remember Tutach. You hanged his hostages; he will catch you before you reach Armenia.'

Now it was my lady's turn to falter; the thought of her daughter in the Turkish camp was more than she could bear.

'Wait, my lord Domestic,' she said, for the first time addressing him with the respect his position demanded. 'We are both in a sad fix. My followers are demoralised, and I can't trust them to man the battlements. But you also are in danger. While we argue Tutach may overwhelm us both. It is my duty to remain with my husband, and I would rather live in the city than anywhere on earth; but I won't arrive there a penniless refugee; better the mountains of Armenia. If the Emperor would give me a decent maintenance, so that I can live like a lady in some respectable convent, then I shall advise my followers to lay down their arms.'

'My dear lady,' Alexius said with a courtly smile, 'I cannot promise money in the name of the Emperor. That is the business of the Treasurer, and anyway the Treasury is empty. But I want to get this business cleared up. I shall myself support you in the city, in a manner befitting your courage and nobility. Will you yield your castle, and live in the city as my guest?'

My lady looked steadily into his face, and nodded. 'To you I yield, my lord,' she said formally, and then continued in the casual tone she used for social affairs. 'We shall be entirely at your mercy. It's the sort of agreement that calls for oaths, and hostages, and silver deposited in some holy shrine as guarantee. I'm not asking for that, and you could hardly give it. But you have made a solemn promise before witnesses, and I trust the honour of Comnenus. Your men will be more comfortable in the citadel; if you ride up now we shall be in time for dinner.'

An hour later we were all dining in the great hall of the castle. It was an odd party. My lord wore a bronze ring on his ankle, a symbol rather than an impediment; Alexius explained that he had been commanded to keep him in fetters, and this was just enough to enable him to swear truthfully that he had carried out his orders. The new lord of the castle sat between his prisoner and his prisoner's wife, chatting amicably to both. Nearby were the three children, nine-year-old Joan using a Roman eating-prong and talking politely about the errors of Italus the Frank, who was unsound in theology, but had received the Imperial appointment of Hypatus of the Philosophers; she might have been a young Roman lady, released from the schoolroom to entertain distinguished visitors. The two boys were more rough; though they also spoke Greek, and could discuss the subjects which interest educated Romans. At the other tables Frankish knights, interspersed with Roman officers, stumbled in their few words of Greek to inquire about pay and prospects in the Roman army. We were all very friendly. Most Franks were relieved that the great adventure was ended. It would have been a wonderful exploit to found a Frankish state so far away, in this desert of infidels; but it was a very difficult and dangerous undertaking. Now we could relax, and the next time we charged it would be at the orders of a cautious Roman commander who never fought unless the odds were on his side.

I did not propose to join the Roman army. I am not really a warrior, and already in those days I was beginning to feel that slaughter and pillage are not so attractive in fact as they are in the ancient poems. When the meal was finished I left my place and knelt before the Domestic. I addressed him in my best Greek, giving the proper titles of respect; these are very complicated, varying not only with the post held by the great man but also with the quite independent system of honorary court rank; many native Romans cannot get them right, but I had just been coached by my neighbour. I said that Messer Roussel was a very great man, accustomed to being waited on since his childhood; if he was to ride on a long journey, and then face the Emperor for judgement, it might make a difference if he was in good health and fit to speak in his own defence; he needed a servant who could speak his own language, and translate into Greek anything that must be said. If I was permitted to travel as his attendant I would swear, by any oath they might impose, never to bear arms against Romania.

Alexius considered. Then he looked up and said: 'I was told the Frankopole had released his oathbound companions. Do you still regard yourself as his man? I understand the theory of these Frankish customs.'

'No, your splendid excellency,' I answered, pleased that he had referred to my lord by his title; it showed that he was regarded as a soldier who happened to have been in rebellion, not a barbarian invader; and the Romans are normally lenient to rebels. 'No, Messer Roussel has no followers, according to the customs of the Franks. He dismissed us from his service when he lost his freedom. But the Frankopole befriended me when I was a helpless orphan; and it would be unseemly if such a great warrior had no one to run his errands while he is merely a prisoner of state, not convicted of any crime.'

'Very well,' Alexius answered graciously. 'While the Frankopole is under arrest and unconvicted the Treasury would allow rations for one servant. I am glad to see fidelity in a Frank; your countrymen have a reputation for deserting the unsuccessful. But don't delude yourself, because I now treat him with respect, that your leader has the slightest chance of acquittal. The best he can hope for is blindness and a monastery. Then what will you do? Take vows and follow him?'

'I shall need someone to manage my stable,' Matilda put in eagerly. 'I would rather have a horse than a silk gown for Sundays. And I never get on with Roman grooms; they *will* starve a lady's horse to keep it quiet. Young Roger can be my steward. A loyal Frank, who speaks good Greek, will be very useful to me.'

'Oho, I see. The young man will not leave his lady,' the Domestic said with that tiresome grin which people always wear when they think they are fostering an illicit love-affair. 'But a man of such loyalty will keep his oath to the Emperor. No, you need not swear on holy relics. If your word is not enough you only insult the True Cross by false swearing. I choose to trust you as a man of honour. This Roger son of Odo will be noted on the ration-strength as personal servant to the prisoner, and when we reach the city he may join my other guests in the convent. There, that is settled.'

All Romans like a friendly arrangement, if it can be made without loss of dignity. It was only common sense for Alexius to keep on good terms with the band who were now to enter his army. But there was more in it than that. The Domestic was in favour with his Emperor; but he had fallen from power before, and it might happen again. Alexius never lost a chance of winning an adherent, no matter how humble. In return he was himself a faithful friend, as the rest of this story will show.

By the end of dinner we were all comrades. Messer Roussel faced a black future, and there was nothing we could do to save him; but he might have been killed in battle on any day of the week, and life goes on when your lord has fallen. We gave over all our mail and weapons, without concealing anything, and my lady helped the paymaster to check our treasure and divide it into packloads.

The only people who were not satisfied with the new arrangement were the burgesses of Amasia. Either they were to be returned to the Empire, in which case nearly three years' tribute would be due to the Treasury, or their defenders would march west leaving them a prey to the Turks; either prospect was extremely distasteful. As a matter of fact they were faced with both. That night the magnates of the town were summoned to the citadel and ordered to raise a very large sum of money at once, since the payment to Tutach had left the Domestic penniless; and as they left they could see we were preparing to evacuate. Romans are so accustomed to bullying provincials that the only public opinion they ever take into account is that of the turbulent mob in the city.

The burgesses of Amasia had been manning their own wall for two years and more, and they were no longer mere fodder for the tax-gatherer. When the magnates descended to the town they called a meeting in the market-place, and all night we heard trumpets and saw watchfires. In the morning they sent the Bishop, a most unwilling envoy, to tell us the gates were closed and the streets barricaded, and that no one would be allowed to leave the citadel until Messer Roussel had been set at liberty. How they thought he could defend them without followers or money I don't know; but burgesses get these irrational ideas in times of stress.

I had passed the night in the little room where Messer Roussel was confined; it was not a dungeon, and we had plenty of blankets, for Alexius was fearful of my lord's popularity and did not wish to excite sympathy on his behalf. In the morning I was allowed out, ostensibly to fetch water for washing; but my real mission was to learn the news, always the principal duty of a prisoner's servant. I found the whole fortress in a state of alarm.

The burgesses, under cover of darkness, had built a drystone wall opposite the gate; archers lay behind it, and we could not leave until they had been dislodged. Of course the troopers could cut a way through if they tried; but they feared the Franks might change sides again. In such a tricky situation any western leader would have murdered his prisoner; but that is not the Roman way. Such a murder would leave a lasting stain on the reputation of Alexius, and his men might refuse to carry out his orders.

The deadlock lasted all morning. Just before dinner the Domestic visited his captive, and we were all driven out, guards and servants, while they conferred in private. Naturally I hoped they were making some friendly arrangement; an easy solution would be for my lord to escape. But when Alexius left, and I was permitted to bring in the dinner, I found Messer Roussel kneeling in prayer. He spoke over his shoulder: 'Eat that yourself, little Roger. I shall fast. I am not hungry, and the physicians say fasting gives one a better chance of recovery after the operation. This afternoon I am to be blinded, in the presence of a deputation from the town. After seeing that they will not hinder our departure. They would have blinded me anyway when I reached the city, and Alexius has promised not to castrate me as well. That's something. It's very painful, but many Romans survive it. I am glad you offered to serve me; I shall need a body-servant until I have picked up the knack of dressing myself in the dark.'

I was appalled; but I was also struck with admiration at the fortitude with which my lord faced his dreadful fate. Not wishing to weaken his resolution I rushed sobbing from the room.

That afternoon a dozen of the chief men of Amasia were admitted to the citadel. The great hall was arranged as a tribunal, with the Domestic and his officers seated behind a table. All the garrison, Franks as well as Romans, were ranged round the walls, though Alexius had the decency to permit my lady and her children to remain praying in the chapel. When all was prepared, with the burgesses in the front row where they had a good view, I was despatched to bring in my lord. He was so weighted with fetters he could hardly walk, but he held his head high, and lay down on the table without assistance. The soldiers bound him firmly; but this was merciful, lest the hot iron should scar his face if he flinched.

A farrier entered, bearing a glowing iron rod. This struck me as strange; my father was a smith, and I know how quickly iron cools when it is withdrawn from the forge. There was a fire in the hall; but for some reason the farrier preferred to use the regulation army brazier in the courtyard. I hoped the man knew his business, and would get it over at the first attempt; my lord, or any other man, would go mad with suspense if the rod had to be taken away and reheated.

The Roman method of blinding does not bring hot iron into actual contact with the eyeball; if that happens, as it sometimes does when the Emperor secretly desires the death of the culprit, it leaves a ghastly open wound, which soon kills by gangrene (such had been the fate of Romanus Diogenes). The correct way of destroying sight without shortening life is to hold the iron very close; heat does the damage without bloodshed. So I did not expect a strong odour of roast flesh; all the same, I was slightly surprised that there was no smell at all. As the iron approached my lord uttered a great bellow of agony, and the spectators groaned in sympathy; one of our knights dashed forward and was knocked down by a guard. There was very nearly a riot, but we Franks were unarmed. When I looked again at the table the Roman physician (there is one attached to every band) was applying a linen bandage, which he wound over the victim's head; my lord was silent, though his body shook with sobs, and the farrier was already on his way out. He carried the iron very carelessly, and I hoped he would burn himself, but he didn't.

That evening we marched. The burgesses did not hinder us, for like all Romans they are practical men who never brood over a setback but at once make the best of a new situation. Alexius had even compelled them to pay some of their tribute, threatening to break down the walls and leave them at Tutach's mercy if they refused. The Bishop and most of the magnates marched with us, and those who remained were already preparing an embassy, offering the Turks a large blackmail if they kept away from the gates.

We were a discontented and almost mutinous army. The Franks were now armed, for we needed all our strength; it was safe to arm us, for we had no leader. We mourned the great captain we had lost. Messer Roussel had not always led us to victory; a wiser chief would have stood a siege on Mount Sophon instead of galloping haphazard after those Turks; but there was no better lord in the world for courage and constancy and kindness to his followers. The Roman troopers also were angry. The Domestic could not conceal from them that he was leaving Amasia to the Turks, and they grumbled that the only result of the campaign had been to weaken the already precarious Christian cause. They had made a dangerous expedition only to remove a Christian garrison from a Roman town. They said openly that Alexius should have been content with a nominal promise of allegiance, which could have been easily obtained, instead of blinding a great warrior when every warrior was needed. All complained, and those who guarded the curtained litter which bore my lord could not be restrained from expressions of sympathy.

I marched on foot, leading the foremost mule of the litter to save my lord from the roughness of the road. No one might see him, but I was in call if he needed me, and the physician had promised that in a few days, when the bandage could be removed, I should do it. Matilda and the children rode apart; when I blamed her neglect of her husband I was told my lord had sent word he wished to be left in silence; the physician added that it would help his recovery, but I thought Matilda should have stayed with him all the same.

From Amasia to the Halys the land paid blackmail to the Six Horsetails, and Alexius had arranged safe passage; I believe he gave a small sum of money to ratify the bargain, but we had not really bought our way through; it was rather that Tutach knew we were poor and well armed, and was glad to see the backs of the last Christian warriors who had disputed what was now his fief. But west of the river lay the pastures of another infidel horde, the Children of Kutlumush. When we encamped on the bank the Domestic sent a slave of Turkish blood to see if he could make a treaty with them, but after dark a barbarian threw into our camp the head and genitals of our envoy, as a sign that they never made terms with Romans. Our little column of eight hundred men, cumbered with women and children, could not fight a way through. There was nothing for it but to leave the great road, striking north through the hills of the Galatians. We sacked a village, because otherwise we would have starved; but Alexius hated it, and his men were unwilling. Romans dislike pillage, and think a really good general should gain his ends by manoeuvre without fighting. It would be pleasant if that were possible, but we live in a fallen world.

After only two days in the hills we continued northward to the coast; this was beginning to be infested with little parties of raiding Turks, but they had not yet crossed the hills in force, and the surviving farmers were glad to sell us supplies. Alexius paid cash, and with money the peasants could make a fresh start in Europe or the Caucasus, instead of waiting helplessly by their barns for Turks to come and cut their throats.

Alexius was a good officer; he wished to gain the confidence of his new mercenaries, and he spent most of his time riding up and down the column, chatting with any Frank who could speak Greek. Several times a day he inquired after my lord's health, though he seemed to take it for granted the news would be favourable. What was done was done, and nothing could undo it; perhaps I should have been gruff with him, yet when a great man took the trouble to be kind I felt I must reply politely. Besides, like most noble Romans, he could be very charming if he wished.

So when on the seventh day of the march he called out to me,

'We are near Castle Comnenon, the home of my ancestors, where we shall sleep tonight. How does it compare with the castles of Italy?' I showed a flattering interest; though I took pleasure in telling my lord, through the curtains, that the place had been built by Alexius's grandfather, born a Thracian peasant. The house of Comnenus is powerful, but not ancient.

Alexius had not visited the castle since Manzikert. I suppose he knew the neighbourhood had been ravaged, but he cannot have foreseen the ruin he would find, or he would not have boasted. The building stood intact, for it was roofed with a brick dome which would not burn; but the whole place had been sacked, and not a stick of furniture remained. The walls kept out the weather, and that was all.

Our officers and knights supped in the great hall, though they had nothing to eat but the salt beef and biscuit we carried with us. I was not grand enough to eat with them, but as my lord's servant I stood in a corner, waiting to take his supper to the little chamber where he lay bandaged. Everyone was in a bad temper; the ruin of Castle Comnenon was worse than any Roman had expected; apparently they had been told in the city that no Turks had come so far north. The officers began to grumble, muttering that if the remains of the army had been better led, even after Manzikert, the countryside could have been saved. Theodore Docianus was especially bitter at the desolation. I saw him go from one man to another, obviously canvassing opinions; then he stood before the tables and began a set speech.

'Cousin Alexius,' he said bitterly, 'you are three times Domestic of Asia, Europe and the Schools, and since our Emperor is a man of letters you have complete control of the army. Behold the results: Castle Comnenon pillaged, and my own estates deserted and valueless! These gentlemen are all clients of the great house of Comnenus. They also own land here. We consider you have failed in your duty, wasting the last resources of Romania to overthrow a barbarian who is after all a Christian. Roussel was the best warrior in Asia, and in mutilating him you pursued the Emperor's private feud, instead of looking to the welfare of the state. My comrades and I will no longer obey you as Domestic; though if you change your policy we shall make you something greater.'

I listened quietly, fearing that if I attracted attention I might be turned out of the hall. The Roman army proclaims a new Emperor whenever it is dissatisfied with the conduct of affairs, and here it was happening before my eyes. They proposed to make Alexius Emperor against his will; but he could not refuse, for once the perilous Purple had been offered Michael must seek his eyes, whether he plotted treason or was faithful. How could he escape? In spite of all that has passed I still liked Alexius Comnenus, so young and brave and charming.

The Domestic heard his cousin to the end, without calling on the guards to interfere; probably they would not have obeyed him, for Roman troopers delight in civil war. The band who first proclaim a usurper will be his bodyguard if he succeeds, and the soldiers in the ranks will probably escape punishment if he fails. When he rose it seemed that he also would make a speech, but he preferred to lighten the tension by talking informally. The Greek language lends itself to these shades of seriousness, for nearly every word has two forms, the old one used in official proclamations and rhetoric, and the modern slang of light conversation. When he addressed his hearers as 'Kavallarii', the slang for horsemen, it was evident that he was not delivering a speech of acceptance to go down in history as the first pronouncement of a new Emperor.

'Jockeys,' he began with a friendly smile, 'my gallant cousin has spoken as a patriotic Roman. The affairs of Asia are in a bad way, and perhaps another Domestic would have done better; though Palaeologus did not cover himself with glory.' (This raised a laugh among these partisans of Comnenus.) 'But all our troubles stem from that disaster at Manzikert, for which I am not to blame; since two years ago I was a student completing my education. Our wise Emperor is not to blame either, for he is still a student at the present day.' (Another laugh.) 'I'm sorry we couldn't hold Amasia, though the order to retreat seemed popular when I gave it. Until the Treasury has been replenished we cannot fight so far to the eastward. My brother owns this castle, and I would hold it if I could. But cousin Theodore is a man with a grievance; he is cantankerous by nature, and when he plays polo the umpire is exhausted while the ponies are still fresh. He says I was wrong to blind the Frank, even if that was the only way of gathering tribute from Amasia. Well, I got the money; it has been spent among your tenants, and you may squeeze a little rent out of them if you are quick about it. Of course it was a great waste to destroy a mighty warrior; but could you, cousin Theodore, think of a better way out of that citadel? If you could, you should have told me. Perhaps I have not inflicted irreparable harm. The Frank invoked St Michael when the iron was applied, and the Archangel may have performed a miracle for a man of such holy and exemplary life.' (Roars of laughter.) 'You there, you're his body-servant. Fetch Roussel. He shall sup with me in my hall.'

As I hurried to my lord's cell I puzzled over this speech. Alexius had deflated a serious situation; he had made fun of Docianus, and Palaeologus, and the Emperor, and put his hearers in a good temper. But if he now paraded my lord among the company his pitiful condition would spoil the effect of what had gone before; it seemed a tactless mistake, and I already knew Alexius well enough to realise he did not make tactless mistakes.

My lord followed with docility, though in his weighty fetters he could hardly walk. When he stood in the hall Alexius called in a friendly tone:

'Lord Vestiarius, for as an untried prisoner you retain your rank, will you remove the bandage before these gentlemen?'

When his head was bared my lord blinked and rubbed his eyes; then he looked round the hall. 'I thought I was to pretend until we reached the Emperor,' he said casually, 'but if you say it's all right I suppose it is. You're a good friend in a tight place, and I shall always take your advice. I don't see my lady and the children.'

There were whoops of delight, and everyone forgot about making Emperors while they celebrated the trick which had been played on the burgesses of Amasia. The iron had been cold. That was a stratagem which appealed to every Roman. Alexius had not lied to anyone, which heightened their pleasure; they excuse lies told in a good cause, but a man who can deceive his enemies without them is considered much more cunning. Of course every Frank was weeping with joy, and my lady came in and got as drunk as the rest. That feast in Castle Comnenon stands out in my memory.

Next morning we were brought back to realities. My lord was still a prisoner charged with treason, and must remain in fetters. Alexius would not accept his parole; he reminded us that perhaps the Emperor would order a real blinding after we reached the city; it would be sad if such a gallant knight broke his word, but too much to expect him to keep it. That is the Roman view of honour, as a strong force but not the strongest in the world; it is more sensible than the high-blown notions of the troubadours.

We were too few to spare a garrison, and Castle Comnenon was left empty to the Turks. We continued towards the Bosphorus, but the Domestic of all the armies of Romania could not even ride through the inner Themes of Bucellarion and Optimaton; the Children of Kutlumush were raiding the valley of the Sangarius, and we dared not encounter them. We turned north to seek refuge in the seaport of Heraclea. The Domestic put us, horses and all, on the shipping in the port, and we sailed to the city. It was a shameful admission of weakness, very unpopular with the troops; the Romans of the city are resigned to the loss of Asia, but the soldiers are not. I thought, and everyone agreed with me, that the Emperor Michael was unlikely to hold the Purple for very much longer.

When we disembarked I was separated from my lord; until the Emperor had leisure to sentence him he was chained in the common gaol, and criminals are not allowed servants. My companions of what had once been the Band of St Michael were absorbed into the Roman army; not as a unit, for obvious reasons, but distributed in twos and threes among the garrisons of Europe. My lady and her household, of which I was now a member, were pensioners on the charity of Alexius Comnenus; though my lady reminded us that we need not be ashamed at taking alms; for it was one of the terms on which we had surrendered, and as much our rightful due as any ransom from a defeated foe.

Alexius was as good as his word, though he might have broken it with impunity. It is worth bearing in mind, when you get to Romania, that he is a man who keeps promises. There was a comfortable and lax house of nuns of good birth, the Convent of St Thecla, at the western end of the city; it was only half a mile from the walls, convenient for hunting. There my lady was installed, as a boarder without vows; her daughter went with her, but even a fashionable convent cannot admit male guests, so Ralph and Osbert lived in a small house just beyond the porter's lodge, and I took charge of them under the grand title of Pedagogue. I must have been the only pedagogue in the city who couldn't read and write. A steward of the Comneni paid our expenses once a month, and gave me a small sum for clothes and pocket-money. We lived as poor gentry, but there were many poor gentry in the city now the Turks had intercepted the rents of Asia; we had enough to eat and horses to ride.

I was not present when my lord was brought before the Emperor. The trial was held technically in open court, but unexpectedly, early in the morning, and I did not hear of it until it was over. Alexius sent word of what had passed; it might have been worse. The military members of the council proposed that Messer Roussel should again be employed in the army; they pointed out that he had refused to join Tutach, or to change his faith to win freedom from Artouch; he could be trusted to hold some unimportant fortress against the infidel, and if his garrison was composed of regular Roman troopers there would be no danger of rebellion. There was a grave shortage of competent officers, and it seemed a pity to waste one of the best of them, just because in the past he had been insubordinate.

Nicephoritzes the Logothete proposed that he should be blinded at once, and later burned alive in the Hippodrome as a contribution to the Easter entertainments. I don't think he was wholly serious, for even the wickedest Romans are very merciful; but my lord was present, and I imagine the Logothete wanted to give him a fright. In the end the Emperor's sentence was a compromise; my lord would not be employed in the army, but neither was he to be blinded. He was condemned to rigorous imprisonment; and, what was really vindictive, his status would be that of a captured deserter, not an unsuccessful rebel. It was unkind, as well as absurd, to pretend that my lord had run away from the army because he was afraid to fight.

Even rigorous imprisonment among the merciful Romans allows of daily exercise in the fresh air; Alexius arranged that my lord should have good food as well, and that his fetters should be removed when he took his weekly bath. He might live for many years. The family of Balliol and their one remaining follower settled down to wait for better times.

CHAPTER FIFTEEN

The City

C

It was known to every Roman that we were under the protection of Alexius Comnenus, and we were treated with respect. Alexius was now a very great man; he was the nephew of a past Emperor, and head of a great family; for his brother Isaac, who had failed to capture Antioch, was neither a leader nor a man of character, and had retired from politics. He was in his twenty-first year, but that was an advantage, because it meant that no one could blame him for the disaster at Manzikert. In the spring of 1074, a few months after we reached the city, he created a great sensation by marrying Irene Ducaina, daughter of Andronicus and granddaughter of the old Caesar. For two generations the houses of Ducas and Comnenus had been rivals, but now the Caesar, sitting blind in his monastery, had given up the struggle. He still hoped that his descendants would wear the Purple, and this marriage gave the future children of Irene a very good chance, though they would not be Ducates. I understand the match was reasonably happy; but Alexius could woo any lady, and he made use of his charm to aim higher; he conquered Maria the Alan, wife of the Emperor Michael. Every politician in the city waited for him to seize power; but he surprised us all by remaining loyal. He was commander in chief under an Emperor who would never take the field, and that seemed to satisfy his ambition. For four years the tangled and exciting politics of the city stood still.

My lady knew city life, and loved what she knew; but for me it was a strange experience. You might think that living by the gatehouse of a convent, with one horse to ride and no enemies to fight, would be dull in the extreme; in fact the days were never long enough for all I wished to do. I was responsible for training my lord's sons, and that meant spending the morning in the saddle; Ralph was twelve and Osbert eight, and of course their father had already taught them how to control a warhorse. But a growing boy needs constant practice, and it is a fascinating job; you must implant deep in his mind the conviction that he can go anywhere and do anything on any animal ever foaled, but if you overdo it he may have a painful fall and lose his nerve for ever. On fine days we rode in the forest beyond the walls, and if it was frosty or very wet there was always polo in the Hippodrome; though habitual polo-players get in the habit of checking their mounts before a collision instead of galloping hard into an adversary, and young men should not spend too much time at it. We would return to our lodging for dinner, and in the afternoon my lady received us in the guestroom of the convent. On Sundays and holidays we heard an early Mass at a Latin church down by the harbour, that the boys might be familiar with the ritual of their ancestors; but nearly every evening we visited one of the great Roman churches, to see the lamps and listen to the singing; Holy Wisdom, of course, has the best illuminations, but many other churches employ good choirs. My lady appreciated Roman music, and her children endured it without complaint; but it is very different from plainchant and I never got the hang of it.

Once a month the clerk who paid our pension brought a sealed report that the Domestic had seen my lord, and that he was in good health; but we never received a message from him; there was no reason to suppose he would leave his prison until he was carried out for burial. My lady was in practice a widow, and it was for her to make her own life, if she was to have a life at all.

Matilda managed very well. She had given up the attempt to use paint like a smart Roman lady; she had never done it with the discretion of a native, and if she dressed like everyone else it only called attention to her accent; now she wore discreet Frankish gowns and proclaimed herself a foreigner; but that made her the more sought after among those bored society ladies, who in any case looked to a foreigner, the Empress Maria, as leader of fashion. To safeguard her reputation she took her daughter everywhere; Joan was now ten, and it was time to betroth her; but it was difficult to arrange a match for a penniless girl whose noble birth meant nothing to a Roman.

The city seemed gay and splendid; the streets were thronged with gallant horsemen, and two or three times a week we visited some great mansion where groups of handsome young men in gauze mitres and pointed beards whispered to painted ladies while eunuchs sang or a scholar declaimed; clean, scented slaves handed round different kinds of wine, and the little cakes were covered with a sweet crust of sugar, a mysterious Arabian vegetable. On feast days the Emperor rode in state to Holy Wisdom, tall Varangians in gilded armour pressing back the loyal crowds, while Our Lady of Blachernae spread her blessing on all who saw her carried before him. (It had been explained that the picture lost at Manzikert was not the real one, but a duplicate copied for just such an emergency. You may believe this if you can.) After the Liturgy the Emperor would enter the Imperial Box in the Hippodrome; there would be displays of trick-riding, and acrobats dancing on ropes. The Hippodrome was originally constructed for chariot races, but the chariots came to be regarded as ensigns of the various quarters of the city, just as Lombard towns reverence the waggons which carry their banners more even than the flag itself; the races were suppressed because they led to bloody faction-fights. So the Hippodrome has lost its function; but it is the traditional meeting-place of the Emperor and his subjects, where by ancient custom they may petition him. Everyone crowds into it, from habit or in the hope of seeing some exciting political event. In fact it is not easy to devise an entertainment in that great arena; trick-riding seen from a distance is dull unless the man falls off, and the clergy will not permit jousting. I went once or twice, but only Romans find it amusing.

The harbour, also, is crowded with the shipping of every land; anything in the world may be bought there, and remarkably cheap; there are no robbers, and a special lawcourt holds merchants to their bargains. All is arranged to give the impression that the Empire is the centre of the world. But when you look again you notice that the best ships are Italian, and even those which fly Roman colours hail from Venice, which only pretends to be Roman to annoy the other Emperor in Germany.

I began to understand that a great deal of what I saw was a sham. The city is not the centre of a mighty Empire; the whole Empire is nothing but the city. Practically every Theme in Asia had been overrun by the Turks, and the Themes of Europe were in the hands of powerful and insubordinate nobles. John Bryennius, for example, brother to the great Strategus of Hellas, conducted a private war against the Scythians of the Danube; the campaign was successful but expensive, since these nomads yield poor plunder; now the powerful house of Bryennius was putting pressure on the Lotothete to make him pay for the expedition. They might have succeeded, if there had been any money in the Treasury.

The real weakness of Romania was poverty; not the grinding parsimony of men who have never been rich, but the sudden shock which comes to a wealthy magnate when his lands are confiscated. For more than seven hundred years the favourite weapon of the Romans had been gold; they had grown used to handling the richest revenue in the world; they paid barbarians to fight for them, they built expensive fortifications round every town, they bought allies by heaping presents on neighbouring rulers. Now there was no more tribute from Asia.

Since it seemed that my lord's only hope of pardon lay in a change of ruler I took as much interest in politics as a native Roman. Of course I dared not speak freely to strangers; but standing at the back of some great church, listening to those nasal hymns which I found so unpleasant, I might talk treason with my lady. She often rode in the private hunting parties, for ladies only, which were the favourite amusement of the barbarian Empress. I remember one evening in the summer of 1077 when I begged her to let me know what she thought of Alexius and his prospects.

'Of course he could seize the Purple tomorrow, if he wished,' my lady answered. 'I myself wonder why he doesn't, and this morning, when we had jumped a stream and got rid of the field, I took the opportunity of asking the Empress. Alexius is a very close friend of hers. Maria was frank, as she always is with me. She finds it a relief to open her mind to another barbarian, instead of keeping up appearances with these staid Romans, who would remember the right etiquette if an earthquake interrupted an Imperial audience. She told me Alexius does not wish to undertake the responsibility of ruling until affairs have become either better or worse. Every taxpayer must hate the Emperor who presses them so hard; they don't hate Alexius, but they would if taxes were levied in his name. When the Treasury is filled it will be time to seize the throne and win popularity by reducing the assessment. Or if the city were threatened by a hostile army the people would insist on putting a gallant young soldier at the head of the state; but then Michael would probably make him co-Emperor, and everything would arrange itself. Alexius has his life before him, and he is willing to wait; but it's odd that the Empress is so confident that no harm will come to her. Franks cannot understand these Roman politics.'

'I see, my lady. One day Alexius will rule, and until then my lord must wait in prison. But what will become of his children, landless boys and a dowerless maid? Will the heirs of Balliol live out their lives as paid soldiers, with no wall of their own to keep out their enemies?'

'They are not the heirs of Balliol. The head of the house holds a strong town in Normandy, and these sons of a landless cadet may visit their cousin if they wish to live as Frankish lords. Or they can stay in Romania and draw ordinary army pay.

"Soldiers, be content with your wages." That's all the Gospel has to say about soldiering. Oh Roger, I'm tired of scheming and fighting, and pillaging to have the ransom ready when we meet bad luck. I never want to see another corpse. That last year in Asia *I* led the band, you drew on *my* courage, *I* kept a brave front and bargained with our enemies when we were helpless. I couldn't go through it again. I never want to leave St Thecla, and the well-ordered city, and the debonair scented gallants of the Hippodrome. I would rather live peacefully in a hired lodging than defend my own land against the infidel, riding through rain and sleeping in mud. I hope my lord is freed, and I'm sure he will be; but if Messer Roussel would then hang up his mail and enter religion my old age would be happy.'

This was not the Matilda whose steadfast courage had won the admiration of Artouch. I was surprised. Middle age often changes the character of a lady, but she was in her thirties and it could not be that. It must be the influence of the city, which can undermine the character of the most courageous Frank. Don't you young gentlemen stay there too long, or you will find yourselves playing polo instead of jousting with sharpened lances. There had once been a Matilda de Balliol whom I had admired as a noble heroine; now she no longer existed, and walking about in her body was a tired old woman who sought happiness in the mild gossip of convent parlours. I sighed, and turned my attention to the squeaking eunuch who sang antiphonally against a choir of basses, that even the queerest of His creatures might give praise to the Lord.

If my lady had retired from the struggle my lord's sons still needed my help. Young Messer Ralph was fifteen, and should already have gone as a page to some friendly baron, that a conscientious master whose correction would not be handicapped by natural affection might teach him courtesy and gracious manners. I did what I could, but I am not a gentleman, and I could not bring myself to beat a youth of such high birth. The Domestic offered to put him in the Varangian Guard, which in Roman eyes is the most honourable position open to a barbarian; but I answered that a wellborn Frank could not walk, even in gilded armour; it might bring him into personal contact with the Emperor, but nothing could compensate for the lack of a warhorse; any pupil of mine must ride against his enemies. It was arranged that in a year or two he should join the Frankish mercenaries. Young Osbert was only eleven, and there was plenty of time to decide his future. A shipmaster from Amalfi, who had known Messer Roussel in Italy, offered to make him a pirate when he was old enough to fight; the pirates of Amalfi win a very good living off the African coast; they seldom rob Christian ships, unless they meet one that is undermanned and carrying a rich cargo, and they are respected in every port of Christendom.

Little Joan wished to pass her life in the convent of St Thecla. But this Matilda would not allow. The house was notoriously lax, and though it made a good harbourage for widows, and wives whose husbands happened to be in gaol, the young novices often produced superfluous babies. In any case the Abbess exacted a rich dowry from every newcomer. Joan was told she might enter religion if she wished, and we would be glad of her prayers; but it must be in one of the strict communities of the west, where dowries are not demanded and men do not visit the parlour. If she chose the world instead her mother would look for a decent mercenary, willing to take a penniless bride for the sake of her noble birth. Like most girls who have free choice in the matter Joan eventually chose marriage; though by the autumn of 1077 Matilda had not yet found a suitable husband.

In those days the whole city began to think that the Emperor Michael had weathered the storm. The Turks seemed content with the territory they had overrun; the Domestic was a model of fidelity and competence, and so long as he obeyed a civilian Emperor the remnant of the Army of Asia followed his example; the very heavy taxes and ingenious confiscations devised by the Logothete slightly exceeded expenditure; when the Treasury was full mercenaries could be hired, and once the Turks began to retreat native recruits would join the army, the taxes could be lightened, and the power of Romania would increase every year like a snowball rolling downhill. It very nearly came off. But as usual the Romans did not pay enough attention to the affairs of Europe.

There the house of Bryennius remained powerful, since Nicephorus was now Strategus of Thrace and Hellas. For the last two years he had remained in his castle of Adrianople, and the Logothete rightly supposed he was plotting treason. If the Empire had been stronger the Strategus would have been appointed to some remote fortress, and arrested if he did not go into exile as commanded. But Michael and his minister wished to postpone the trial of strength until there was more money in the Treasury. It was a tense situation, just the kind of thing Roman politicians enjoy; every Roman who has reached eminence by his own efforts is certain that he is the cleverest man in the world, and it amuses him to watch his enemies prosper until it is time to crush them. About harvest in the year 1077 Nicephoritzes thought the time was ripe; but he had left it just too late. The Bryenii were strong enough to wage war with the city.

In that September the Strategus was far away in Durazzo, burning the lairs of the Sclavonian pirates. Here was a good opportunity to arrest him while he was parted from the main body of his troops, and the Logothete sent a Varangian with orders to put him on a ship and bring him to the city. It was a good plan, typically Roman; the Strategus must think himself safe at that extremity of the Empire, while the Army of Europe lay at Adrianople, a shield between him and the Emperor; but the messenger carried bribes for his bodyguard, and his followers could do nothing to rescue him from a ship.

The plan miscarried through the incompetence of the Varangian. These men enjoy a very high reputation, and certainly they are brave, and skilled in arms; but they are utterly reckless, and though faithful they do not bother to obey orders which they find inconvenient; their real job is to guard the

Emperor's person, and they are unfit for more difficult tasks. They all tell you that in their own fatherland they are of excessively noble birth, but they can't ride, and they get drunk whenever they feel like it, instead of waiting for an appropriate time. I could never regard them as gentlemen.

This Varangian broke his journey at Adrianople. There, in the ancestral stronghold of the Bryennii, the foolish barbarian drank in a low tavern and got it into his muffled head that the troopers round him were not treating the Emperor's guardsman with sufficient respect (these northern savages are always on the lookout for slights). He began to boast that he carried orders for the arrest of the Strategus. That got him all the attention he wanted. The soldiers took him before John Bryennius, who cut off his nose and proclaimed Nicephorus Emperor of Romania.

At first this revolt of the unfashionable and second-rate Army of Europe was not taken seriously in the city. But when the Logothete looked round for the mighty Army of Asia he found that since Manzikert there was very little of it left. A force had to be gathered from the garrisons of the Black Sea, and by the time it was levied Nicephorus Bryennius was back in Adrianople. The loyalists marched north under the command of the Strategus Basilakes, and that was another mistake; for the Treasury owed him a great deal of money, and the pay of his men was in arrears. On reaching Adrianople he joined Bryennius.

It was agreed that Nicephoritzes seemed to be losing his touch, and there was speculation about the prospect of an Emperor from Europe, the first for more than two generations. But no one thought civil war would affect the private lives of undistinguished citizens; this was the normal way in which the Purple changed hands, and nobody would suffer except Michael and his ministers. The Emperor ought to enter religion, and Nicephoritzes should take the ready cash in the Treasury and sail to Italy or some infidel land. Then Romania would have a competent ruler who could get on with the pressing business of pushing back the Turks.

But Michael made a fight of it, and to everyone's surprise Alexius remained loyal. I think fidelity to his oath had something to do with his decision, though no Roman politician would give that explanation for his conduct, from fear of the derision of his colleagues; but in fact, though Alexius is now Emperor, he succeeded on the abdication of his predecessor, and in all his career he has obeyed his lawful superior. Whatever the reason, when Alexius backed Michael everyone saw that the Emperor had a chance after all; there was a pause in the campaign, because neither side wished to incur the reproach of shedding first blood.

The established pattern for a peaceable change of Emperors would have been for Michael to retire, or for the populace of the city to rise against him and open the gates to Bryennius. But Michael was obstinate, and the populace feared Alexius. The rebels waited in Adrianople, but when November came and Michael still reigned they advanced gingerly, hoping their approach would set off the revolt. Both sides had tried to hire barbarian mercenaries. But the Turks, who were doing very well in Asia, scorned the meagre pay offered by Nicephoritzes; while Bryennius was in touch with the Patzinaks, poor men who were delighted to cross the Danube unhindered. John Bryennius was a dashing leader of horse, though not really a skilful commander, and he brought a cloud of nomad archers right up to the city, while his elder brother remained with the regular bands in Adrianople.

Crowds of frightened refugees poured in through all the landward gates. The Patzinaks were in the suburbs. It was useless for a peasant to sit at home and cheer for Bryennius; that would have been all right in a civil war between Roman troops, but these barbarians pillaged without inquiring into politics, and cut the throat of anyone who grumbled. Since Bryennius could not pay them his officers had no control; and Romans from the backward Themes of Europe are jealous of the city; the rebels were secretly pleased to avenge a long memory of slights and insults on the élite of the capital.

The city was in despair. Politics were interfering with the private lives of law-abiding taxpayers, Bryennius and his ridiculous Europeans were plundering the home of civilisation; in a night the whole mob of porters, day-labourers and craftsmen became intensely loyal to Michael. The gates were closed, and puzzled householders thronged the office of the Eparch to find out whether they should march under the banners of the Greens or the Blues, in the old organisation for home defence which had not been called out for generations.

In the middle of a wintry night I was roused by a hammering on the door of our little house. I had long ago made arrangements for an emergency, and the stout door stood firm while I hustled the boys through a big drain which came out in the garden of the convent. Then I picked up my sword and went down to interview the callers. The street was a blaze of torches, and I was too dazzled to recognise anyone, but a well-known voice called:

'Hallo, surely little Roger is in ambush behind that beard. Will you be my man for this campaign? Alexius has freed me, and I'm glad to fight for the man who saved my eyes.'

I fell on my knees before Messer Roussel, and renewed the fealty which had never left my heart.

The eunuch who guarded the convent knew my voice and opened at the first summons. Naturally the Rule lays down that everyone must be in bed from supper to Matins, but the whole of St Thecla was gathered in the hall; these nuns never keep their Rule, even in time of peace, and with all these exciting goings-on in the city they were still discussing politics. My pupils had joined them, and were playing cat's-cradle with a pretty young novice.

Now I could examine my lord by the light of those excellent Roman lamps; he seemed very much altered, for during his long imprisonment his hair and beard had grown untrimmed; it was now more grey than red, and the bushy effect made his head so large that his body appeared smaller. But he was not really shrunken; thanks to Alexius he had been allowed sufficient food and a walk in the open every day; when his hair was clipped to go under the hauberk he would look a gallant knight. I blessed the tender-hearted Romans; how many brave knights in the west never recover after a few months in a foeman's dungeon.

His children hung back; they recognised him, but for four years they had thought of him as someone from the past who would never return. They enjoyed life in the city, and remembered with aversion the hunger, the cold, and the long marches which had made up their days when the house of Balliol was trying to conquer Asia. But Matilda, after one gasp of astonishment, flung herself into his arms.

'Oh, my lord,' she cried, 'when do we march, and which side do we help? Or shall we bar the gate and hold this convent for ourselves? The chapel is full of silver, and if we hire mercenaries we might get Bryennius and Ducas bidding in competition for our support.'

'No, sweetheart,' my lord said firmly. 'Five years ago we tried to found a realm, and it's really too difficult. Besides, young Alexius has been very good to me. I shall stick to the Emperor he supports. That's Michael at present, though of course he may change his mind. I have been released to help in the defence of the city, and tomorrow I shall start to recruit Franks from the Italian factories. The Logothete has promised horses and mail, and an advance of pay. It's a come-down, after being lord of Armeniakon, but at least I'm no worse off than when we first landed in Romania; that's really a triumph for a simple Frank after eight years in the east. Now I've been alone for a very long time. It would be tactless to ask the Abbess to provide a marriage-bed; let's go back to that little house where I found young Roger. The children can stay here, and we'll all meet at breakfast.'

My lord never cared for his children, and they repaid him with indifference; he was kind to chubby infants, and a good comrade to the knights who rode beside him in the charge, but raw youths betwixt and between got on his nerves. It seemed a little surprising that after so many years of solitude he should seek out his own wife for his first night of freedom. But I discovered later that he feared it might bring him back luck if he went straight to a brothel and fell into mortal sin. For a long time he had been in a State of Grace, but a dungeon provides no opportunity for anything else. Anyway, it was the right way to behave.

As they left the Abbess wished them joy, but there were none of the coarse remarks you would get in even a well-regulated western convent; Roman nuns are lax, but discreet in speech; the standard of what is funny and what shocking varies from country to country in the most surprising way. The rest of us sat around until dawn, drinking and discussing the campaign.

It was the general opinion that Michael must now beat Bryennius. He had the support of the city, and Alexius was wholeheartedly on his side; it was obviously the Domestic who had released my lord. Everyone was pleased, for after victory the convent would merit a good thank-offering for its shelter of the Frankopole's family. Only young Ralph was depressed.

'I hope father has learned his lesson,' he said to me aside. 'It was all arranged that I should be an officer in the regular army. But if father gets up to his old tricks again he will really be blinded, and no one will trust me, either. Do you think, uncle Roger, that for once he will be faithful to his paymaster? He seems faithful now, but after he has won a battle I bet he hoists the banner of St Michael and challenges all comers.'

It only shows what can be done by a constant drip of slander. People had somehow got it into their heads that Messer Roussel rebelled against his employers, the worst fault in a mercenary; here was his own son believing that malicious gossip. Young Ralph was too big to be beaten, but I took him by the ear and led him into the courtyard, where I spoke to him as though I really were an uncle.

I pointed out that my lord had displayed astonishing fidelity to every one of his paymasters. In the early days in Italy he served Roger fitzTancred without the slightest hint of disloyalty; he had left the west quite openly, with the goodwill and consent of everyone who had a right to be consulted; in Romania he had been faithful to Romanus Diogenes, doing his duty as long as there was a Roman army to command his allegiance; he had never sworn fealty to Michael, and when Isaac Comnenus hanged his followers without trial he had been obliged to go to war in their defence; even then he had put himself under the orders of John Ducas, and had continued faithfully to uphold his losing cause until Alexius captured him by treachery. My lord had been taken in war, and he was lucky to be alive and unmutilated; but his honour was spotless, and anyone who understood the customs of the west would see that he was an exceptionally loyal mercenary.

Privately I thought it likely that my lord had learned discretion; at least while Alexius commanded the Roman army Michael was too strong to be overthrown, and Messer Roussel would serve him.

In the morning my lord set out, in borrowed mail, to raise a band for the war against Bryennius. Most Franks in the army were content with their status, and did not wish to jeopardise promotion by joining an irregular unit; but the port was full of Italian ships, and some bad characters in the regular bands were glad to make a fresh start where their records were unknown. Neither these men nor the Italian pirates were a good class of recruit, but they could fight very savagely if there was no way of retreat. The Emperor issued horses and in the east every Frank has arms hidden somewhere. By midday my lord was at the head of two hundred and fifty of the worst rascals in Christendom, as brave and well-armed as any Varangian and better trained for warfare among complicated fortifications.

The fortifications of the city are very complicated. There is a triple line, first an outer wall six feet high, embanked within to form a breastwork for archers; then a curtain forty feet high set with sixty-foot towers; behind that a sixty-foot wall set with eighty-foot towers. In front is a wide ditch lined with masonry, furnished with pipes by which it may be flooded; but the machinery had been neglected, and in fact the ditch remained dry. Every tower carries catapults, and in theory no besieger can approach.

But John Bryennius nearly got in, for the city was defended by a very small garrison which was not expecting an assault. By a sudden surprise the Patzinaks carried one sector of the outer breastwork and the middle wall behind it. They held a tower of this middle wall, and nothing barred their way except the last curtain; which was the strongest, but would soon be breached if they brought up engines under cover of the outer works. They could be seen fetching timber. Here was the obvious place for Franks to attack; the enemy must stand and meet us, instead of keeping out of reach and shooting arrows.

Although at least his throne and probably his life were at stake the Emperor took no part in the war. I admired his self-restraint in refusing to meddle with a business he did not understand. Most princes would have waved a sword in the background, giving futile orders to the reserve just when it was needed for some urgent task. But even he could not bring himself to trust all his forces to a Comnenus and a rival; as nominal colleague to Alexius the Emperor's brother Constantine had been dragged from the second-rate palace where he amused himself by drilling a sulky guard. The real second in command was of course Messer Roussel, but the Caesar Constantine had to be kept harmless and occupied near the Golden Gate, three miles from the point of danger.

By nightfall the Patzinaks were back beyond the ditch. Nomad archers who have been compelled to dismount are no match for mailed Franks. Young Ralph drew his sword for the first time, though his brother Osbert was considered too young. Even Matilda and Joan were there to keep order in the ranks, for we had no respectable knights whom we could appoint as subordinate officers. But it was not really much of a fight, though it increased our fame among the ignorant burgesses of the city. These Romans were all on our side; for John Bryennius by plundering the suburbs had brought politics into their private lives in a way that made him very much disliked.

The rebels hung about the neighbourhood until the middle of Advent. They were too weak to blockade the city, and the loyalists were too weak to drive them away; for the oddest thing about this slow-moving and half-hearted war was the very small number of warriors available to fight it. Here was the richest city in the world, dignified by the oldest crown in Christendom; John Bryennius had nearly won it with a thousand heathen light horse, and the Emperor was safe on his throne because in the nick of time he had taken into pay less than three hundred Franks.

Of course both sides had other troops at their disposal; but even in this crisis they behaved like good Romans. Nicephorus Bryennius kept most of the Army of Europe in Hellas and Dalmatia, to check the Sclavonians; and what was left of the Army of Asia held the diminished eastern frontier against the Turks. This was partly because in a civil war both sides must please public opinion, but partly because Roman nobles, even in rebellion, care deeply for the welfare of the state.

My lord was again Frankopole, and the Treasury owed him a generous salary, though it could not be paid until the war was won. But in his own city the Emperor's credit is good, and we lived in considerable state; my lady was at last mistress of those private female apartments which had so charmed her as a guest in Roman mansions, and we did not see much of her. Usually she had the nuns of St Thecla, and all the other female friends she could think of, eating cakes in her private room. It was rather restful to be free of her driving energy, and my lord did not complain.

But campaigning from the city, though it meant warm beds and good food when the jousting was finished, brought us no plunder. We were glad when, just before Christmas, the war moved westward to Thrace. All the Patzinaks suddenly went home; they had pillaged the suburbs until nothing was left, and Bryennius had no money to pay them wages. He fell back towards Adrianople, where his brother Nicephorus kept the meagre state of an unsuccessful claimant to the Purple. That should have ended the war; a usurper must go forward; when he retreats his supporters lose heart and try to buy forgiveness from the established ruler, as had happened when John Ducas withdrew from Chrysopolis. What kept the struggle alive was the rivalry between the two halves of the Empire. Bryennius was head of the only European house on a par with Comnenus, and Palaeologus, and Ducas, the great families of Asia; at last the despised Army of Europe had a chance of setting their commander on the throne; they would not submit until they had been beaten in the field. Meanwhile Alexius was ordered to lead an expedition against the rebel towns of Thrace, and he took Messer Roussel as second in command.

Before we set out, between Christmas and Epiphany, a council was held in the mansion of the Domestic. Matilda and her sons were invited to be present, and I came along because no one forbade me. Alexius wished the proceedings to be known in the city; he was so powerful that he must always be under suspicion of aiming at the Purple, and he dared not hold secret discussions with prominent military leaders. But what was really in doubt was the fidelity of Messer Roussel. There was no reason why he should join Bryennius, who was in constant straits for money, while Michael controlled the temporarily insolvent but well-managed Treasury of the city; but he might try to found an independent realm in Thrace; as he had done in Asia. The Domestic was frank about it; he is a man of many moods, who can fit his demeanour to his company; on this occasion he chose to be a bluff warrior with no time for politics.

'Lord Frankopole,' he said cheerfully, 'we are to march against John Bryennius, who holds Athyra in Thrace. I know we'll beat him easily, though if these stubborn Europeans defend every fortified town the campaign may last for years. I might be called back to the city, since the pay of the Army of Asia is heavily in arrear, and they may revolt when they think I am busy. Then you will command in Europe. But the Logothete doubts your loyalty. I told him you are an honest knight, who has never yet broken his engagement. You know exactly how true that is, and I need not dwell on the subject. Anyway, here are a company of holy monks, with the genuine image of Our Lady of Blachernae. The Emperor commands you to swear fidelity on that holy relic before you leave the city.'

This was insulting, however you looked at it; but Alexius had put it as gently as he could, pretending that the whole idea was a whim of the hated Nicephoritzes. My lord hesitated; I think he intended to be loyal, but no one likes to be publicly singled out as less trustworthy than his comrades. My lady intervened, seizing the picture from an embarrassed monk and kneeling before her husband.

'Come on, Roussel, swear,' she said briskly. 'We tried to found a Frankish state when we led disciplined sergeants who had followed us from Italy; and we failed. We won't succeed now, with a gang of scoundrels picked at random from the harbour. Earn your pay and save it for your daughter's dowry. The Balliols will never be independent rulers.'

My lord put his hand on the panel, and repeated the usual oath. He spoke impressively, but I could see him change as he did it. When he had finished his head dropped and his mouth grew slack. He was an old soldier, still good for a few more campaigns, but looking for security and a warm hall for his old age; no longer the gallant captain who had been prepared to meet the world in arms to found a realm of his own. The great adventure was over.

CHAPTER SIXTEEN

Nicephoritzes the Eunuch

We marched before Epiphany. The Domestic brought the Schools of the Guard, the only regular troops in the city, and the Varangians, who are not properly troops at all but who might be useful in the escalade since they are trained to fight on foot. The Frankopole now led more than four hundred mailed horse, for every Frank in Romania was eager to join his banner.

Athyra is an unimportant place, but our army was not strong enough to invest it in form. However, Alexius brought first-class engineers from the naval arsenal, and after less than a fortnight we battered down a gate. We tried an assault, though the Romans dislike that bloody method of winning a town. At the end of a long day's fighting we got in, and John Bryennius fled with his horse, leaving his foot to be cut down in the streets; he had more foot than most Roman armies, for his Sclavonian mercenaries had never learned to ride. In fairness I must admit our Varangians were useful; in their own homes they rule Sclavonian peasants, and both races fight in the same way, with great two-handed axes; but the Varangians do it very much better.

In the little port of Athyra we waited for the spring. We would not move until we received our arrears of pay; but we must remain faithful to our defaulting paymaster, for no one else in the eastern world had any money either. We lived in the castle; but the Domestic lodged there also, and saw to it that my lord had no dealings with the burgesses. We were tired and bored. This was a nagging, petty war in a plundered land, where

241

four hundred horse made a great army and every farm had been burned by the barbarians; less than seven years ago we had marched with sixty thousand horse through the smiling untouched countryside of Asia. It was melancholy to witness the collapse of a great Empire, and we could not decide whether our futile and cautious warfare made things worse, or whether the only hope for Romania lay in the suppression of Bryennius.

My lord's children were a trial to him; in early youth they had been flattered as the heirs of a great man who might become a mighty prince; now they were of no particular importance, and they blamed their father. Ralph was nearly sixteen, and already rode with the band, though it was one of my duties to jostle him out of the front rank if the enemy looked like meeting our charge. It was difficult to foresee his future; he did not take kindly to discipline, and Roman officers dislike recruits who will not obey orders; but he was not a good enough jouster to win fame among the turbulent champions of the west. He thought common troopers should follow a Balliol, but mercenaries care very little for noble birth and only obey the captains who lead them to rich plunder. As we gossiped in the hall after supper (this Roman hall had no hearth, for the hot-air pipes were in good order; it was warm, but gloomy to a fire-loving Frank) he would make catty remarks about the danger of negotiating with infidels or the discomforts of a Roman prison. He was a cheeky cub who would have been improved by a thrashing, but in his heart my lord agreed that he had ruined his family. Ralph was not rebuked, and grew more impudent every day.

Joan was thirteen, and during the coming year she must be married or shut up in a convent; men and women mix very freely in Romania, and those mansions have so many little private rooms that a seducer has more opportunity than in a Frankish castle where the ladies sit together in a crowded hall; a damsel of fourteen easily loses her reputation, if not her virginity, and then good communities, where the nuns are ladies, will not have her even with a large dowry. But Matilda, who should have been negotiating with suitable young men was unwilling to commit herself during the war. Messer Roussel might win promotion; it would be rash to betroth his only daughter to a younger son, when next year she might be worthy of an heir. The girl herself was obedient, though a little sulky; she desired the freedom of marriage, and did not care who might be her lord; for once she was the mother of a son she might choose a friend from among the gallants of the city.

Osbert was only eleven, and his elder brother compelled him to behave meekly. Besides, his career was settled, and a pirate is never a nuisance to his family and may one day bring home useful plunder. He was a cheerful child, always climbing trees, and learning to fence without a shield as sailors must when they board a hostile ship. He obeyed me, and I liked him.

The head of the family was undoubtedly Matilda. She had resumed her habit of giving orders, because when a decision had to be made we all asked her opinion. Without her guidance we would have sat all day in the comfort of Athyra; she kept us up to the mark by demanding every evening where we proposed to ride next morning, and telling us where to go when my lord answered that one direction was as good as another. For many miles round we protected the peasants, so that they could get on with their winter ploughing and contribute their quota of land-tax when the harvest was reaped. Money is the most important weapon in civil war, and Alexius was continually increasing the areas which paid taxes to the Emperor Michael. He was pleased with our activity.

Riding against the rebels my lord displayed the old dash which had made him famous in Italy. The hauberk hid his grey hair, and mail conceals a middle-aged paunch better than the most cleverly-cut tunic. The common sergeants, who only saw him on horseback, followed him with devotion. But in the evenings he relaxed, an old tired warrior who knew his life was ending in failure.

'When I first came east it seemed quite simple,' he said to me one evening, while the rest of the company were shaking dice for a silver jug, too finely made to be chopped into equal shares.

'I intended to set up for myself when I got the chance, though naturally I did not propose to make treacherous war on my employer. Romanus Diogenes had the finest army in the world, and after I had helped him to beat the infidels there would be room for a Frankish county beyond the frontier of Romania. Frankish ways are better than Roman. They build fine churches and castles, and the city is the wonder of the world; even these blasted pipes of hot smoke warm the hall better than a hearth, though it means that people sit about in corners instead of gathering round the fire to listen to the head of the family. We can't make anything like that. Our food and wine are not so delicate, and we dress like peasants beside their silk robes and gauze mitres. But when all's said and done they are taxpaying slaves; eunuchs tallage the most noble families, and they won't even fight unless someone pays them; the Patriarch serves the Emperor as though he were indeed the Equal of the Apostles, instead of putting Kings to the ban in defence of the liberty of God's Church; they accept the decisions of hired judges in their lawcourts; even the villeins in Balliol would revolt if their suits were not decided by a jury of their peers. And the Emperor at the head of it is nobody in particular, just some lord who has come out on top in their everlasting civil wars. They have neither loyalty nor freedom. When I showed them the decent Frankish way of doing things I knew they would be my faithful subjects. So they were; wherever I ruled the burgesses were content. But these blasted lumps of gold and silver which they continually handle got the better of me in the end. You can tell my ungrateful children, next time they raise the subject, that I was beaten, not because I am not the best knight in the east, but because these Romans are moneygrubbers, unfit to be ruled by a warrior. But they pay generously. I am content to serve them. My sons can found their own realms if they are men enough to do it. Why should I risk my eyes for their benefit?'

I soothed my poor lord by agreeing with everything he said. If he had lost heart he might as well end his days in a comfortable castle. But of course Messer Roussel was no longer a gallant knight; it is the hope of independence which makes gentlemen charge so fiercely that they cannot be withstood; a hireling who fights for pay is no better in the mêlée than a Roman trooper, and not so useful on campaign because his commander cannot trust him to obey orders.

The Franks were still the most valuable band in Michael's service, though most of them were unemployed mariners who would not be deemed good horsemen in the west; but an Italian sailor rides well enough to shine in a Roman army, and though they thought more of winning booty than of defeating Bryennius they could scatter horse-archers, or ride down Sclavonian foot, whenever they went on patrol. We might have finished the war before spring if Alexius had advanced and brought Bryennius to battle. But there was no money in the city, and after harvest the taxes would come in; we hung about because the Domestic had received a sound military training as the Romans conceive it, and would not lead out his men until he was assured of supplies and a well-filled paychest.

These scientific Roman strategists forget that other things happen while two armies face one another in idleness. Some time in Lent a eunuch of the Domos rode in with an urgent message for the Domestic. We Balliols were lounging in the hall, listening to a stray jongleur who had sailed east to see the world, and walked from the city when he heard of a Frankish audience kicking their heels in Thrace; he was a second-rate performer, as one would expect so far from home, but some of his jokes were broad enough to make a mule blush, and he could dance upside-down; he was better than nothing, and much better than a family quarrel.

Suddenly the Domestic entered, accompanied by half a dozen Varangians. Evidently this was an official call. He carried a despatch in his hand; as he spoke he occasionally glanced at it, to make sure he got his facts right, and I reflected how easy it must be to make an impressive and cogent speech if you can read without effort.

'Lord Frankopole,' he began formally, 'tonight I must ride

for the city, and the regular troops with me. You will carry on the war as you think fit, until I send more definite instructions. Nicephorus Botaniates has been proclaimed in Pontus; he has already defeated George Palaeologus, and the whole Army of Asia obeys him. Worse still, he has given the great town of Nicaea to the Turks in payment for their help. The Asiatics must hate Nicephoritzes more than the infidels. I have been summoned to defend the city. Just to settle any doubt, I shall fight for Michael Ducas; not perhaps to the death, but so long as he has a chance of victory. Tomorrow you will be a free agent, but I advise you to do the same. It is Michael who holds the Treasury. Don't risk a battle; just keep on pushing back the rebels gently, and when we have enough money a great army will reinforce you. I trust you; don't spoil my record as a judge of fidelity.'

Alexius had probably intended to make a formal declaration that it was the duty of every soldier to support the reigning Emperor; but Messer Roussel was his intimate friend, and he could not keep back his own estimate of the political situation. In fact he passed on the hint that Botaniates would probably win; but no matter who held the city a captain who fought against Bryennius would be rewarded.

When we were once more alone, a roomful of Franks who could discuss in our own language these confusing Roman politics, young Ralph was the first to offer advice. 'Listen father,' he called impudently, 'St Michael has given us another chance, in spite of your failure at Amasia. Botaniates has let the Turks into Nicaea! That means that in the next few days he must conquer or yield, for he has no fortress behind him. Meanwhile Bryennius holds Europe, and we hold eastern Thrace. No Themes obey the city! Never mind who rules there; he will be provost of a wealthy market, less powerful than the Duke of Venice. Come on. Tomorrow we ride against Adrianople. May I be the first to salute Count Roussel of Thrace!'

My lord was always calm in council; now he spoke without

open rudeness. 'Messer Ralph,' he said quietly, 'the times are disturbed, and you are my most trusted follower. I appoint you castellan. Until daybreak you should visit the sentinels every hour. You may begin your rounds at once. Report when you have inspected every post.'

To a lad of that age the opportunity to inspect veteran sentinels and report them if they were idle was more attractive even than giving advice to his betters. Ralph went willingly.

After he left we were a little nervous of my lord's temper, and kept silence until Matilda spoke. 'My dear, I know the boy's a trial,' she said. 'I dare say you also were a nuisance at his age. But what he says is reasonable. Botaniates has sold the remnant of Asia for a chance to reign in the city, and if you open negotiations with Bryennius he will divide Europe with us.'

'Of course he will, at this minute. It gives him the summer to collect the taxes of the west and hire a strong army. Alexius saw that, and he was warning me against it. Supposing next year Romania is divided among three rulers, Botaniates in the city, Bryennius in Thessalonica, and myself at Adrianople between them? How long do you think I would last, with two Romans intriguing against me? And where does Alexius come in? He could seize the Purple tomorrow. At present he is content to command in the city, but if he tried he could capture me again, and next time I would really be mutilated.'

'Then you will draw pay and obey orders, like a common sergeant?' answered Matilda. 'I know you were beaten once, and unlike your sons I don't think it was your fault. We none of us allowed for the energy of Alexius Comnenus. But it isn't like you, or worthy of your blood, to give up just because the first attempt was unsuccessful.'

'You haven't been strapped down with the blinding-iron before your eyes. I knew it would be cold if Alexius kept his word, but that might have been a trick. It was very easy to imagine what it would feel like white-hot. I shall never risk that again. I shall say so publicly to the whole band, and those who wish to serve a more dashing leader may seek him elsewhere.

Would you, madam, care to join Bryennius or Botaniates? I can offer you safe conduct this evening.'

My lord strode restlessly up and down, his head averted, trying to keep back his tears. Joan began to cry, and the rest of us felt horribly embarrassed. When all values were collapsing after Manzikert my lord had shown himself the greatest captain in the east; now this great leader had declined into a faithful servant, broken by fear. Later we explained his conduct by saying he was loyal to Alexius who had granted him mercy; but at that moment the truth peeped out. Well, no one has ever put the iron to my eyes. But then I am not a knight of ancient descent; the son of a smith is expected to run away rather than go down fighting. It was because we thought Messer Roussel was different that every Frank in the east was proud to follow his banner.

Matilda began to chatter, attempting to pass off an awkward situation, like a well-bred Roman lady. 'Be careful of that embroidery, Joan. If you must cry don't drop tears on the silk. Osbert, sit still. You'll wear a hole in your chausses if you squirm like that. Now then, Roussel, the band will expect orders to march. If we do nothing half of them will desert to Botaniates, to be in at the sack of the city. Without the Domestic we are not strong enough to assault Adrianople. Where shall we go? Roger, you've been sitting in silence like a well-trained pedagogue; God knows you aren't that, whatever you may be. What shall we do to keep the men busy?'

As a rule when my lady turned to me suddenly I found myself tongue-tied, but on this occasion I had a bright idea. 'That lazy eunuch of the Dromos took all day to cover twenty miles,' I said at once. 'It is important to know what passes in the city. I suggest we march south-west and occupy a better harbour. Then we shall hear the latest news from the ships in the Marmora.'

'That's sound. We don't want to find ourselves fighting gallantly for Michael three days after he has been blinded,' my lady said briskly. 'I hate asking these Romans to explain a map, and I'm never any wiser when they do. Roussel, can you think of a handy seaport which we can capture without help from the Domestic? It must be in rebel hands, to make it obvious we are fighting in Michael's cause when we march against it.'

'Oh yes, Selymbria,' my lord answered without hesitation. No matter how upset he felt he could always plan a campaign.

'Then we march there tomorrow,' said Matilda with decision. 'Will you give orders tonight? Roger, go and tell the servants to prepare to move. I shall ride Swallow if his back is quite cool, but see they give him a fresh saddle-cloth. I shall need six reasonably honest sergeants to guard our baggage. Remember, Joan, to fold your dresses tonight; if you keep us waiting in the morning I shall marry you to an infidel Patzinak.'

This last remark was intended to relieve the solemnity of the occasion. My lady was always giving orders, because she made up her mind more quickly than anyone else; then she would realise she was taking too much upon herself, and try to smooth things over by making some very unfunny joke.

When we reached Selymbria the little garrison who held it for Bryennius embarked on local fishing-boats and sailed west. The Roman navy nearly always adheres to the ruler of the city; but their real job is to enforce the regulations of the Treasury and protect the sea from pirates; they never seek out Roman ships in the service of a usurper, and avoid fighting if they can. Though in theory Michael controlled the sea, the men of Bryennius could sail near the coast if they were not too ostentatious about it.

Selymbria is a decayed fishing-port, without even a proper castle. The inhabitants own no cattle, and the only supplies we could seize were fish and cabbage. It was the middle of Lent, and of course such food should have sufficed. But the eastern church has so many fasts unknown to the west that Franks get into the habit of eating beef every day, just to show their independence. Our men demanded to be led against some other town where there would be a comfortable castle and better plunder.

It was bad policy to move away from the city when great events might take us unawares; but our men were a poor lot of unemployed loafers, and they might desert, or worse still change sides, if we did not carry on the campaign as they wished. Twenty miles to the west lay the flourishing town of Heraclea-in-Thrace; it was the centre of a rich district, whence fat cattle were shipped to the city. We marched west along the shore, and once again the rebel garrison fled by sea and the burgesses opened their gates to us.

We now occupied a district sixty miles long, whence all administration had vanished; the people brought their disputes to the Frankopole, in default of any other authority, and it seemed that we would found our county by accident. But Messer Roussel would not judge civil causes, or take any step except the routine hanging of thieves; he said it might give the Romans an excuse to charge him with disloyalty. We could all see that the war against Bryennius had been shelved while the greater struggle was decided; presently the Schools of the Guard, under whichever leader came out on top, would march west and restore order. I wondered that Bryennius did not collect what treasure he could and sail to Italy; but most Romans would rather be blind in the city than free anywhere else, and I suppose he thought he had a chance. Civil war can bring surprising results, and a great territory obeyed the court of Adrianople.

By the harbour of Heraclea there was a Latin church, for Italian ships sometimes put in to wait for a fair wind; on Easter Sunday I persuaded my lord and his family to perform their duties. In Asia we had never bothered; for there were no Latin priests and it is very difficult to find out which of the Roman clergy have incurred excommunication by supporting a schismatic Patriarch and which adhere to the True Faith; even those who are unsuspended delight to tease a Frank by pretending they have never heard of the dispute, or of the Pope either. But here was a well-educated Italian priest, who kept the correct ritual; he had only left Apulia because his Bishop had caught him embezzling the vessels of the altar. It was too good an opportunity to miss. It is evident, when you consider what came after, that my lord was under the special protection of his patron St Michael. That was only fair, for he must have killed more infidels than any other knight of his generation.

The castle of Heraclea is built on a hill, only to be reached by a stiff climb. So that fasting men should not have a tiring walk in the heat of the day my lady had breakfast prepared under an awning in the market-place. We had just taken our seats at the long tables when the lookout on the mole set fire to his beacon, so close that the wind drove smoke into our faces. That meant hostile ships heading for the port; though Bryennius had no fleet we were on the borders of the enemy, and my lord left nothing to chance. The men were ordered up the hill to arm, and a groom went to fetch my lord's sword and shield; but the gentry strolled down to get a look at the attackers and estimate their numbers.

There was a stiff breeze from the east, and the water was too choppy for galleys. All we could make out was a fast Roman despatch boat, with all sail set; she was reaching for the narrow mouth of the harbour at a very good speed, which would wreck her if the helmsman made a mistake. These fast two-masted boats are seldom used in battle, on account of their light construction; she might shoot off the famous Greek Fire; but although there was a strong wind the houses by the port were roofed with tiles, not thatch. We all cursed the nervous lookout who had spoiled our gala breakfast.

I like watching a ship make harbour on a windy day. It is satisfying to see something difficult done well, and Roman seamen are nearly as skilful as Italians. As the boat gained shelter inside the mole her yards came down with a run, the sails were neatly furled, and the anchor splashed overboard. While she still had way on her the dinghy plumped into the water, and three men sculled hurriedly to shore. We felt a little flat; what had seemed a hostile assault was nothing more than an urgent message from the city.

But the two men who climbed out of the dinghy (the third immediately sculled away) were not ordinary couriers of the Dromos. One wore gilded armour, crowned with an elaborate helm whose crest caught the wind and must have been a great nuisance to the wearer; he carried no shield, and his officer's mace flashed with jewelled ornaments. The other was the biggest man I have ever seen, more than six foot tall and very fat indeed; that colossal paunch could only belong to a eunuch, but no courier would wear so many necklaces and bracelets. Between them they carried, very awkwardly, a small ironbound casket. I could think of only one explanation of this ostentatious display of wealth. 'Be very careful, my lord,' I called. 'Bryennius, or maybe Botaniates, wishes it to be known that he is offering you a bribe, so that the Emperor will doubt your loyalty. Take anything they give you, but send half to the Treasury; and be public in all your dealings.'

'All right, little Roger,' he answered cheerfully. 'I welcome bribes, but two men can't carry enough to buy my honour. Ask these gentlemen if they are seeking the Frankopole. And since there are at present three Emperors in Romania it would not be indelicate to inquire whether they support one side more than another.'

After all these years my lord spoke fluent Greek, but army regulations assume that the Frankopole will need a linguist, and he took advantage of that to make the strangers declare themselves in public.

The eunuch drew himself up and spoke in the high-pitched voice which to Roman ears denotes a great servant of the state; you must remember that in this queer country he was accustomed to the deference of bearded men.

'I am Nicephorus, Logothete of the Dromos, and my companion is the Hetairiarch David. Two days ago we were faithful servants of the Emperor Michael, but yesterday the little rat abandoned the Purple. Nicephorus Botaniates now reigns in the city, and I may as well tell you frankly, before you hear it from someone else, that he has offered a reward for my arrest.

Luckily a tower by the harbour was held by Alans who spoke no Greek, and no one had remembered to tell them of the change of rulers. They opened their postern to the Hetairiarch and the master of that despatch boat was bribed to get us away. I am being open with you. We thought Heraclea was held for Bryennius, but in any case the sailors would take us no farther. We have brought nothing but our own savings, and we had no thought of bribing you. But you also were in the service of Michael Ducas, and if we discuss the situation in private we ought to arrive at some profitable arrangement.'

'That is honestly told,' answered my lord, no longer bothering to keep up the pretence that he needed a linguist. 'You may come to my hall for a private discussion, though I make no promises. What part was played by the Domestic, and which lord does he now serve? But we can go into that round the council-board.'

By the time we climbed the hill the band were armed and standing to their horses. They had heard rumours, and were very excited. It looked as though they were in the position that every mercenary dreams of; the lord to whom they had sworn allegiance was out of the fight, and they were free to sell their swords; but there were still two rivals in the field, who must continue the bidding. Even if the worst had happened and the war was at an end, they might sack Heraclea without punishment. They wanted to fight someone, anyone, at once. To keep them busy my lord sent them down to the market-place, where they arrested prominent burgesses and held them to ransom until they had collected all the money and wine in the town. That is the best way to rob a place where you intend to remain; if individual sergeants are allowed to rummage by themselves they nearly always end by burning the houses, and then you must bivouac in the open.

We were still fasting after our Easter Communion, and the fugitives also were hungry. We gathered round a table, munching bread and cold beef; just my lord and my lady, the

Logothete and the Hetairiarch, and myself, the old friend of the family who was admitted to every council.

The first thing to find out was how Botaniates had won the city. The Logothete told us, for he knew it is futile to open a council with lies; the time for deception is at the end, when you have persuaded your hearers that you are exceptionally truthful. The change had been effected by a typical Roman arrangement; the Patriarch had begged Michael to abdicate, while the Domestic pointed out that he was unlikely to win. After the Emperor had been persuaded it only remained to safeguard his dignity. He was the legitimate heir of Constantine Ducas, and everyone was anxious to ease his fall; he got an oath that if he went quietly he would be permitted to join the secular clergy, unmutilated. (These Romans keep their promises; Michael is now a respected Archbishop.) Even then it was considered too humiliating for a legitimate Emperor to hand power direct to a usurper; Michael abdicated in favour of his brother Constantine, who protested his unworthiness and abdicated in his turn, naming as heir the eminent soldier Nicephorus Botaniates. If you heard nothing but official proclamations you would never gather that this eminent soldier was encamped outside the Blachernae Gate, building siege-engines, when he was offered the Purple.

What mattered to us was that Alexius Comnenus had played a great part in the change of rulers; the Schools of the Guard took orders from him alone, and he might have named himself successor to Michael; but he had chosen to serve the Emperor Nicephorus. When my lord heard this he said: 'Alexius is my lord. He saved my eyes, and succoured me in prison. I follow where he leads.'

'Very proper,' answered the Logothete, 'but I have not yet finished. Hear me to the end. There was no saving Michael Ducas, and Botaniates was at the gates. The Domestic submitted to the nearest claimant, but who knows which of them he prefers in his heart? I am a patriot, who submitted to a great deprivation that my mind should be undistracted in the service of the state. To me Bryennius seems the more worthy ruler. He defends Europe, while Botaniates sold Nicaea to the infidel. Besides, we have nothing to sell to the Emperor in possession. But Bryennius had a second-rate staff; many of them, I understand, are whole men, always trying to find jobs for their sons. He should welcome a trained eunuch of the Dromos. And he has not yet appointed a Domestic. There is not much money in this chest, but no one else has any at all. Send a messenger at once to Adrianople, and when Bryennius marches south I can buy a way into the city. I offer you the opportunity to be the first barbarian Domestic of all the armies of Romania.'

'What about my lord the Hetairiarch?' asked Matilda.

'I am not ambitious, lady,' David answered with a smile. 'I am no warrior. What I really understand is keeping order in the city. I would serve under the Frankopole.'

'You know, my dear,' said my lord timidly, as though genuinely anxious to learn her opinion, 'this sounds a sensible proposition. I cannot understand why Alexius always takes second place. I thought this scramble would end with him in possession of the Purple. But if he won't move, Bryennius is the better master. He must buy my support at a good price, while Botaniates will merely continue to owe me the pay which Michael owed me already.'

'There is one point to be cleared up,' said my lady. 'The Domestic still holds his office. Why must the Logothete and the Hetairiarch flee for their lives?'

For the first time Nicephoritzes seemed embarrassed. 'Oh well, when these changes occur there are always men to be rewarded. Someone wanted my place, I suppose.'

But David, a stupid brute whose only qualification for his post had been his savage repression of discontent in the city, blurted out: 'The scoundrels would not let us join their plot. They put a price on our heads without trying to win us.'

'Don't bother about that price,' said my lord. 'Times are hard, but I can get along without blood-money.'

'Of course they are free to go,' Matilda said sharply, 'but

don't you see what this means? You never understand Romans. I tell you the only man they hate worse than David the torturer is his master the Logothete; if you can call that a man. Whichever side has Nicephoritzes automatically loses every other Roman. That's why poor Michael was beaten, and if Bryennius accepts him Bryennius will be destroyed. You must tell the two of them to be out of Heraclea by sunset, though I agree that a gentleman cannot earn blood-money.'

I could see that my lord felt uncomfortable. He liked to be liked, and it cost him a great effort to be stern in council. But he always followed my lady's advice.

'You see how it is, gentlemen,' he said awkwardly. 'I had one very lucky escape, and I can't afford to be on the losing side again. You had better continue your journey. Since you have money I can sell you good horses.'

The Logothete heard him with a fixed smile, but David's face was a picture of consternation. These rogues were at the end of their tether. Their last chance had been to bring Bryennius a substantial reinforcement; if they reached his camp as helpless fugitives he could earn popularity by handing them over to execution. But no one rises in the tangled jungle of Roman politics unless he has the courage to face the consequence of failure. The eunuch struggled from his chair, and when at last his great bulk was upright he strolled over to a side-table and brought back a flagon of wine. 'In these troubled times friends meet to part again,' he said with a gallant effort at gaiety. 'You will at least drink to our journey. Success to the Emperor Nicephorus, whether his surname be Bryennius or Botaniates. May the war be bloody, and the vengeance ruthless!'

When he picked up the flagon it had been hidden by his bulk. I was slow to understand, but the Balliols were slower; Frankish assassins use steel, but I am half Roman. My lord drained his cup at one gulp, at the same time as I threw my wine in the eunuch's beardless face, shouting 'Don't drink. It's poisoned.'

My lady leapt for the Logothete's shoulders. She got him down and sat on his head, while I tapped the Hetairiarch over the ear with his own jewelled mace before the unmilitary creature could tug out his sword. But by the time the Romans were bound hand and foot my lord was dead.

Matilda shed no tears. She herself unclenched the teeth and straightened the twisted body for burial, but all she said was, 'Messer Roussel was lucky to the end. He was usually in mortal sin, yet death took him at breakfast after his Easter Communion. We may pray for his soul, confident that it is bound for Heaven. I'm glad he died with two hundred men under his banner, but really his life ended years ago, when he yielded to Artouch. My duty is finished. Now I may live to please myself.'

Then she became very practical, giving orders for the safe keeping of the Logothete's treasure chest, and mustering the band for their return to the city. We all had different ideas about what to do to the murderers; my own plan was to permit them to drink poison as they struggled to do, that they might burn for ever in Hell as suicides. But my lady insisted on handing them over to the new Emperor. He was as stern as a merciful Roman can be; first they were flogged in the Hippodrome, to make them destroy their own dignity by screaming in public; then they were taken to an island in the Marmora, where they died ten days later. Presumably they were tortured to death, but the facts were hushed up; for the Romans of the city dislike cruelty, and it might have made Botaniates unpopular.

Our leaderless band dispersed in the city. Alexius continued my lady's pension; she went back to St Thecla, and in the end made her vows there. Ralph enlisted in the Roman army, carrying a bow into battle as though he had never been a knight. Osbert went to sea; but he never came back, and I heard a rumour that he had wandered all the way to Scotland, at the other end of the world. Joan ran away with a Venetian sailor, though I don't think he married her. I came here, to St Benedict. I had long sought the opportunity, but while my lord needed my service it was due to him.

If Messer Roussel had possessed half of his wife's wisdom and resolution we might have founded a decent Frankish state, and kept the Turks from the Bosphorus. He was a very gallant knight, but the east cannot be ruled by courage alone.

HISTORICAL NOTE

Roussel de Balliol was a genuine historical personage, who performed all the exploits here narrated. Ducange, in a note to his edition of Anna Comnena, identifies him with a Norman conqueror of Sicily in the service of Roger fitzTancred. The contemporary Byzantine historians, Anna Comnena, Bryennius, and Attaliates, describe his actions as they occur; but of course what interested them was the downfall of Romanus Diogenes, and the exciting adventures that marked the rise to power of Alexius Comnenus; they do not give a connected account of the adventures of a barbarian mercenary. Thus we know that Roussel was blockading Chliat when the Emperor was defeated at Manzikert, and he subsequently seized Ancyra, rebelled against the Domestic Isaac Comnenus, proclaimed John Ducas and won a great battle at the Bridge of Zompi. His two captures by the Turkish leaders Artouch and Tutach are also historical. There are conflicting versions of his obscure death at the moment when Botaniates had achieved the Purple, and I have followed that given by Bryennius. The bogus blinding is mentioned by more than one contemporary historian.

We also know that he had a wife and children; his wife was sent to make peace at Zompi, ransomed him from Artouch, and with her children arrested his murderers. But no contemporary bothers to give her name, or even to indicate her nationality; she may have been a Greek, or a Norman of Normandy. Thus Matilda is a character entirely of my own invention; so are her children, and little Roger the narrator. Every other character, except the Bishop of Amasia and a few minor members of the Norman band, is a genuine historical personage, who in fact performed the actions attributed to him in this fictional biography.

All Orion/Phoenix titles are available at your local bookshop or from the following address:

Mail Order Department
Littlehampton Book Services
FREEPOST BR535
Worthing, West Sussex, BN13 3BR
telephone 01903 828503, *facsimile* 01903 828802
e-mail MailOrders@lbsltd.co.uk
(Please ensure that you include full postal address details)

Payment can be made either by credit/debit card (Visa, Mastercard, Access and Switch accepted) or by sending a £ Sterling cheque or postal order made payable to *Littlehampton Book Services*.
DO NOT SEND CASH OR CURRENCY

Please add the following to cover postage and packing

UK and BFPO:
£1.50 for the first book, and 50p for each additional book to a maximum of £3.50

Overseas and Eire:
£2.50 for the first book plus £1.00 for the second book and 50p for each additional book ordered

---

BLOCK CAPITALS PLEASE

name of cardholder .... *delivery address*
.... *(if different from cardholder)*
address of cardholder ....
....
....
....
postcode .... *postcode* ....

☐ I enclose my remittance for £ ....

☐ please debit my Mastercard/Visa/Access/Switch (delete as appropriate)

card number ☐☐☐☐☐☐☐☐☐☐☐☐☐☐☐☐

expiry date ☐☐☐☐ Switch issue no. ☐☐

signature ....

prices and availability are subject to change without notice

Zehnow 2/17